Praise for *When Hope Sank*

Intriguing from page one, *When Hope Sank* pu'' ⸻ y, hard decisions, real-to-life emotions, and ⸻ ⸻eimer sprinkles painful circumstances with the ⸻ ⸻t miss this beautifully told historical tale.

—Hannah Lin⸻ ⸻-winning author of
Beneath His Silence ⸻ *Garden of the Midnights*

Peril and adventure are woven with a fine hand for detail into a satisfyingly sweet love story in this Civil War-era tale. Weimer's passion for history shines through and does not disappoint!

—Shannon McNear, 2014 RITA® finalist, 2021 SELAH winner,
and author of the Daughters of the Lost Colony series

Denise Weimer has penned a poignant tale of tragedy, intrigue, and romance that will keep readers turning the pages. Her attention to detail immerses the reader in the time period. Action scenes are balanced with emotions and reactions that leave the reader pulling for the characters. It's a well-written historical romance spawned from the pages of history.

—Pegg Thomas, award-winning novelist

When Hope Sank is a poignant romance that will captivate you to the very end. Daring rescues, a love triangle, and the perfect mix of espionage and danger help bring the destruction of the steamboat *Sultana* to light. Filled with hope and faith, *When Hope Sank* reminds us to love as Christ loves and that sometimes family can be found in the unlikeliest of places.

—Candice Sue Patterson, author of
When the Waters Came and *Saving Mrs. Roosevelt*

Denise Weimer's captivating tale, set during the aftermath of the Civil War, has startlingly contemporary meaning. *When Hope Sank* is a well-written journey through the past to a highly desirable destination readers still seek today—the triumph of good over evil, faith over doubt, and sacrifice instead of selfishness.

—Rhonda Dragomir, award-winning author of
When the Flames Ravaged

A DAY TO REMEMBER

When Hope Sank

DENISE WEIMER

BARBOUR
PUBLISHING

When Hope Sank ©2024 by Denise Weimer

Print ISBN 978-1-63609-829-6
Adobe Digital Edition (.epub) 978-1-63609-830-2

All scripture quotations, unless otherwise noted, are taken from the King James Version of the Bible.

This book is a work of fiction. Names, characters, places, and incidents are either products of the author's imagination or used fictitiously. Any similarity to actual people, organizations, and/or events is purely coincidental.

Published by Barbour Publishing, Inc., 1810 Barbour Drive, Uhrichsville, Ohio 44683, www.barbourbooks.com

Cover Design by Faceout Studio

Our mission is to inspire the world with the life-changing message of the Bible.

 Member of the
Evangelical Christian
Publishers Association

Printed in the United States of America.

DEDICATION

This one is for my agent, Linda S. Glaz, from whom I have learned so much, and who patiently persisted until I got that contract.

When thou passest through the waters, I will be with thee; and through the rivers, they shall not overflow thee: when thou walkest through the fire, thou shalt not be burned; neither shall the flame kindle upon thee.

Isaiah 43:2

Chapter One

∽

MID-APRIL 1865

"Free Arkansas."

The unexpected phrase, whispered a stone's throw away at the inn's back alley door, froze Lily Livingston's arms in mid-swing. The dirty dishwater she'd been about to fling from the entrance to the kitchen swirled and settled in the pan, all but a defiant trickle. The speaker's head swiveled in her direction. He'd removed his gambler-style hat, providing a glimpse of long, center-parted black hair despite the drizzly night. Something in the slash of his frown, the alertness of his posture, caused Lily to withdraw into the doorway.

Who was entering River Rest's private room the back way, and why was he offering such a strange greeting to whoever answered the door? Experience had taught her to use caution where patrons of her uncle's establishment were concerned. Some of the worst sorts of shirkers and criminals slaked their thirst and sought their slumber at inns along the Mississippi these days. *These days.* She sniffed. Even before the Civil War made Arkansas a haven for guerillas and bushwhackers, river ruffians had abounded—gamblers, thieves, swindlers. And worse. Much worse.

"Miss Lily, what you doing?"

The question shot through Lily with the urgency of an alert on a telegraph wire, straightening her spine.

Behind her stood Martha, Uncle Thad's cook. She held a dishcloth in one fist on her bony hip and plowed a furrow in her forehead with a raised brow.

Lily lifted her finger to her lips. "There's a man out there."

"There's always a man out there."

"This one seemed…like trouble."

"Ain't they all?" Martha rolled her eyes. "I declare, Miss Lily. You be scared of you own shadow. 'Course, I guess I can't blame you, young and pretty as you are." With a huff, she made to take the basin, but Lily peeked out the door. The alley had emptied.

"He's gone." Her pulse returned to normal.

"Good. We got another load of dishes."

Lily finished emptying the pan and then fetched fresh water from the well behind the inn. Martha and her daughter, Mika, would never understand if she told them she'd trade her golden hair and fair skin for their dark features in a moment, if only it would purchase her permanent invisibility. But the freedwomen—Aunt Susanna's former slaves—and Martha's husband, Joss, who worked at the livery next door, had suffered far more than invisibility. She could never envy their position in life, even though the Union conquest of this portion of Arkansas in mid-1862 had lent local colored folk a measure of dignity and opportunity.

As Lily came back inside, Martha examined the remnants of stew on the inner rim of her Dutch oven. "Close that door. It's letting in an awful draft."

Drying a saucer, Mika gave a little snort. "You wouldn't be so cold if you got a little meat on your bones, Mama." The thirteen-year-old had just started to develop curves. Lily had caught her admiring her silhouette in the guest room mirrors more than once lately.

"Too busy doing my magic tricks." Martha flung her dishcloth down and reached for a corncob. She started scouring the pot with the vigor of a chimney sweep. "Coming up with something to cook from nothing."

Lily carefully lifted her washbasin next to a stack of dirty dishes on the counter. "It's true that our navels are about touching our backbones. It's been a long four years and an especially hard winter, with most of the farmers driven off their land." Mika sidled closer to take over the washing, but Lily smiled and shook her head. "I'll do it."

A grateful light sparked in the girl's eyes. "Thank you, miss."

"Of course." Aunt Susanna assigned Mika the worst tasks, from emptying chamber pots to scrubbing stained sheets. The poor girl ought to enjoy a few moments of relative peace at the end of a hard day—though it be but one in an endless and thankless chain. Lily added soap flakes and plunged the first dish into the water. "And remember, you don't have to call me *miss*."

"If you say so, Miss Lily." Taking up a serving platter and swiping it with her drying rag, Mika leaned over and whispered, "I got that package you been wanting." She tilted her head toward a large oval basket near the door. "Under the tablecloth that needs mending."

Lily's lips rounded. "Thank you," she whispered back. "Have any trouble?"

Mika shook her braids, the calico cloth that covered them flapping in the back. They both bent their heads over the sink. "The general's man met me at the provost office as planned. Said there'll be more—"

"You two find some kind of secret writing on those dishes?" Martha stared at them over her shoulder.

"No, Mama." Mika shot her a grin. "We were just talking about the good the Yankee-men do around here—'specially now that the Southern boys are surrendering."

Well, that was true. Lily pressed her lips together, smothering her smile. The presence of Union officials made it possible for her handiwork to earn some extra greenbacks and Mika her usual tip, so long as they kept it secret from the family.

"Don't let the missus hear you talking like that," Martha mumbled. Her gaze snapped up as the door from the dining room banged open, but it was only Jacob, Lily's twelve-year-old brother.

He darted across the room, looking like a stick in high-waisted breeches and suspenders topped by a mop of tawny hair. Grabbing the broom, he wended his way back out, calling to Lily as he went. "Uncle Thad says he needs you at the bar, Sis."

When Lily's shoulders sagged, Mika assessed her with sympathy. "Maybe he just needs you to mind it while he goes to the privy."

Lily drew her lips in. Doubtful. "He usually just closes the window for that." The bar sat near the front door, where it serviced both walk-up and dine-in customers. No, he'd want her for a chore of some sort, one that would no doubt expose her to the notice of the less savory patrons who lingered over their mugs this time of an evening.

"I'll go." Mika met her gaze. The girl was unusually insightful for her age. But then, she would have already learned the value of staying out of the way of certain types of men.

"Thank you, but no. I can better fend off the difficult ones. And you know Uncle Thad doesn't let you handle spirits."

All in all, Uncle Thad, her late father's brother, was a decent sort, hardworking and respectable. He watched out for the women of his household, and despite his wife's protestations, usually countenanced Lily's preference for back-of-house work—or at the most, serving food to the tables in the dining room. That meant the need must be legitimate.

Lily wiped her hands and rolled down her sleeves, then straightened her stained white apron over her tan-checked muslin work dress. A short walk up the hallway brought her to the entry, where Uncle Thad greeted her from behind the enclosed bar.

"Lily-love, I need you to run this tray of whiskeys to the back room." Sliding said tray toward her, he headed off any questions with an explanation. "Beth is busy serving their supper, and your aunt has retired with one of her headaches."

Biting the inside of her cheek, Lily refrained from remarking that Aunt Susanna's headaches always struck on the busiest nights, and Beth hadn't been seen in the kitchen since disappearing through its doors with the first servings of stew and cornbread. Instead, she merely asked, "Who do you mean by 'their'?" If that sleazy man from the alley was part of the company, she might leave the drinks on the sideboard.

Uncle Thad's salt-and-pepper brows rose. He put on a jolly smile, although his heightened color told her he'd overdone it again today. The very notion shuddered in Lily's chest like the report of a cannon. Without her father's brother, where would she be? Not to mention, Jacob?

Cutting his gaze to where several blue-coated soldiers lingered over chicory coffee and sweet potato pie in the adjoining dining room, Uncle Thad leaned closer and lowered his voice. "You'll be pleased to know, it's Timber Sutton and some of his friends."

"Timber Sutton? He hasn't been seen in these parts since…January?"

The gangly old man had once frequented Mound City and the nearby towns of Hopefield and Marion, as well as Memphis, Tennessee, a ferry ride across the Mississippi River. Everyone knew he'd acted as a courier and scout for Confederate guerillas. But that was before Union officials had tightened their grip on this portion of the state, punishing the partisans and any who supported them. Those who hadn't been flushed out were now being bribed to lay down their arms. General Robert E. Lee might have surrendered the Army of Northern Virginia to Ulysses S. Grant earlier this month, but Joe Johnston still had almost ninety thousand Confederates in North Carolina—not to mention the other smaller armies remaining in the western states. Until those regular forces made peace, the most hardened partisans would die fighting.

And the presence of Union officials in the dining room while Southern sympathizers held court only feet away also explained why her uncle wouldn't abandon his post.

He winked. "I reckoned you'd want a quick word with Sutton."

If anyone knew where Lucky Cecil Duke—her late twin brother's best friend and the man who laid claim to her as his future bride—could be found, Sutton would. Lily forced an answering lift of her lips. Even Uncle Thad assumed she'd hung her hopes on the dashing young captain who'd long defended her honor. Was there any point in saying him nay? Thaddeus Livingston couldn't shelter her forever, no matter how kind his heart.

"I'll get these right in." So saying, she whisked the heavy tray as quickly as possible through the dining room.

At her approach, Jacob glanced up from sweeping cornbread crumbs from beneath a table at the far end. He stopped with a bright smile and reached for the private room's doorknob with a gentlemanly flourish. "Let me get that for you, Sis."

With no hand free for her customary ruffle of his hair, she passed on Thad's wink. As she entered, he closed the door behind her.

"…leavin' the coal barge north of Memphis," a nasal voice was saying. "Once they shovel it in, *ka-pow!*" A paunchy, middle-aged man Lily didn't recognize threw his hands wide and expelled an explosive breath. "Hundreds of paroled Yankee prisoners, blown to kingdom come."

A second man snickered. "So much for their dreams of home." From the side, even through the haze of his cigar smoke, Lily identified his hawkish face and greasy hair. And next to him, her hand on the tasteless burgundy coat of the man from the alley, her cousin Beth sat, facing the other way.

Lily bit back a gasp. Her swift motion toward the sideboard possessed all the subtlety of a spy balloon, for the fourth individual across the table cleared his throat and lunged to his feet. "Miss Lily. So good to see you again."

"And you, Mr. Sutton. I trust you are well." With a nod in his direction, she altered her path, approaching the table despite the lascivious gazes of the two strangers.

Sutton remained standing, a silent, unnoticed rebuke to his companions. "It's not my welfare that's important, Miss Lily, but yours. And his whom I just saw over a week ago." His tone took on an undercurrent of meaning as deep as the whirlpools that snared small crafts near the riverbanks.

"Thank you, Mr. Sutton." Lily's face heated as she delivered the drinks. "Compliments of Uncle Thad. You gentlemen have a good night." She turned away, but a hand shot out from below, snagging her hip.

"What's your hurry, Lovely Lily?" Like a hungry python, the burgundy-coated man's arm slid up and around her waist, drawing her down.

A flash of horror hotter than General Sherman's fires engulfed her whole body. "Stop it!" She rocked on the heels of her boots, losing her balance and tumbling onto the skinny knee the man from the alley had pressed against Beth's skirt. Her cousin squeaked, the man laughed, and

Lily floundered to regain her feet. A faint sour smell leached from his clothes, alcohol from his breath. The orange tip of his cigar smoldered inches from her cheek as the fingers of his other hand curled around the boning of her corset.

The sensation of those fingers, hot little circles penetrating the fabric of her dress, corset, and chemise, nearly undid her. "No! Let me go." She tore his grip away and clambered up, finding Timber Sutton at her side, offering her his arm. She sucked in a shuddering breath. Righting herself, she smoothed her skirt. And her revulsion. This was why she didn't serve bar customers.

"There now, Miss Lily. No harm done." But Sutton turned narrowed eyes upon his companion. "Find another woman to manhandle, Frenchie. This one's taken."

"Taken? By who? You?" The man scoffed, then casually took another puff on his cigar.

"By Cecil Duke," Sutton answered succinctly.

Lily stepped behind him.

The stranger gave a low whistle. "Captain of Duke's Partisans? Lucky Cecil, indeed…" He eyed Lily with fresh regard, but her skin crawled wherever his gaze touched. Finally, he looked away, banking his cigar on the edge of his dirty plate. "He'll be surrenderin' his famed company soon enough, but I s'pose I mustn't rile a man I hope to work with."

What did that mean? And Cecil…here? Her heart gave a heavy thud. Lily moved toward the sideboard to search Sutton's face, and he offered her a single, firm nod.

"That's right. Your worries will soon be past, Miss Lily. Cecil should be back within the month." He refocused on his companion. "And nobody wants on his bad side."

In a single blur of movement, the Frenchman's chair scraped, and a knife flashed from his boot to Sutton's neck. One stumbling step back, and the edge of the sideboard dug into Lily's hip. Beth jumped up with a cry and grabbed her arm.

Frenchie held Sutton by a fistful of his wool vest and stained ecru shirt. His mouth turned down as he fairly spat onto Sutton's gray goatee.

"If there's anyone's bad side you don't want to be on, old man, it's mine. Understand?" He pressed the tip of his blade near the courier's bobbing Adam's apple—the only indication of his distress.

"Yes." The single syllable hissed out between barely parted lips.

Frenchie released Sutton and stowed his weapon in another fluid motion. His reptilian mannerisms turned Lily's stomach. He grabbed a glass from the tray she'd brought in and bolted down a swallow, then slapped Sutton's forearm. "You'll quickly learn what motivates me. Not threats. Not fear. Certainly not pity." He eased back into his seat.

Sutton remained stiff as a ramrod, his chin almost as high as his color, but the other man who'd been speaking as Lily entered strained the buttons of his tapestry waistcoat as he leaned forward. He offered a tittering suggestion—"Profit?"

"Profit?" Leaning back, Frenchie expelled the word like a plug of tobacco. "Surely you of all people recognize my undyin' dedication to the cause, even in the face of apparent defeat." He glanced over his shoulder. Jerked his chin toward the table. "Sit down, Sutton. No bad blood. Not between true patriots. Let us toast…" He raised his glass. "To our fine brotherhood."

"Come on, Beth," Lily whispered into her cousin's hair. She drew her toward the exit before the awful man could again take notice of them. Sutton obliged them with a nod, moving to block Frenchie's view.

With her thin lips pressed together, Beth followed Lily out the door. Lily closed and leaned against it, willing air into her lungs and battening emotional shutters down on the panic. She squeezed her eyes shut, but the flashing of memories made them pop open again. Thankfully, the dining room had emptied of customers. She took a deep, whistling breath.

"Are you all right?" Beth took her hand. "You're shaking."

"Am *I* all right?" Snatching her hand away, Lily pinned her with a hard stare. "I should be asking *you* that. Why did you stay in that room with those men? Isn't it obvious what they're capable of…at least that Frenchie?"

Beth sniffed. Angled her chin away. "He's never touched me. He wouldn't have hurt you either. You didn't have to be so dramatic."

Lily clamped down on her lower lip. Any explanation that didn't cost her dearly would only risk hurting her cousin. Instead, she asked, "And the prisoners they were talking about? I guess they won't hurt them either."

A high-pitched, shaky laugh tumbled from her cousin's lips. "Oh, Frenchie's forever hatching one crazy plan or another. None of them ever come to anything. For all his threats, he's a liar and a braggart, Lily—another sad Southern boy who refuses to believe the war is over."

Lily's retort popped out, harsh and cold. "He's anything but a boy." Indeed, the malevolence in those dark eyes had shaken her to her core. But he possessed the brooding sort of looks her lonely cousin—considered an old maid by many at twenty-five—might find intriguing. "What is his real name, anyway?"

Beth lifted her shoulder. "I've only ever heard him called Frenchie. He's not from around here."

"No good comes of a man who's only known by a nickname. Why were you even in there with them, Beth?" Even if Beth was right about them not being saboteurs, for her cousin's safety, she couldn't let it go.

The older girl wrapped skinny fingers around Lily's upper arm, pulling her farther into the dining room. "Because when they think they have an admiring audience, they tip well. And I need the money. Who knows?" The laugh returned, and she circled her hand in front of her face, where the flickering oil lamps only partially concealed her pockmarks, the cruel residue of childhood smallpox. "Maybe they just feel sorry for me."

"Beth." Lily grasped her cousin's hand. "Sutton's fine, but the others are dangerous. You heard what Frenchie said. He doesn't pity anyone. You're wrong to think your scars will protect you. Better to be alone than to keep company with the wrong people."

"As though you would know." Beth pulled away, averting her face. A bitter play acted out there, its encore a twisted smile. "You have Cecil."

"And you have Judge Winkler." Even as she said it, Lily's voice wavered, for she was far more likely to fall in love with Cecil Duke than Beth was with the man her parents had chosen for her.

"Ha. Winkler. Even his name sounds fat and middle aged."

Lily scrambled to throw a cloak of dignity around her cousin. "He's wealthy and respected, and Uncle Thad says that as a moderate, he'll be able to resume office. He should return from Ohio soon, and you won't ever have to worry about serving uncouth men again."

"No. Just my husband, whom I'll despise." Her face set, Beth started toward the hallway.

"Beth, he's a good man. He's very fond of you."

"Fond of me?" Her cousin whirled, her mask dropping again. Disgust twisted her features. "Do you think that's all I want? All I deserve?"

Lily took a step back. "Of course not."

"Hiram Winkler is not the only one who will be home soon. Our dashing local hero will also be coming for his bride."

It was true. The last time Cecil Duke had ridden through with his band of raiders, he'd sworn to wed Lily as soon as the war ended. Lily's lips quivered but refused to produce the expected response. The bonds between them had been too deep for separation and conflicting loyalties to sever. She'd needed Cecil. But he was a stranger now.

She could never make Beth understand. She had to leave—and soon. But she couldn't risk telling anyone what she'd just heard in case Aunt Susanna discovered her treachery and threw her and Jacob out before her plans were in place.

Chapter Two

After three and a half years at war, he was going home. But to what?

Cade Palmer lay on his cot, hands folded over his sunken chest, as the steamboat churned north on the Mississippi River. He'd been unable to settle into sleep since the *Sultana* had pulled away from the barges a mile above Memphis, Tennessee, around midnight. The songs of the roustabouts as they trundled coal on board had mingled with the merrymaking of the soldiers—Union prisoners of war just paroled from Andersonville in Georgia and Cahaba in Alabama, giddy with the rush of freedom. Delirious in their eagerness to return to their homes in Indiana, Kentucky, Michigan, Ohio, Tennessee, and West Virginia.

They celebrated the news that General Johnston had agreed to peace terms with General Sherman only the day before, effectively ending the war, even while many spoke with shock and grief of the recent assassination of President Lincoln. The steamer had carried the news downriver on its way to Vicksburg, its bell tolling, its decks draped in black bunting and its flag at half-staff.

Relative quiet now reigned in the main saloon where the officers slept.

Well, save for the occasional cough or snore—or snort, squeal, or bray from the condemned horses, hogs, and mules in the stern cargo room behind them, a deck below. Cade had only a short while before James came to switch out watching the sick men forward of the main cabin, over the boilers where it was warm, but he couldn't make his mind shut off.

James Caldwell might not be an officer, but his experience as an orderly had secured his place in the main saloon, helping Cade care for the ill. Not that Cade thought of himself as an officer—a lieutenant—anymore. Not after nine months in captivity. But a doctor, yes. The deprivations of prison camp might have made a sick joke of his position, but being a physician was so much more than a title. It was part of who you were.

Thank You, Lord, for delivering me.

Cade tried out the prayer as a beggar tries on a new coat—in awe but unable to quell the sense of unworthiness. It had been so long since he'd wanted to talk to God.

But now…the nightmare of Andersonville was over. He could finally practice medicine the way he'd always intended.

Could he, though? After they were mustered out at Camp Chase, Ohio, James would return to the Caldwell family farm outside Cincinnati, but what awaited Cade? Would his former professor welcome him into his medical practice? Even knowing Cade's family did not approve? The war had provided a temporary solution after Cade's graduation, but letters from his mother and sister had betrayed their belief that the brutality of life as a field surgeon would end his medical aspirations. Little did they know how his time in Andersonville had only hardened his resolve.

No, he would not waste this second chance. One way or another, he would save lives in the future.

Cade turned onto his side, and his hand almost hit the face of a man sleeping on the floor. Paying passengers and officers alike crowded into the main cabin rather than brave the cool mist and wind on the open decks where the enlisted soldiers huddled together. Not only were the two rows of double-stacked cots filled, but bodies crowded into every conceivable space. A fight had broken out earlier when one man tried to save a bunk with his hat and another had claimed it. Some slept in chairs. One civilian passenger had given up on slumber and sat reading a book by the light of a single oil lamp. Not a bad idea, if one had a book to read.

The overcrowding of the boat had become apparent even before the third train bearing prisoners arrived from Camp Fisk, the parole camp outside Vicksburg, Mississippi. The sagging upper hurricane deck had been braced with heavy wooden beams. Rumors quickly spread that the quartermaster at Vicksburg, Colonel Reuben Hatch, and the captain of the *Sultana*, Cass Mason, had profited from the government payment by adding men beyond the steamer's capacity.

Indeed, the overloading had almost already caused disaster when they'd stopped that day at Helena, Arkansas. Spring flooding meant the Mississippi River overflowed its banks by as much as three miles. Levees normally maintained by the Army Corps of Engineers had broken. The soldiers had gathered on deck to take in the spectacle of Helena, so flooded that residents had to use rowboats to traverse the streets. When a photographer had set up to make a picture of the *Sultana* from shore, so many men had rushed to one side that the boat had started to tip. It had taken frantic effort from the senior officer among them, Major William Fidler, to redistribute the soldiers.

If Cade was any judge, over two thousand souls now traveled on a boat meant to transport less than a quarter of that number. It didn't help ease minds that when the Ohio men had boarded first and settled mainly on the hurricane deck and around the opening of the stairway that led down to the enclosed saloon, a steady banging from the boiler below attested to some sort of repair taking place.

James had joked that maybe Mason had blown out a boiler earning those antlers posted between the two massive smokestacks, indicating the *Sultana* was the fastest steamer on the Mississippi. That was James—always finding humor in even the grimmest situation. He was the son of a farmer and Cade the son of a minister. While they'd grown up together in Cade's father's church, he'd never claimed the faith Cade had. But James' determined grip on life had kept Cade afloat more times than he could count since they'd been captured together.

Thus far, according to a member of the crew, the *Sultana* had maintained the standard, respectable pace of nine miles an hour. No indications of distress. Cade's shoulders relaxed, and his breathing evened out.

He must have finally drifted off, for he was next aware of a slight listing to one side—and someone calling his name. A voice that had become the one he most valued. He opened his eyes. James lightly shook his foot as he leaned over the end of the cot.

"My turn?" The familiar sense of helplessness caved in Cade's stomach. Dread.

Men relied on him for help and comfort when he had so little to give, not even the herbal remedies they'd tried at Andersonville. A surgeon had inspected the paroled men before they boarded, but many of those sick had circled around and snuck on, anyway. They weren't prepared for twenty cases of the same type of diarrhea that had decimated the prison population.

"Most of them are resting."

"As should you." Cade rolled forward to get a leg into the small space between his cot and the soldier on the floor.

A sound louder than the fateful cannonade at Lynchburg the day of their capture blasted through the boat. A blast blew Cade off the bed and atop of the man sleeping below him. Debris rained down.

"Rebels!" someone yelled.

Then someone screamed. And another.

Not Rebels. A wave of hot steam swept through the saloon. Cade hunkered as it seared the shirt off his back. But rather than crying out, he managed to hold his breath against the super-heated air. The boilers! They must have exploded.

This couldn't actually be happening.

The creaking and cracking all around confirmed reality. Metal screeched. Steam hissed. Men howled and cursed.

Cade rolled off the soldier who'd cushioned his fall and groped in the smoke. His fingertips contacted chunks of timber and objects he could not identify. He cracked one eyelid open. Was that a light burning in the ladies' cabin, aft of the saloon?

He drew a tiny test of a breath. It burned but could be tolerated.

"James?" Then louder. "James!"

Amid the ruckus, a voice wheezed, "Here."

Cade crawled in that direction, but terror weakened his limbs. For ahead, he could see…nothing. The front of the cabin was gone. The sick men gone. And into the hole where they had been, debris and cots fell as the floor disintegrated.

But there—James, lying face down. Cade had just grasped his friend's leg when a tremendous groan shuddered through the boat, followed by a sound that could only be the smokestacks and the upper deck collapsing. From above, a large shape hurtled down—straight toward James' head.

"No!" Cade flung out his right arm.

His hand absorbed the impact of the massive timber. Something gave way in his wrist. Pain splintered through every finger and down his forearm, wrenching out a cry. But the timber landed just to his friend's side rather than atop him.

Cade clasped his injured hand to his chest. This was bad. His medical mind made instant calculations. The palm throbbed, the fine bones likely damaged. His fingers didn't want to curl. The index finger was crooked. Definitely broken, then. And his wrist? No protrusion, but the distal radius could still be fractured.

James propped himself up. In a sudden flare of light, his torso gleamed bare, his back scalded red. Much like Cade's own?

The meaning of the light registered when someone shouted, "Put out that fire! Put out that fire!"

The debris from the collapsing decks was feeding the open furnaces a level below. As if from Dante's inferno, flames leaped upward, and men who were able raced to the racks that should have held the red fire buckets. But they found none, for they'd been used earlier for drinking water and slop.

Cade closed the fingers of his left hand around James' arm. "We have to get out of here."

James nodded. "To the stern."

Not that they had much choice, with the boat blown open a third of the way back from the bow.

They helped each other stand, then began to pick their way through the saloon, littered with debris, bodies, and parts of bodies reminiscent of those they'd carted away from the surgical tents after major battles. Passengers from the staterooms that lined the saloon emerged wearing lifebelts, including a woman, a man, and a little girl in a pink nightgown. They all hurried toward the stern. Fire already leaped like crazed lizards along the crosspieces of the roof, gobbling up the paint.

Across the room, a man had made tourniquets of his suspenders for both his legs, broken at the ankles with the bones protruding. He begged for help from a man whose face appeared in a hole in the ceiling above. "Throw me in the river is all I ask, else I shall burn to death here."

His would-be savior called back, "I am powerless to help you. I can't swim!"

Cade had spent much of his boyhood with friends on the Ohio River, but how many were filled with that same terrible choice—burn or drown? "We should help him."

"Yes, but first, we should find something that floats." His friend looked around.

James was right. A drowning man would pull them down. And there would be hundreds of drowning men out in the river.

At last, Cade located a splintered stateroom door among the debris. "Help me with this. We can put him on it."

James stooped to help him bear the weight, but when they turned toward the man with the broken ankles, another soldier was carrying him toward the promenade. Many others, however, cried out from the rubble. On their way aft, they worked together to free those they could.

By the time they reached the back of the main cabin, half a dozen followed. Several helped each other, badly burned or with broken limbs. Cade's heart constricted. To come this far, only to face death again when they'd thought they were free at last…

He couldn't think about it, or none of them would make it.

Passengers, including the young family Cade had noticed earlier, lowered themselves from ropes through the narrow stern windows at the cabin's aft, onto the lip of the main deck that protruded below. But with the wounded and the door in tow, Cade and James accessed the small section of stern deck behind the paddlewheel through the rear stateroom.

The scene from the railing stopped them in their tracks.

"God preserve us," James muttered.

The blast that had rent the main saloon had torn through the hurricane deck to the crew's Texas cabin and the pilothouse. Dark figures leaped from the hurricane deck above. The right smokestack had apparently fallen on whatever might have been left of the pilothouse—without which the ship could not be steered. The left smokestack had collapsed onto the front of the hurricane deck. The counterweighted left paddlewheel tilted out. Likely the other one did as well, leaving the boat at the swollen river's mercy.

On the deck below, horses and mules had gotten loose from the stern cargo hold and trampled any passengers unfortunate enough to fall in their path. Some people attempted to push them over and then to follow and cling to the animals as they swam. Men who jumped over with timbers found them seized and submersed.

In the dark water, what looked like a hundred men fought over a capsized metal lifeboat. Every time it righted, it was quickly flipped, burying half the people who tried to scramble aboard. Finally, someone jumped from the deck with a stick and poked a hole in the craft.

Cursing, screaming, and sobbing filled the air.

"We should get off." The urging of one of the more able-bodied men they'd brought from the cargo area drew Cade's attention behind him.

Explosions shuddered the deck beneath their feet. Cade and James grabbed the railing. The paddlewheel fell away, barely clinging at the bottom as the flames licking the main cabin flared higher and blew toward them.

The man repeated his panicked warning. "We must get off while we can!"

"Not yet." Cade firmed his tone even though his heart pounded with the same terror. "Too many are jumping now."

"Cade's right. If the other paddlewheel comes off—"

James never got to finish his statement, for the wild-eyed man rushed them, grabbing at the door they'd propped between them.

"Give me that!"

"No!" James maneuvered the door like an unwieldy shield. "You can wait, or you can jump without it."

Another man they'd rescued joined the fight. Cade struggled to hold on to his edge with his left hand. Attempting to use the right sent excruciating pain along his arm.

The door flipped sideways, knocking their initial attacker over the railing. He fell with a scream onto a mass of flailing bodies below and was quickly churned under.

The private who'd helped him stared overboard, and his throat worked. "You were right."

Cade eyed him. Each labored breath burned going down. The steam had done tissue damage. "You should take off that coat."

"Water's bound to be freezin'."

"You won't need help getting pulled under."

The soldier set his mouth and shrugged out of his uniform jacket, the standard-issue kind they'd been given at Camp Fisk to replace the rags that had endured prison camp.

The boat began to turn. As James had predicted, the right paddle-wheel must have come off. A chorus of screams from the bow indicated that the wind carried the flames toward the front of the steamer, now shifting downriver.

The pivoting meant that not only had the fire cleared but somewhat less crowded water opened up below. Cade turned to address their group. "We should try our luck now. James and I will go first, after we throw over the door. But jump far out." He met his friend's gaze until James gave a brief, somber nod.

James waved his arm behind him. "Stand clear, men."

Their comrades obliged. Cade and James slid the door onto the railing, Cade using his right shoulder rather than that hand. After exchanging a glance, they shoved with all their might. Then they scrambled onto the railing. In the inky water, men were already splashing toward the door. Cade aimed for an open spot, sucked in a deep breath, and launched himself with all the effort remaining in his trembling legs.

He struck the water face forward, his hip slamming into the edge of the door. He resisted the urge to cry out, lest he inhale a lungful of river water.

He came up a moment later, spluttering, and spun about in search of the door. A half-dozen bodies already covered it, and a dozen more fought to take hold. Many of those men probably couldn't swim. He could. But given the flooded state of the river and the pressure of the current, even the strongest swimmer could perish before making it to shore. Not to mention his injured hand, which he could only cup weakly. The more he used it, the more damage he would do. His only decent chance of survival was to get on that door.

Was he willing to fight off drowning men to do so? Cade treaded water as an agony of indecision swept over him. Had he not pledged his life to saving others?

Then a body floated up beside him, arms akimbo, face white and eyes closed.

"James!" Cade grabbed his friend under the shoulders with his right arm and smacked his cheek with his left hand. "James, can you hear me?" He must have hit his head on something—or someone—when he entered the water.

A moan from the man allowed Cade's heart to resume a steady beat. Thank God. But he had to get James onto the door.

Tugging his friend's form behind him, Cade swam toward the wood. A strength possessed him he hadn't thought remained in his body, already wasted from nine months in prison camp. But he and James had fared better than most on the extra victuals afforded the medical staff. And now Cade used that advantage to push his way to the door.

"Move! Move aside. This man is unconscious."

Those in his path kicked and pushed. But he hadn't come this far to let his most faithful friend surrender to the river's numbing embrace. Finally, with the help of one other man who retained some presence of mind, he got James on the door.

Hands grasped wildly at what remained of Cade's clothing, his burned back, his arms and legs. His instincts shouted for him to shove the men away. Kill his own comrades to survive. But conviction grasped his chest and seemed to squeeze any extra air from his lungs.

He grabbed a flailing hand and placed it on the door. Then another, giving up his place. Treading water behind.

If any of them were to survive, they had to get away from the burning boat. And they couldn't take on any more people. The door was already submerged.

Cade sucked in enough air to shout. "We must get to shore! Everyone has to kick. Now!" He pushed the soldier between him and the door and waved his arm forward.

"He's right," another man shouted. "Swim! Swim for the Arkansas side."

Whatever happened, Cade had to see James to safety. But how far could he swim with a fractured hand and wrist? He needed something greater than himself, stronger even than his deepest reserves.

Lord, help us. Help me.

Would God even answer him—when they were barely on speaking terms?

Chapter Three

People yelling—inside the inn as well as without—woke Lily. Lights flickered even through her third-story window. She sat up in bed. The curtain partition to her little brother's nook remained closed, so he must still be asleep. But now the bells of steamboats downriver, across at Memphis, began to clang. Something was very wrong.

Lily padded barefoot across the braided rug and held aside her window's muslin curtain. Dark figures ran along the streets carrying lanterns, and lights also dotted the flooded Mississippi River as a variety of crafts launched from Mound City. Crafts that had apparently been hidden two days prior when, in an effort to stop guerilla warfare, the Union picket boat *Pocahontas* had prowled the local waters on a mission to destroy any civilian-owned yawls, rowboats, skiffs, rafts, and canoes. But where were they going?

"Wake up, Jacob. Something's happened." Lily called to her brother as she pulled her wrapper over her cotton nightgown. She hurried out of their room onto the narrow landing, then through the door to her right that led onto the small third-floor balcony. There her breath clogged in her throat, and her heart nearly stopped.

About a mile up the river, which was lit for miles in all directions, flames engulfed a steamer. The paddlewheels had fallen away, and the boat turned around. Hundreds of figures crowded the main forward deck, many jumping off—or pushing each other. Bodies and debris darkened the surrounding water. And were those people in the trees? Yes, clinging to the tops of the cottonwoods and willows submerged to the point that they resembled bushes.

"What is it?" Jacob stood in the doorway, rubbing his eyes. His sandy hair stuck up in all directions.

"A boat is on fire. Lots of people in the water." Without giving him time to gawp at the view, she nudged him back toward their room. "Get dressed."

"But what can we do? Uncle Thad said the Yankees hacked up our canoe."

"We'll ready the inn. The steamers will send out their rowboats, and once they've built up steam, they'll go too. The people they rescue will need places to stay."

"Lily?" Her uncle's call up the stairs stopped her at the entrance to her room.

"Yes, Uncle Thad?"

"You and Jacob get dressed and come down. I need your help."

"We'll be right there." She grasped the door and shooed Jacob to his alcove.

Uncle Thad raised his voice once more. "Bring some extra blankets and meet me at the livery."

The livery? That had nothing to do with cooking breakfast or making up beds. Yet Lily called her consent and hastened to change into her chemise. The many layers of a lady's clothing never seemed more ridiculous than in an emergency. But she daren't leave off her stockings, pantalets, corset, under-petticoat, or the corded petticoat she wore to keep her skirts from dragging in lieu of the wider hoops. Not with the strange men who would shortly flood their inn.

She was donning her navy cotton one-piece dress with its practical fitted coat sleeves when Jacob demanded, "Are you ready yet?"

"Yes." She'd no sooner answered than he snatched the partition aside and marched into her area in his old boots, wool pants, suspenders, and a striped shirt.

Jacob grabbed an armload of quilts from their chest. "Let's go."

Lily fumbled with the top two hooks of her bodice as she followed him down the stairs. They met Beth descending from the second story. In the wavering light of the oil lamp mounted on the wall at the landing, her dark braid was disheveled, her face pale.

"Martha is already in the kitchen." Beth spoke breathlessly. "Father insists we get the rooms ready, although I say, let the Yankees in Memphis take care of their own."

"Their own?"

"Yes. That steamer was carrying prisoners of war."

Lily's steps faltered as the voice of the gloating stranger in the River Rest's private room came back to her from a couple of weeks before. *Hundreds of paroled Yankee prisoners, blown to kingdom come.* "Oh no, Beth. No..." Had they really done it? Blown up a Union steamer?

Beth whirled to face her, her eyes narrowed. "Don't make a scene, Lily. We know nothing more about this than anyone else."

"But we do. Your friend Frenchie and that other man—"

"You don't know what you heard, Lily. And we don't know what happened on that steamer." She grabbed Lily's arm. "Now, come on. If I have to make up beds for the enemy, you can at least help me out."

"Uncle Thad told us to meet him at the livery." Jacob spoke up from the foot of the stairs.

"The livery? What is he doing?" Beth's sharp glance toggled between them.

"I don't know, but we have to go." Jacob snatched Lily's hand, and she allowed herself to be pulled away—out the front door and down the street. A wagon clattered past, followed by a woman with a stack of linens, before they turned into the alley between the inn and the livery.

As they entered the stable from the side door, the familiar scents of hay and manure hit Lily's nose. Horses shifted and snorted from stalls on both sides, while a soft golden light burned in the rear.

Joss, Martha's tall, dark-skinned husband, led a bridled draft horse into the walkway. "Evenin', Miss Lily. Jacob."

Lily stopped to peruse his somber face. "Joss, what is going on?"

"Go help your uncle. He'll explain." He gestured toward the back of the stable, from which gasping and grunting emanated, before opening the double doors to a cool rush of April air and leading his animal into the dark courtyard.

Jacob rounded the last stall before Lily and cried out, "Uncle Thad! Our canoe!" He plunked their quilts on top of a crate.

"You hid it from the patrols." Lily rushed to join him as their uncle straightened and turned from the long dugout craft, half wrapped in canvas and covered with straw.

His ample chest beneath his wool vest heaved, and moisture glistened on his flushed face. "As did many others. The Yankees will thank us now. Help me get it outside while Joss is hitching up the wagon."

They hastened to do his bidding, dragging the craft free of its coverings, placing the quilts inside, and spreading out along its length to carry it from the stable. Joss and Uncle Thad hefted it into the back of the waiting wagon. Joss and Jacob climbed in alongside it while Uncle Thad helped Lily onto the spring-loaded seat and gathered up the reins beside her. With a call to the horse from her uncle, the wagon rumbled forward.

He glanced at her as he drove them to the riverfront. "I want you both to wait with the wagon while Joss and I bring in survivors. We'll have to make several trips. Do all you can to make the men comfortable until we can take them to River Rest."

Lily nodded. "We've got the blankets you told us to bring, but won't they need water?"

Joss' deep voice came from behind her. "We brought a couple of canteens."

The warehouses lining the street gave way to the ferry landing. A man waved to them from the riverbank, where several people were launching canoes and skiffs. "Livingston! Over here."

Jacob popped up from the back of the wagon. "It's Sheriff Berry. And Louis."

Jacob sometimes played with the son of Mound City's sole law enforcement official. Berry was not the only discharged Confederate coming to the aid of the burning steamboat's survivors. Lily recognized Captain George Malone and Franklin Barton, formerly of the 23rd Arkansas Cavalry, among the men on the shore. Louis Berry and his cousin fed kindling onto a small fire that struggled against the predawn dampness.

When Uncle Thad stopped the wagon nearby, Berry explained their plan to navigate the dense brush along the shores, by boat and by foot as need be, to rescue the men trapped in the trees. "John Fogleman is doing the same from his place upriver," he said of a local timber baron who rafted logs to New Orleans. "Between us, we'll get as many as we can until the steamers can go out."

"My niece and nephew will wait here. Once we get a wagonload, we'll take them to River Rest." Uncle Thad set the brake and handed the reins to Lily.

Sheriff Berry lifted his hat to her. "We can use the help, miss. My cook is bringin' coffee once the boys get the fire goin'. Young Jacob might want to help gather kindling."

He'd no sooner made the suggestion than Jacob dashed off into the trees.

"Stay close by," Lily called after him.

The wagon shuddered and the horse pranced in place as the men removed the canoe from the back, but she held the reins tight. Then the men, too, disappeared into the shadows, and she was left alone on the seat, shivering against the cold, damp wind. She'd have brought a shawl had she realized what her errand would be.

The chorus of moans, cries, and screams that became audible after the searchers splashed into the river drew her back even straighter than her corset. How could she think for one moment of herself? The treetops out in the flooded water swayed with forms like locusts. Calls for help drifted to her ears. Some men prayed, while others cursed. A quavering tenor sent a chill down her spine. "Rock of Ages, cleft for me..."

A sob rose from the depths of Lily's being. Men were dying. Dying, even now. And was she partly to blame? Why had she not reported the conversation she'd overheard to the provost?

"Boys! Miss Lily!" Sheriff Berry had returned in his canoe, paddling to shore with the craft weighted down almost to the waterline.

Lily wrapped the reins around the brake prong and clambered down from the wagon just as her brother and the Berry boys burst from the woods. They dropped their armloads of sticks on the fire and ran for the riverbank, where they met the sheriff. He grounded the canoe and helped the first survivor disembark.

Lily stumbled to a halt. The man wore nothing save the sheriff's coat tied about his midsection. The current—or other people—must have torn his clothing away. The dim light from the lantern revealed burns all the way down one side of his body. Shreds of flesh hung from his one arm. Lily's hand flew to her mouth, and her stomach threatened to revolt.

"The quilts, Lily!" Her brother leaped into action where she had failed. He ran to the wagon and back again before she could unglue her feet, shoving the load of material against her before he offered the shivering man a covering.

God, help me do what I must. Lily had never volunteered in the Memphis hospitals as many girls from the city had. Her aunt had strictly forbidden it, unwilling for her daughter or niece to be exposed to "indecencies," as she called them. More like, exposed to Union soldiers.

Lily had never argued. She had her own reasons to avoid men.

But Christian compassion demanded her involvement now. These poor souls had nowhere else to turn—at least, until they could be ferried across to the hospitals. She set the quilts on the ground, took up the one on top, and went forward to offer it to the next soldier who staggered toward her in naught but a long, sopping-wet shirt. She averted her gaze as best she could until he was covered.

"Go warm yourself at the fire." She gestured to where the Berry family had a nice blaze going. "The cook has brought a big boiler of coffee."

"Thank you, ma'am." The man stumbled toward the promise of warmth.

Jacob was gaping at a one-legged prisoner of war, the last man from the canoe whom Sheriff Berry helped to hobble their direction. And no wonder, for he was so skinny that every rib stuck out like the folds of an accordion. Had they fed these men at all in prison? Lily hurried forward and slipped her arm beneath the soldier's shoulders.

"You got him, Miss Lily?" the sheriff asked her.

"I've got him."

"Then I'm headin' back out." He was already running toward the river before he finished his sentence.

The urgency of the situation took hold of Lily. Men in this condition would die—if not from their wounds then from the icy shock of the river—if they weren't rescued and cared for immediately.

She offered the emaciated man a tentative smile. "Let me help you to the wagon, and we'll see what we can do about that cut of yours." Lily nodded toward the bleeding gash on his forehead, then glanced back at her brother. "Jacob, bring the blankets."

He followed and placed the quilts on the wagon bed as Lily helped the soldier scoot onto it. She swaddled the trembling man, tucking the edges of the blanket tight around him. "There, now. You'll warm up soon enough. Jacob? Bring some water?"

Her brother scrambled into the wagon to oblige. The soldier's eyes stared past her, hollow and unseeing. Deep compassion washed over Lily. What horrors had he just beheld, to render him as stunned as if he'd endured an artillery bombardment?

"You poor thing." She chafed his hands. Nothing to fear here. Her adolescent brother's grip held more strength. "You didn't deserve this. Not after all you've been through. Where are you from, soldier?"

For a moment, he focused on her, but he did not answer. Even so, she took the opportunity to offer him the tin cup her brother handed her.

"Will you drink some water?" When he still didn't move, Lily lifted the curled metal edge to his lips. She tilted the cup, and he sipped.

He'd no sooner swallowed than he gagged, lurched forward, and emptied what must be a stomach full of river water all over Lily's dress and the ground. She leaped back with a cry.

He coughed and gagged, and she stepped forward again to thump his back. Liquid drooled from his mouth. At last, he found his voice, soft and raspy. "I'm sorry. I'm sorry."

Lily shook her head. "No, I am the one who is sorry. It was stupid of me not to think about all the river water you must've swallowed." Her patting turned into soothing circles. The man began to weep. "Jacob, pour a little more water into the cup."

"But, Sis—"

"For his cut, Jacob."

"Ohhh." With a slow nod, he complied.

"And give me your kerchief."

While her brother was still pouring the water, Louis Berry ran up, out of breath. "Frank Barton just brought in another load. Can I use those blankets?"

"Certainly." Lily's stomach clenched as the boy took the quilts and ran off.

"Where is Uncle Thad? Shouldn't he be back by now?" Handing her the cup, followed by the kerchief from around his neck, Jacob voiced her own worry.

The waters near the shore were treacherous with submerged trees, debris, and unseen eddies. What would they do if Uncle Thad and Joss failed to return?

Lily shook off her anxiety. "I'm sure he's coming. Why don't you run down to the riverbank and see if you can spot him?"

Jacob sprung from the wagon bed with the grace of a panther and scampered off.

Lily dipped her brother's kerchief in the cup of water, then lifted her patient's chin. First, she wiped his mouth, then she flipped the cotton material and dabbed gently at the abrasion on his forehead. The man's clouded gaze now followed her every move with gratefulness. She pressed the kerchief into his hand. "Here. Hold this to your head, and then lie back and rest. We'll take you to our inn in a few minutes."

She was still helping him get settled when Jacob ran back to them.

"Lily! Lily! There's a man near the shore calling for help. I think he's stuck in a whirlpool." He practically jerked her from the wagon. "He's got a door or something with another man on it."

They thundered to a stop on the riverbank. Sure enough, on the other side of a cottonwood tree out in the chute of the river that ran between Mound City and Hen Island, she could make out a man clinging to a door.

His arm was flung over a prone form atop the wood—barely holding it on as an eddy circled them round and round. Every few minutes, the head of the man in the water went under. When it came up, he'd cry for help.

Lily's heart wrenched. She looked around in desperation. No boats approached. Everyone ashore but her and her brother stood yards away at the fire. This man and the one he was fighting so hard to save would drown before anyone else came if she didn't help them.

She bent and unlaced her boots. "Take off your shoes and pants."

"What? We can't go in there! Uncle Thad told us to stay on shore."

"Do as I say, and quickly." She shucked off her own shoes, then glanced up at Jacob, who was still standing there frozen. "Do you want the deaths of those men on our heads?"

Her shouted question galvanized him. He started undressing as she reached under her skirt for the button of her under-petticoat. Then her corded petticoat. They dropped with a *poof* onto the ground.

The dress too.

The voice in her spirit told her it would weigh her down. She hesitated only a second before undoing her bodice hooks.

Jacob was already splashing into the water.

"Wait! Wait for me." Lily shoved her dress down over her hips and tore open her corset hooks. In her chemise, pantalets, and stockings, she bounded after Jacob. "Stay with me. Head for that tree." She couldn't risk her brother's life to save those of strangers. Thankfully, their father had taught both of them to swim at an early age.

She waded until the water encircled her chest in an icy embrace. She gasped, then launched out and swam, parting the dark river with bare white arms. Her stockings were tugged down her calves and off her kicking feet. She and Jacob reached the cottonwood at the same time. They grabbed on to a limb and held on, breathing hard.

Upriver, the burning steamer had floated to the head of Hen Island near Fogleman's Landing.

The door still circled in the nearby eddy. The man clinging to it had stopped calling out for help. The other one didn't move at all. Was he even alive?

"We work our way around, right?" Her brother could hardly get the question past his chattering teeth. He was so young, not nearly a man. Was he strong enough for this?

"Yes, but you don't let go of the tree. Ever. You understand?"

His head bobbed. "But how are we going to get to them?"

"You'll hold on to me, and I'll see if I can get that man to grab my other hand as he comes around." With both of their arm spans fully extended, she should be able to just reach him. Hopefully, the man was still conscious and could help her.

Lily and Jacob moved from branch to branch, sometimes above the water, sometimes partially immersed, crouching, swimming, jumping. What a mercy she'd discarded her dress. Even her chemise billowed around her and caught between her legs, threatening by turns to be whisked away or to drag her down. At last, they made their way down the branch nearest the eddy.

Lily clung on to the end and shouted to the men. "Hey! Over here."

The slumped dark head of the one in the river lifted. His eyes widened.

"I'm going out, Jacob." She eased herself farther into the water, glancing back. "Do *not* let go of the tree…or my hand. Not for anything."

Jacob's eyes were rounder than the soldier's as he nodded. Her poor brother was terrified. But Lily felt only purpose—such as she had not for as long as she could remember. Maybe since before the war. Finally, she was doing something to save someone besides herself.

The sucking motion of the whirlpool hit her sooner than she'd expected. She clamped on to Jacob's hand until her knuckles could tighten no more. He groaned with the strain. The men on the door spun in her direction.

Lily extended her free arm as far as she could. "Give me your hand!"

An agonized expression came over the man's face. Then he thrust the door toward her with the arm he'd used to hold the other man atop it. What was he doing? She had only a second. He'd left her no choice but to grasp for the edge of the wood. But just as her fingertips made contact, a timber came out of nowhere, breaking her hold on Jacob and sending her spinning into the whirlpool.

Chapter Four

A cry ripped from Cade's throat when the timber tore the woman from the boy's grasp and into the same eddy from which he'd been too weak to free himself and James. He'd just about accepted the fact that they would perish within feet of shore. Then someone had called to him, and he'd beheld what surely must be a figment of his imagination—a blond woman in white undergarments, perched in the limb of a tree. Maybe God hadn't abandoned him, after all.

As the water swirled over her head, Cade lunged for her. He hadn't been able to offer her his broken hand. The force of the whirlpool against the fractured bones, not to mention her grasp, would have been more than he could bear. He could never have held on to the door in that kind of pain. But he could now if he crooked his right arm around her neck and kept his hand immobilized—which he did. He pulled her face above water, and she came up spluttering.

"Grab the door."

She did as he said.

The adolescent in the tree was yelling, "Lily! Lily!" His terrified cries rose into an unnatural octave.

Cade had to reassure him. Somehow, he got enough air into his lungs to call out, "I've got her." But now he'd just trapped another person in this vicious cycle of swirling. Once the woman was secure, at least for the moment, he firmed his grip on James.

Lily shoved back strands of hair come loose from her braid to look up at his comrade. "Is he dead?"

"Unconscious. He hit his head on something when he jumped from the boat."

"He's your friend?" Water splashed into her mouth, and she spat and smacked.

Cade nodded. "He's burned bad. Maybe with both of us kicking..." Even as he spoke, the muscles in his arm cramped. He'd had it raised, clinging to the door, for too long. A gripping pain in his right calf corresponded. He stiffened as his face contorted.

Lily threw her arm around him—across burns that would have agonized if his whole body hadn't been numb with cold. Her gesture gave him courage. What kind of woman shed her layers and swam out into a flooded river to rescue a stranger? He wouldn't be the cause of her perishing in the attempt.

"Thank you." For an instant, their eyes locked even as the world whirled by—a bizarre dance, more dizzying than a waltz, for two people meeting under the worst of circumstances.

"Lily!"

Another cry from the boy drew the woman's attention. Her head swiveled. "Don't leave the tree!" The tension in her voice revealed that she was more frightened for the youth than herself.

"Your brother?" Cade rasped.

"Jacob."

"No. Look!" Jacob demanded. He clung to the limb with one hand while in the other he held a broken-off branch.

Lily glanced back at Cade. "It might be long enough for one of us to reach, if we both swim for it. You willing to try?"

"I am, but you have to grab it. My right hand's broken. Probably my wrist too."

Understanding dawned in her eyes. "All right. I'll hold your arm. When we get close, kick when I say kick."

As the eddy swirled them toward the cottonwood, Cade prayed for strength. His body was shutting down. And despite what he'd said about James, for all Cade knew, *unconscious* could be a generous term. If they didn't get out now, it might be too late for both of them. And for their angel of mercy.

"Kick!" Lily yelled and lunged forward, pulling him by the elbow.

Cade kicked and somehow held on to the door with James aboard. When Lily's fingers closed around the branch her brother held out to her, relief jangled through him.

"Pull, Jacob! Pull!" Panic lanced through her strangled command.

The boy's face contorted with effort, and he leaned back on the branch. A groan erupted from his throat and escaped from between his clenched teeth.

The decreased pressure on the door told Cade the moment they'd broken free of the eddy. "We're out!"

"Not yet." Despite Lily's words, her face lit as she drew him near. Jacob held on to her, and she held on to Cade, her bare arm around his neck. A deep shudder punctuated the relief of her impulsive embrace.

He grasped her close, his heart thudding as her soft form reminded him he was alive. But not by much. He held on to her as much to keep from sinking as to celebrate his rescue.

"What's your name?" Her whisper tickled his ear.

"Cade." He couldn't manage any more.

"Cade." She pulled back to study his face. "We have a fire on shore. A wagon to take you to our inn. But you'll have to help us just a little longer. Can you do that?"

For a blonde, she had the deepest eyes. Dark brown? He drew strength from them. He gave a nod.

Paddles splashed. Voices shouted.

Lily turned toward the sounds as a long canoe approached. "Uncle Thad?"

The man on board was her uncle?

A dark shape rose from the front. A big man with a booming voice.

"What are you doing out here, Lily? Jacob! I told you to stay on shore."

"These men were stuck in an eddy, Uncle. They would've drowned." Lily's shivering thickened her words, as though her tongue got in the way, negating her effort to be emphatic.

Blackness swam before Cade's eyes. Not yet. If he passed out…

He focused long enough to understand that the canoe was already loaded and could only hold one more person.

"But we'll come right back," the uncle added.

Cade lifted his head. "Take James."

"No. You've been in the water longer." This time, Lily's reply came out sharp. Did that mean she thought James was dead?

He wasn't taking that chance. "Take him."

A dark head poked around the owner of the canoe. "That's the lieutenant. The one who made sure we was all in trees before he swam off with his friend."

When Lily swiveled toward Cade, he met her eyes. "I had to get him out."

"All right. We'll send your friend." Lily grabbed the door, and she and Jacob floated it toward the canoe. "Jacob and I will stay with you."

As soon as they pulled the door from his grasp, Cade started sinking like an ironclad with a cannonball in its hull. He had no more fight left. But Lily's arms grasped him and lifted his head back above water.

"Help me, Jacob."

More hands clasped his shoulders, his arms. A branch rasped against his waist, its pointy tips sharp as fingernails. Lily and her brother struggled with him toward the tree trunk, where they huddled on a thick branch with their arms around him.

Lily bent her wet head against his. "Stay with us. We can't lose you now. It seems you're a hero, Lieutenant Cade whoever-you-are."

"No." He'd only done what James would have done for him. He wanted to touch her cheek, but he lacked the strength to lift his good hand. "You are."

They returned to shore only to be told that the Berry family had already sent Uncle Thad's wagon filled with former Union prisoners ahead to River Rest. They would have to wait, along with Cade and the other men Joss and Lily's uncle had rescued on their second trip.

Joss and Uncle Thad carried Cade as carefully as possible over to the fire. Meanwhile, in the shadows near the river, Lily wrung out her chemise as best she could with her stiffened hands. Then she hurried into her dress. She kept stepping on the skirt and tripping. Mud stained the hem. Without her corset, the bodice fit poorly, and she was all thumbs, anyway, and shaking so badly that fastening it took twice the time it should. But she didn't give up until she'd secured every last hook. Lily rolled her corset, boots, and under-petticoat into her corded petticoat and hastened to the fire.

Cade lay on an old blanket facing the flames in only a pair of long underwear bottoms. Even though shadows cloaked his back, the raw, burned flesh glowed as red as if heated by the fire. Lily moaned as she sank to her knees. No telling what debris had already embedded in his skin. She pulled her petticoat from her bundle and draped it over him. When they wrapped him in the blanket to place him in the wagon, at least the clean cotton might provide some protection.

She smoothed a lock of dark hair back from his forehead—something she would never have dared to do under circumstances any less traumatic. But those swollen waters had washed away the normal walls of propriety and reserve.

As painfully thin and darkened with a couple of days' growth of beard as his face was, his bone structure hinted he'd been a handsome man. But it was his devotion to his friend, not to mention how he'd put all the other men her uncle had picked up ahead of himself, that drew her to his side.

He moaned softly. "James?"

Lily leaned down, her hand on his shoulder. "Already taken to the inn. Don't worry."

The fingers of his good hand inched across the blanket to grasp her skirt. "Thank you."

"You're welcome."

At least they'd heeded her warning about his broken wrist and right hand, which lay across him with the fingers crooked.

His gaze followed hers. "How bad is it?"

She swallowed hard. "It's swelling."

He convulsed as the chilled state of his body seemed to register. "Lily?" Her name came out from between clenched teeth.

"Yes?" She draped her arm around the top of his shoulders where he wasn't burned. Not that she had much warmth to share.

"I need...a surgeon." Cade trembled violently.

Uncle Thad was accepting a cup of coffee from the Berrys' cook just across the fire, watching them. She withdrew her arm from Cade's shoulders. "I'm sure Dr. Courtner will come as soon as he can. He lives in Marion but serves Mound City." And had served Hopefield, which had once been her home before the Yankees destroyed it. And now, the flooded Mississippi completely covered its remains. Lily put aside those painful memories. "Someone will have sent for him." With any luck, he was already here.

"Not a local doctor. Army surgeon. From Memphis." He gasped out each short phrase softly, but somehow, with the firmest of cadence. He was an officer, after all. He must be used to being decisive.

She frowned. "Dr. Courtner should be skilled enough at treating burns."

"My hand. Has to be set...before it swells...too much."

"I'm sure Dr. Courtner—"

"Please, miss!"

She sat back on her heels. Had she misjudged him? Was this Yankee as cruel as those the commanders in Memphis had sent against them? She met her uncle's gaze across the fire. His thick brows hovered low above his dark eyes as he took a swig of coffee from a tin cup.

"Please," Cade whispered.

Something in his desperation wrapped around her heart. "D–do you want me to see if the ferry will be coming for survivors from this side of the river?" After his dramatic rescue, after all she'd risked, she was not ready to let him go. Who was the selfish one? For he was right—he'd receive better care at the Officers' Hospital at the corner of Front and Court streets. Or at any of the many wartime hospitals in Memphis.

He gave a tight nod. "Yes."

Her chest tight, Lily got up.

Uncle Thad tossed the remaining coffee from his cup and hurried over. "Where are you going?"

"To the landing, to ask about the ferry." She shoved her boots on her bare feet without tying them.

"For him?" He spoke in a low tone and jerked his chin toward Cade. "What makes that one special?"

To be fair, he was only being protective. Her uncle was accustomed to her avoiding men, not coddling them.

Lily looked away from the shivering figure on the ground. "Nothing." Maybe everything, because even with his strange request, she trusted him. "But he's right. Some of these men should be taken to Memphis." When she started away, Uncle Thad caught her arm.

"The wagon will be back in a minute."

"I know." She lifted her chin.

"Don't miss it. We can't wait for you."

"I won't." Lily tugged free and headed for the landing. Her feet had gone numb, sliding around in her shoes, and her legs tingled. She stumbled several times. It didn't help that her skirts dragged without her corded petticoat.

She found Sheriff Berry talking with some local officials at the dock. When she asked him about transporting the critically injured, he shook his head.

"No time soon, Miss Livingston. *Rosedella*, along with all the other steamboats, is helping collect *Sultana* survivors." He gestured to the other side of the river.

In the faint first light of dawn, the boats that had gotten up steam made trips from Memphis to Hen's Island, where the fated steamer had almost disappeared beneath the waters. Rowboats and rafts and people clinging to debris still dotted the river.

"*Sultana?* That was its name?" If tales she'd heard from sailors rang true, hadn't a number of previous steamers also called *Sultana* met the same fiery fate?

Lily wrapped her arms around herself. Her dress now felt as wet as her undergarments. She shivered as the cool wind whipped her skirts about her legs.

"That's right. They're saying over twenty-one hundred souls were aboard. I'd expect the hospitals in Memphis will be filled before anyone from Arkansas can arrive. If you want to care for the wounded at River Rest, you'll have to rely on Dr. Courtner."

How would Cade react to that news? Probably not well. What was so important about his hand, even if it was his dominant one? Men lived without the use of whole limbs—indeed, without the limbs at all. 'Twas an all-too-common thing these days. She was much more concerned about his back. And there would be at least a dozen men at the inn injured worse than him. She squared her shoulders to return to the riverbank, pivoted, and gasped.

A wagon she'd circled earlier had blocked her view of the levee. Scores of bodies wrapped in blankets lay atop it, and from the wagon, the local cabinetmaker unloaded coffins. From the looks of it, all the coffins in Crittenden County. Lily's heart sank as guilt tugged her to a deeper, darker place than a river eddy ever could.

This was her fault. If Cade knew this tragedy had occurred as a result of her silence, he'd call her something other than a hero.

Chapter Five

Cade finally could empathize with the injured men who'd moaned and screamed as they'd been transported in ambulances from the battlefields. Even the short drive into the little town was excruciating, though Lily had made sure they laid him on his good side before she climbed up onto the seat. Every bump jostled his shattered hand and shot pain through his pelvis. The fall on the door when he'd jumped into the water—it must have fractured or at least contused his hip. The icy water had masked the pain until now. And the rasp of material against his burned back grated like sandpaper. Still, he bit back any sound.

Some of the men in the wagon were injured far worse. Their groans and weeping brought anguish to his soul. He shouldn't be lying here among them, once again unable to help. Why had God allowed him to become adept as a surgeon if he was never again to be allowed to use his gifts and training?

Cade insisted the others be taken inside first. It was the least he could do. While Lily's uncle and the black man who accompanied him helped them to the porch and through the front door one by one, Cade propped himself on his elbow. The motion made fire ripple across his shoulder blades, and he quickly dropped back onto his side but not before receiving an impression of a sizable frame inn badly in need of whitewash.

Double verandas ran the length of the front with a smaller porch on the third half story. When it had been built ten or twenty years ago, it probably offered the nicest accommodations this side of the Mississippi. A hanging sign visible from the wagon bed swayed slightly in the breeze, creaking softly. RIVER REST.

These wounded men, broken in body and spirit, would find little rest here. They needed to be in the hospital and to receive immediate care, the latest advances the war had taught doctors. But Lily had told him, with apologies she had no reason to offer, that no steamer would come this morning—and maybe not today at all.

Cade attempted to flex his fingers. He could barely move them even though the numbing effects of the icy river had faded. Maybe the cold water had bought him some time with the swelling, though. How long would it take for this Dr. Courtner to arrive?

"Cade?" Lily spoke from the side of the wagon. Her fingertips grazed his bare shoulder. "Can I help you up? It's your turn."

He grunted and struggled back up onto his elbow. She slid her arm beneath his until he came to a sitting position. The blanket fell away, but her petticoat stuck to the raw flesh of his back. Very gently, she pulled it free. He sucked in a sharp breath. As she draped the cotton undergarment about his shoulders, her lovely face creased with pity. The light of early morning revealed that she was as young as he'd first thought her—younger than him. Early twenties, maybe? Her skin was flawless, her figure petite.

Tears rushed to film his eyes. Why couldn't he have met her a year ago, when he could have swept off his hat and bowed to her in his lieutenant's uniform with its green medical trim, sash, and dress sword? But even then, admiration might not have lit her eyes. For weren't most of the residents in this part of Arkansas Confederates? Another reason he'd have been better off across the river in a military-supervised hospital.

She might have saved him. She might even pity him. But she might still regard him as her enemy. He should be careful.

"You should change out of those wet clothes." His suspicions made his tone sharper than he'd intended. "Get by a fire."

Lily took a step back but quickly came forward to assist again as he struggled to the end of the wagon. "I'm helping get the men situated. Then I'll change."

A slender young woman with her dark hair in a braid hurried out onto the porch. She raised her voice to address Lily. "Mama says all the beds are full."

"Well, find another one. We have one more man."

Lily's uncle appeared behind the girl who must be his daughter. "It's true. We've filled all the rooms not already occupied by guests."

"The guests can check out. This is an emergency. We need their beds." Lily clamped her eyes on Cade with a challenge in them, motioning to him to scoot to the very edge of the wagon. She was not giving up on him. But Cade didn't move.

"Lily, where are they to go?" the big man asked. "All the steamers are busy."

"I don't care. They can take a wagon somewhere or rent a horse from the livery. Now please, Uncle Thad, come help the lieutenant inside."

Cade almost smiled at the determination in Lily's voice. He caught her eye as she turned back to him. "You can put me on the floor."

Her brows drew together. "I'm not putting you on the floor."

Thad lumbered down the steps, the sag of his shoulders portraying his weariness. His daughter trailed at a distance. Pausing beside the wagon, Thad rubbed his chin and surveyed Cade. "Maybe the Foglemans have room. I heard they have taken in some people—and that the doctor is there."

He sucked in a breath to speak, but Lily cut him off. "No. Do you know how far that is? And with no guarantee they'd take you in." She stepped back for Thad to assist. "Help him up to the room next to mine. Jacob and I will move Jacob's bed over there."

"No." The emphatic protest from the dark-haired girl stopped Thad from shouldering Cade's weight. She took a step closer, her hands clasped tight in front of her. Were those pox scars on her face? Hard to tell with her bitter expression creating so many lines. "That's my room."

Thad puffed out a scoffing breath. "That's not your room. Your room is on the second floor."

"But it's the only place I can go for quiet to write and draw. To get away from the customers and…and everyone." She wrung her hands. "Now more than ever."

Cade held in a groan. Maybe he'd just drop onto the dirt street and wait for the horses and wagons to finish him off.

Lily rounded on her cousin. "You're worried about writing and drawing when men are dying?"

"Yankees!" The word screeched from the girl. She might as well have said *vermin* or *demons*. Outright hate contorted her face. "I'd just as soon they all perished in the river."

Cade's stomach muscles clenched. It wasn't enough that he'd been starved in prison, burned off the steamer that was supposed to take him home, and almost drowned in the river. Now he was to accept care from the hands of those who wished him dead? If that was the face of mercy, he'd take his chances on the street.

But Thad's complexion reddened, and he roared at his daughter, "Get out of my sight!"

At least he had the decency to act offended.

The girl hesitated, her mouth opening and closing and tears flooding her eyes. "At least let me—"

"Go!" The man flung his hand toward the inn. "You shame me, girl. I did not raise you to be so hateful."

His daughter turned and scurried away.

Lily touched Cade's shoulder softly, as though she feared his response. "We don't all feel that way, Cade."

Her equally gentle tone indicated he'd find compassion on her face, but he couldn't meet her eyes. Or even bring himself to nod. He'd been treated as less than human for too long to excuse prejudice here, at his most vulnerable, at what was supposed to be the end of his journey.

Thad shook his head. "It's her mother's doing. Run ahead and fix the bed, Lily."

"Yes, Uncle." But she lingered, watching Cade.

Even if Thad was a moderate, this girl came from a family of Southern sympathizers. A community of Southern sympathizers. That kind of loyalty didn't die an easy death. It would take years to burn out. Decades, if not centuries. Whatever bond he thought his rescue had established between them meant nothing.

Only when he still refused to look at her did she turn and go inside.

Lily fed the fire in what was now Cade's room. She'd come over as soon as she'd gotten changed and eaten a bowl of the porridge Martha had prepared for breakfast. She'd brought Cade some, too, but it went untouched on the small table next to Jacob's narrow bed. She'd expected to find Cade lying down, probably on his stomach, but he'd been seated on the edge of the mattress when she'd knocked and entered at his summons. Begrudging summons, judging from his mumbled "come in" and his continued refusal to meet her gaze.

Why was he holding Beth's rudeness against her? Perhaps an explanation was in order.

"I know Beth did not make you welcome, but I hope you can forgive her." She poked another couple of sticks she'd brought over from her room between the small rounded logs on the narrow hearth. "This area might have officially fallen to the Union in '62, but that doesn't mean the local folk surrendered." Satisfied with the orange flames beginning to devour the fodder, she brushed off her hands and glanced at Cade. "Where did you fight?"

"Virginia." He remained bent over, the fingers of his good hand working slowly and tentatively down his swollen right wrist.

Lily gave a grunt of recognition. As she'd thought—he'd know nothing about what had transpired in these parts. And she knew equally as little about him. "And where are you from?"

"Ohio."

She waited until he looked up.

"Cincinnati."

"You were shipped to the Eastern theater." Lily ran her hands over the skirt of her checked work dress. "Where you fought, the rules of traditional warfare would've held sway."

He held her eyes a minute, his dark with pain. Emotional or physical? Certainly, both. "I wouldn't say that."

She nodded. Fair enough. This war had been anything but civil, no matter where it was conducted. "Well, here not so much either."

Cade went back to examining his own wrist.

Lily drew in a draft of air, which, oddly, seemed in short supply. "I say that because the regular Confederate troops got pushed to the far south of the state early in the war. North of the Arkansas River was guerilla territory. The commander of the Mississippi District, Thomas Hindman, called for the raising of independent companies of ten, led by a captain." A captain like Lucky Cecil Duke. The thought of him seemed an intrusion on her conversation with this man who was a stranger but not a stranger. She pushed it away. "Men drifted in and out of regular troops and these partisan bands. Eventually, the Confederates lost control of them. Things got really bad." She swallowed hard.

Cade glanced at her. Something flickered in his eyes.

Lily stuck her hands behind her back. Even though the warmth of the small fire touched her skin, it didn't seem to penetrate. She shivered. "Some of them made their headquarters in these parts...until the Union started making reprisals. They kept lists of anyone known to even have association with the guerillas. The things they did to those families...to whole towns...well, they turned even neutral parties against them."

He blinked at her. "Is that what happened to your family? To you?"

Her feet started forward of their own accord. Better to act than answer. She reached for the pitcher she'd brought in and started to pour some water into a cup, but Cade's voice stopped her.

"No." He gestured to the wide ceramic basin. "Pour it in there."

With a slight frown, she did as he requested.

"Set it on the bed next to me." When she hesitated, he added a gasped "Please."

She settled the basin of cool water on the quilt by his right side. "I'm sorry." How could she have been so insensitive?

"For what?"

"Explaining local politics while you're in pain. I just wanted you to understand Beth." Her sentence trailed off when, with agonizingly slow and careful movements, he laid his hand, fingers curled, in the water.

As he bit back a moan, sympathetic pain lanced through her. Lily's own fingers tangled in the material of her skirt. "Lieutenant? What else do you need?"

His gaze met hers again, sharper this time. "Not to understand Beth. Not to chat about my enemies."

Her breath shuddered from her throat. "I'm not your enemy."

"Is the doctor here?"

She shook her head, more in confusion than denial. "No." And they both knew that up here in the eaves, he'd be the last one seen even when Courtner did arrive.

"The Foglemans...are they Confederates?"

Lily spluttered. Why was he back to that? "John...Fogleman...did not fight for the Confederacy, but he did supply..."

"A sympathizer?"

"Well, yes, but he was in the river this night like every other good man from this shore." Indignation firmed her response. "Or are you forgetting all those who risked their lives to save yours but hours ago? Including myself."

"No. I'm not forgetting." Cade's face twisted, and he started to hold out his good hand, then abruptly lowered it. "If I'm staying here, and the doctor's not coming soon, I'm going to need your help. Unless there's someone else you'd suggest. Someone who doesn't hate Yankees, preferably?"

His mercurial shift back to veiled sarcasm roused her own long-buried humor. Lily lifted her hands. "I'm afraid I'm it. How can I help?"

"Ice. I'm going to need ice."

She nodded. "I can get that." Before she could move, he spoke again in the same flat tone.

"And I'm going to need you to pull my index finger back into place."

"Wh–what?"

"It must be done before the swelling prevents the bones straightening.

And carefully. I don't feel a fragment in the wrist, but that doesn't mean it's not fractured. We'll have to take care not to pull on it when setting the phalange. You'll need to find something about the size of my finger to use as a splint, and some unbleached linen or cotton you can tear into strips to bind it. I'll have to wait for the doctor to assess the metacarpals."

"The what?" Lily's heart hammered. The sudden flow of words after the stoicism he'd exhibited left her addled. And such specific words.

"The smaller bones in the palm—never mind." Cade made a dismissive gesture with his left hand.

"But how do you know all this?" When he leaned forward suddenly, putting his hand to his hip, she stepped toward him. "Are you all right?" What a stupid question. Of course he was not all right. A sudden fear gripped her. He was probably aware of injuries she could have no idea he had. Injuries of the most dangerous kind, those that went unseen. "I'll get the things you need." Although she had no idea how she was to become a nurse, without even a doctor to supervise her.

Or was Cade a doctor? No. He'd fought as a lieutenant—hadn't that man in the canoe said so? But maybe he'd received some medical training before the war. Was he old enough for that? It was the only explanation. That, or perhaps a physician in his family. Because the Confederates would not have held captured medical personnel as prisoners of war. That went against the universal rules of civilized warfare.

He released a puff of air and looked up at her, but his eyes rolled so far beneath the fringe of his dark lashes, she feared he might faint. "Quickly, Lily?"

She jumped into action. Her many questions about this man would have to wait.

Chapter Six

Cade would be the last person on earth right now to judge a man based on his appearance or accent, but both put him on guard against Dr. Courtner—for medical, not personal, reasons—from the moment he arrived late the evening of Cade's rescue. Yet he'd hold his counsel until the stout, white-bearded doctor gave his.

He did, however, ask, "Where are you from, Dr. Courtner?"

"I've lived here most of my adult life, but my parents came from Pennsylvania." Over his wire spectacles, Courtner's faded blue eyes flicked to Cade's. At least he wasn't a Southerner. "You?"

"Ohio."

While the man examined him, Cade attempted to focus on the low-ceilinged room, crowded with shelves of books and pads of drawing paper, dried herbs, and bric-a-brac. In addition to the narrow bed of her brother's Lily had moved in, there was a straight-backed chair before a small chipped desk and a couch of faded green velvet. A painting of the Lady of Shallot hung on the wall next to the window, which was covered by a lace curtain. A woman's rustic retreat—one he'd taken over just as surely as he'd taken over young Jacob's bed.

Where would the boy sleep? With Lily? On the floor?

"The handle of a palmetto fan." The physician chuckled while he examined the splint Lily had fashioned for Cade's finger. "Not a bad job, if I do say so myself."

Cade managed a smile, though the memory of the setting of that once-crooked digit brought anything but amusement. Lily had appeared in more danger of passing out than him. But she'd managed to line up the bones while he held his palm flat against the table. Then she'd quickly wrapped the finger with a strip of linen and reinforced it with canvas—her idea, and quite inventive, given the lack of plaster—before binding the fan handle to his finger with more linen.

"We can be thankful no fragments seem to have been displaced in your wrist, lest you have called upon her to reset your radius as well." The physician clucked his tongue and shook his head. "Bless her heart."

Bless her heart? Obviously, Lily was tougher than she'd let on to folks around here.

"I am, however, more concerned about the potential damage of the fine bones and soft tissues in your hand." Very gently, Dr. Courtner manipulated Cade's palm, making stars twinkle before his open eyes. "It's too swollen as yet for me to judge."

"When it goes down, perhaps…. Well, have you ever tried to set metacarpals?" Even as he asked it, he grimaced. Not from pain but because even young, ambitious doctors rarely attempted such a thing. It would be like working blind.

Or with a broken hand.

"Young man…" Dr. Courtner gave him a scolding glance. "You do not know what you ask."

Oh, but he did.

"No." The physician drew a rolled dressing from his medical bag. "Indeed, once the swelling goes down, the best we can hope is that more aggressive treatment should not be required."

"Aggressive treatment?" The phrase practically croaked out of Cade—he who had performed more amputations than he could count. He had nightmares of piles of limbs and the results of his own "treatments"—the harsh reality of battlefield or prison camp interventions, especially where gangrene was concerned—that once-virile men now had to survive with. But his injury was not a result of a gunshot or shrapnel wound. There wasn't even a compound break.

The elderly doctor patted his good hand. "Don't take on, now. I doubt such measures will be required as long as healing progresses as it should. But I've seen one too many a man forgo surgery only to live with part of their body permanently frozen and in pain to discount the possibility. Later, they regret their caution, their vanity, deeply."

"This isn't vanity. This is my livelihood." Cade ground out the statements. "Everything must be done to restore full functionality—not to reduce it."

"Of course. And it will be. Now let me wrap that wrist of yours." Dr. Courtner waited until Cade slowly extended his arm, and then he set to work. "I'm afraid I've used all my manufactured splints I brought today, but I have a friend I can get more from. When I return, I'll bring both a curved palmar splint and a straight dorsal splint to immobilize the wrist and hand all the way to your fingers. In the meantime, let's ask your hosts if they can provide a flat board to use instead. With your back injury, we'll leave off the sling for now so that you can rest—"

Cade grunted. "You're wrapping that a bit tight."

He got a glare in exchange for his protest.

"And I don't need any splints, although I'll ask for the board."

"Don't need any splints? I'm afraid you don't understand the imperative to keep this arm immobilized, son." Still frowning, Dr. Courtner tied off the linen.

"What I understand is that splints will make the swelling worse, as will these wrappings if they are too tight. And what's imperative is that I exercise this hand as early and as often as possible, or it *will* remain frozen." Cade's cursory tone chafed even his own ears, but his unaccustomed helplessness combined with the elderly physician's antiquated methods created an elixir too bitter—and risky—to swallow.

The man sat back on his chair, his tummy rolling out from beneath his black silk vest. "And just where do you come by this knowledge?"

Cade ducked his head. "The Cincinnati College of Medicine and Surgery."

Dr. Courtner let out a gusty sigh. "Well, that explains your opinionated demands, if not your progressive notions. You served in the war?"

"Thirty-fourth OVI." It was a designation he could speak with pride—and would, regardless of what side this man had been on.

The older doctor rubbed his beard. "A man tends to lose objectivity when it's himself he's treating." But his tone hinted that he was listening now.

Cade's hope rose. "Just let me see how I do without the splints. I read a case in one of my medical books of a man older than me with a hairline fracture three-quarters of an inch above his wrist joint. Crepitus and motion distinct, no displacement. Wrist as swollen as mine, and the bone knit perfectly with no splints applied."

"Which medical book was that?"

A smile tugged on one corner of Cade's mouth. "*A Practical Treatise on Fractures and Dislocations*. 1860."

One of Courtner's eyebrows winged up. "You *are* a young know-it-all, aren't you?"

"I'm not a know-it-all, but I do need to practice again, Dr. Courtner."

"That I understand. We'll do it your way. For now."

Cade's heart surged. "And you'll reexamine my hand again when the swelling goes down?"

"Of course, but I'm not performing surgery on it. And before you ask, I don't know anyone in Memphis who will either." This time, his firm tone brooked no argument.

Cade allowed his shoulders to drop for a moment. He was back to relying on a power greater than himself. The jury was out on how that would turn out. Looked as though he'd have plenty of time to shore himself up with prayers, though.

Dr. Courtner tapped his index finger on his knee. "Now, is there anything else you intend to fight me about?"

"That depends on how you plan to treat my burns." Cade tried to inject a teasing tone into his pronouncement but utterly failed. This was too important.

"Lie down and let me take a look." After Cade struggled onto his stomach, the physician pushed his glasses up on his nose and hovered over him. "Did Miss Livingston debride your back as well?"

The mattress muffled Cade's attempt at a chuckle. "She tried."

"Well, she did a good job of it. I'm going to have to enlist her help as a nurse."

"Good luck with that." Cade had convinced Lily that removing any obvious debris with tweezers and her sewing needle would save Dr. Courtner precious time, but she'd gone so chalky during the procedure that he'd sent her off to bed. For her efforts, he did indeed bless her heart. "Is it too much to hope that you're a proponent of carron oil?"

"Lime water liniment and linseed oil? The stuff the ironworkers used in Scotland?"

"That's it." At least the man knew what it was.

His blowing sound deflated Cade's hopes. "No. Dr. Samuel Gross is the expert on burns." As Cade had feared. Gross had grown up among the Pennsylvania Dutch and earned his degree in Philadelphia—probably not far from Courtner's family. "He proved that the creamy consistency of white paint mixed with linseed oil diminishes fluid loss."

Cade almost came off the bed. "But the lead in the paint can be toxic."

"Easy, son." Dr. Courtner placed a steadying hand on his shoulder. "Tense as you are, I'd be concerned about contracture."

Was that his attempt at a joke?

"I won't live long enough to worry about my skin healing too tight if you kill me first by painting it with lead. The burns cover too much of my back. It can't be done!" His voice rose louder than he'd intended, not just cross but commanding.

Was this how Dr. Courtner had treated all the men in Mound City? Cade had to get on his feet—and quickly.

A rapping at his door prevented the physician's reply. "Yes?" The man's rather testy response brought the door open a crack, with Lily's anxious face peeking in.

At least Cade was somewhat decent now. The doctor had helped him into a pair of army-issue trousers the Sanitary Commission had delivered, and soon, bandages would wrap his torso.

"Is everything all right, Doctor?" Lily asked.

"No, everything's not all right." The older man huffed. "This uppish young man thinks to instruct me on how to conduct business I've been conducting since before he was out of swaddling."

Cade couldn't back down on this. "It must be carron oil." He spoke in a soft but firm voice.

Dr. Courtner didn't bother to lower his. "I don't have carron oil mixed up!"

"Then give me what supplies you do have, and I'll mix it." He levered himself onto his good elbow. "For myself and everyone else."

The older man waved with so much vigor it was clear he would have pushed Cade flat if he wasn't injured. "Stay down! I'll go prepare it." Dr. Courtner shoved to his feet and stomped across the room, muttering under his breath. He jerked the door open and glared at Lily. "I'd suggest you sit with *Doctor Palmer* lest he attempt to do himself more harm than he thinks I'm going to do him."

"I'm sorry..." A *V* of a crease between her fair brows, Lily looked from Dr. Courtner to Cade. "*Who?*"

———————————◆•◆———————————

"So he's a doctor?" Standing with Lily in the foyer, Beth handed her the tray of beef broth and bread she'd prepared.

"Apparently." The revelation still stunned Lily.

She'd sat with Cade until Dr. Courtner had finished applying the dressings Cade had requested—or demanded. He hadn't argued when the older physician instructed her to change the strips daily, though Dr. Courtner had said a lot about granulation and sloughing, which made just enough sense for her to cringe. When she'd walked him out, he'd shown her where he'd left extra bandages and liniment in their storeroom.

"What kind of doctor?" Beth's eyes narrowed. "What else do you know about him?"

"Only that he's from Ohio."

"So he *is* a Yankee."

"Of course he's a Yankee." Lily shifted the cumbersome tray to her hip.

"I mean, he was in the army, right?"

"I—I don't know, Beth. I assume so." Her cousin fired off questions with the persistence of a Gatling gun, some she longed to pose to the man herself. But only after he was fed. "I should take this to him, see if he'll eat some before he sleeps."

He'd been so exhausted from the painful treatment of his injuries, her heart had wrenched. And yet, he'd emphatically refused the dose of morphine Dr. Courtner had offered. The physician had also showed all the women where he'd left them a vial and told them how much to administer should any of the men need a dose during the night.

Beth's lower lip drew up in a moment of indecision. "Maybe I should take it."

"Why?" Suspicion overflowed the tiny word, but surely her cousin wouldn't be interested in a Yankee. Even if he was a handsome doctor.

Beth glanced upstairs, her lashes fluttering. "I was rude to him earlier. If he spends his life saving people, he can't be all bad, can he? Maybe I should apologize."

"Yes, you should. But not now." Lily mounted the stairs before Beth could get ahead of her. She climbed the steps fast, without looking back.

What was this strange protective instinct? Was that normal when you'd saved someone's life? Cade should know...not that she could ask him.

She knocked softly and found Cade just as she'd left him, on his stomach with his right arm bent at the elbow and secured on the board they'd found to support his wrist. His eyes opened as she approached but just as quickly closed again.

"I brought beef broth and bread. You must be hungry."

"Can't move."

Lily slid the tray onto the bedside table and drew the chair close. "I can help."

"Please go."

She closed her fist against her heart as if to draw out the unexpected splinter of pain. "How long since you've eaten?"

No response.

Lily sat down and folded her hands in her lap. The gray shadows of evening lengthened as the sun set behind the inn. A mourning dove called softly from the eaves. The sound calmed her. She leaned forward. Was that a tear easing from one corner of his eye?

If her heart twinged before, it threatened to burst now. Of course he didn't feel like eating. Or speaking. The pain of his back, arm, and hip—for Dr. Courtner told her that might be injured as well, and Cade should remain abed to allow it to knit—must be nothing beside the pain in his heart. Lily longed to absorb it into herself. She knew only one thing that might help. She'd long since given up on praying for herself, but maybe God would honor her prayers for another, for a man like Cade.

She rested her hand on his shoulder and closed her eyes as she did so she wouldn't lose her courage if he looked at her in surprise or irritation. "Father…" she began. Lily swallowed. Her throat was dry, and the intimate address didn't seem to fit. She tried again. "God, I lift Cade before You now. He's been through so much. Much more than any human should. And he's in pain, and I know he must feel alone, when he just wanted to go home." Her voice broke. *Home.* This inn was not her home either. She couldn't remember the last time she'd truly felt safe and at peace. "But I ask that You give him rest and relief and comfort. And that he knows we will take care of him. Help him to heal quickly and thoroughly so he can go back to whatever it is that You would have him do. In Jesus' name. Oh, and maybe help him eat something. Amen."

When Lily opened her eyes, another tear had tracked from Cade's, and his mouth trembled, but then it twitched upward.

"I've never met anyone so convincing."

She drew on all her remaining boldness to wipe the trail of moisture from the side of his nose. Then she smiled back. "Does that mean you'll eat?"

"Don't think I can sit all the way up again right now, but I'll try if you help me."

She stifled a tiny laugh. "I bet that's hard for you to say."

"You have no idea."

"Not really, but I'd love to know more." Lily reached for a pillow, and when he lifted himself on his good arm, she slid it under his head. In that fashion, he remained mostly on his stomach but facing her enough that she might offer him some food.

"Can the questions wait?"

"Of course. But at least I understand now why you were so worried about your hand." And at least her prayer had gotten him talking to her. Perhaps it was already working. She gestured to the tray. "Broth or bread?"

"You could dip it."

She tore off an inner morsel of bread and sopped up some broth with it. "I should tell you, Beth prepared this for you. She meant it by way of apology. She was going to bring it to you herself."

Cade's eyelids sagged as he let out a little breath. "Thank you." He spoke both words with soft but distinct emphasis.

Cupping the bite, Lily leaned forward, then hesitated. He opened his mouth, and she slid the food between his lips. The motion was oddly disconcerting. It shouldn't be. Should it? She kept talking to distract from the flush that must surely be spreading on her cheeks. "She's not all bad. People don't treat her very nicely. Men especially."

The irony of that statement hit her as she prepared another bite. She could say the same for herself—for a totally different reason.

"Because of her scars?"

"Yes. She's a very private person. She hides up here whenever she can." Lily offered the next pinch of bread.

He chewed and swallowed without responding.

"I'm sorry. You said you didn't want to talk."

"I said I didn't want to answer questions. I don't mind if *you* talk. And…tell your cousin I'm sorry to have taken her space."

Lily shook her head. "There's no need for apologies. Except maybe hers." When she gave him a third bite, a tiny trickle of broth squeezed over his lower lip. Her fingers darted out to wipe it before she thought.

When Cade's gaze met hers, she quickly drew her hand back, and standing, she smoothed it against the cloth napkin. She blinked quickly as she glanced out at the hazy gray sky. "Would you like some water?"

"I should drink some water."

She returned to his side, the glass in her hand. But getting the water into his mouth was even more challenging than the bread had been. It required sliding her free hand beneath his jaw on the pillow side to help him straighten, then pressing the rim of the glass to his lips still somewhat sideways. But with slow, steady swallows, and her tilting the cup a corresponding amount, he almost drained the contents.

"Good." A smile of satisfaction settled on Lily's lips, and this time, she used the napkin to wipe his.

Cade's head sagged back on the pillow. "I'm done." His statement came out on a breath that sounded as though it could be his last.

Poor man. "Do you want me to take the pillow?"

"Leave it."

"All right. I'll be across the hall if you need anything. Just call out. I'll also leave the…" When soft breathing issued from behind her, Lily turned back from straightening the tray.

Doctor Cade Palmer's lashes made a dark crescent against the sunken space above his high cheekbones. His lips had parted slightly. She smiled again—until he jerked in reflexive pain. Unfolding a sheet from the foot of the bed, she spread it over him lightly. Then, after stirring up the fire one more time, she went to the door.

Exhaustion called for her to shed her corset and her layers and finally warm herself under her own covers. Not that she'd rest well, with the way her brother kicked in his sleep. And she'd probably get up to check on Cade during the night.

As she passed across the landing, a moan from the floor below drew her up short. Somehow, she'd been so focused on one particular patient that she'd forgotten they had a whole inn full of them.

Chapter Seven

"Fire! Put out that fire!"

The terror-stricken cry levered Lily to a right angle. As the covers slid off Jacob, he groaned a protest.

She shook his shoulder. "Get up. There might be a fire."

Had she left a lamp burning in Cade's room? Had a spark popped out from the hearth? She bolted from bed and across the floor, snatching open the door to the landing. No smoke, no flames greeted her. But the entrance to Cade's room stood ajar, and voices came from inside.

Lily halted on the threshold, her mouth dropping open as her cousin turned toward her. Unlike Lily, Beth wore a modest wrapper over her gown, and her hair had been neatly plaited into its customary night braid. The fire on the hearth had burned down to soft orange embers, and yet, the faint moonlight from the window illuminated Beth's anxious expression.

"What are you doing in here?" Lily gasped out the question.

"That's what I asked her." Cade's voice rumbled from the bed, though in the shadows, she could only make out a dark form as he propped himself up on one side. "I thought at first it was you."

Beth tossed her hand in his direction. "He was moaning, calling out. I came to check on him."

"I wasn't," Cade said. "I woke to find her standing over me."

Golden light flickered into the room along with the pungent scent of kerosene as Jacob arrived with an oil lamp. Lily rested her hands on his shoulders to direct him to the bedside table, where he placed the light. "Thank you, Jacob. As you can see, there's no fire. You can go back to bed."

With a grunt, her brother turned and shuffled out.

Lily faced Cade. "You must have been dreaming. I heard you shouting about fire."

Cade's expression clouded. "Maybe I was." When he struggled to a sitting position, Lily hurried over to assist. Yet the moment he got both feet on the floor, he aimed a glare at Beth. "But she was already in here when I woke. How did she get up here that fast?"

Beth backed up a step. "I told you, I heard you moaning. My room is right under yours."

"I don't believe you. After drugging me, did you come to finish me off?"

"What?" Lily and Beth both asked at the same time.

Cade's gaze swung to Lily, his eyes narrowed. "Which one of you put morphine in that broth?"

Lily laid her hand over her throat. "What are you talking about?"

"The broth. I know it was drugged."

"That's ridiculous. You had three, maybe four bites of bread soaked in it."

"And if I'd eaten it all, I would never have known this girl was in my room." Cade pointed a shaking finger at Beth. "I never have nightmares like those."

A puff of air escaped Lily. "You've never almost died in a steamboat explosion either. Why would you even suggest we might be capable of something so horrible? What reason would we have to drug you?"

"Maybe you should ask the one who said she'd rather all the Yankees had drowned." Cade's cold accusation drew a gasp from Beth, who whirled and fled the room. Her soft crying trailed her down the stairs. Lily had sucked in a breath to scold Cade when he cut her off. "Tell me—in all honesty, do you share her sentiments?"

Her spine stiffened. "How can you ask that? After the prayer I prayed for you?"

Cade stared at her a moment before he blinked rapidly. Letting out a groan, he scrubbed his face with his good hand.

When he swayed, Lily put her hand on his shoulder. "Get back in bed. You've been through too much, and you're not yourself." At least, she was going to choose to believe that. But when she attempted to take his arm to help him lie down, his left hand flew out and grasped her wrist.

"How can I trust you? How can I trust any of you?" Suspicion twisted his features.

Lily's chest constricted, and she blinked back the tears that sprang to her eyes. "How can you trust the woman who risked her life to save yours?" She'd meant the question to be indignant, but her voice wavered.

He released his grip on her, turning his face away. "Please...just leave me alone."

------------◈------------

He was an idiot. He'd sent both Livingston girls from his room deeply offended the night before. Lily had warned Cade about the reasons for Beth's sensitivity, which should have been enough to moderate his tone if not his suspicions. But there was something in the young woman's manner that raised his defenses. And the dark world he'd battled last night, so unnatural in its lurid details.... The phantoms he'd fought had seemed so real, as if he faced them in another realm. He'd never had nightmares so vivid. But could Lily be right? He'd never lived a nightmare before, only witnessed the carnage of other men's.

The silent, composed manner in which Lily had heeded his command to leave still haunted him. Tears and protests would have been preferable. Before she'd departed, taking the lamp with her, her face had gone as white as if he'd struck her. As if he'd betrayed her trust. But how could that be? He hardly knew her. Couldn't she understand—his world had been blown to smithereens? If he couldn't trust his own government to safely deliver him home after almost dying for the Union in a prisoner of war camp, how could he trust anyone in this riverside nest of Rebels?

Yet he found himself listening for Lily's step on the landing all the next morning. He got up long enough to relieve himself and use the water remaining in his basin for drinking and washing. Pain and exhaustion drove him back to bed, the dressings pulling tight across his back.

Cade stifled the growl that rose from deep within. His prison might be more comfortable now, but he was every bit as captive as he'd been at Andersonville—and far more helpless. He could do nothing to speed his own healing process. And what of the men below? How was James faring? Fragments of murmured conversations and footsteps from the second floor confirmed he was not as alone as he felt, but he had to check on their welfare. One way or another.

If he could talk to other survivors, maybe they could piece together what had happened to cause this tragedy. Had it been a faulty boiler? The overcrowding? Soon enough, someone would investigate. Findings would be reported. The truth would come out, and justice would be served. But for now, he would settle for hearing James' voice and seeing the comfort of a familiar face.

At last, a little before noon, someone climbed the steps to the third story and knocked on his door.

"Come in." Cade prepared his contrite expression. Lily was his only link to the outside world, and she'd shown him nothing but kindness. He owed her an apology for the paranoia that had overwhelmed his better judgment in the depths of the night.

But it was Jacob who stepped through the door with a glass of milk and a bowl of what smelled like oatmeal on a tray. "Sorry this took so long. Had a lot of people to feed."

And he was last on the list, by his own doings. Cade's already empty stomach shriveled just a bit more. "Where's Lily?"

The boy slid the tray onto the table. "She said maybe you'll trust that a twelve-year-old won't poison you."

"I never said..." Cade blew out a breath as he worked his way off his stomach—a process slower than the movements of General McClellan's army. "Never mind. Thank you for breakfast." Or the midday meal. Whatever it was. "So she's not coming?"

"She's with the doctor."

"Dr. Courtner?" He'd returned already? "Lily is assisting him?"

"Yep." His errand dispatched, Jacob turned to go.

"Wait," Cade gasped. He wobbled as he came to a sitting position, breathing heavily. Dr. Courtner had agreed to the carron oil for Cade, but he'd never said he'd use it for the other men. "I need you to take a message to her."

Jacob wavered on the threshold. "They'll come up later."

"Later will be too late. I need you to tell your sister something where Dr. Courtner can't hear."

A frown knit the boy's forehead.

Cade waved him closer. "Trust me. This is important." When Jacob finally approached with halting steps, Cade explained how Lily needed to watch for the application of what looked like heavy white cream to patients with extensive burns. "If she sees that, she's to come tell me. I'll instruct her how to prepare the carron oil."

"What if she won't come? She seemed pretty mad at you after you yelled at her last night. She kept sniffling under the covers. Kept me awake for an hour." Jacob tucked one corner of his mouth into a wry bow as he eyed Cade with unveiled disapproval.

So he *had* made her cry. Cade closed his eyes briefly against the sinking sensation. "Tell her I was an idiot." He looked back at the boy. "And I'm sorry I took your bed and ruined your sleep."

"Yeah. Fine." Jacob's face cleared, and he sprang away before Cade could say anything else.

After his boot steps faded on the stairs, Cade reached for the oatmeal. The comforting scent of cinnamon sprinkled on top put him in mind of his mother's kitchen, and his chest squeezed as tight as it had with remorse over Lily. He ate several bites until his stomach threatened to revolt. Then he drank some milk and eased himself back down. What he wouldn't give to lie on his back.

He hadn't seen his mother in three and a half years. Would she even recognize him now? Did she have any idea where he was?

He'd been angry at her when she'd not shown the same pride over his decision to become a doctor as she had when, as a boy, he'd told his parents he wanted to be a preacher. He'd expected disappointment from his father, but he'd hoped Mother would support him. And she had written regularly after he'd enlisted. Said she prayed for him. After all he'd been through, the service he'd given to his country, surely she would be proud now. Would welcome him home with open arms and understand why he needed to help heal the broken people in the wake of this war.

Thinking of which, what was taking Lily so long? Had Jacob given her the message? Did the fact that she didn't appear mean Cade worried without cause? Or…maybe she was still ignoring him. Surely, either way, she'd understand the importance of his summons and at least come reassure him.

Unless the older physician had somehow convinced Lily his treatment was superior. What if Dr. Courtner was applying a second coat of toxic white paint to James even now?

With a groan, Cade rolled to his side. The movement rippled a path of fire across his back. He sat a few minutes on the side of the bed, his throbbing head resting in his cupped palm. The light through the window punctured his eyeballs like a bayonet through a training dummy. His fingers came away from his forehead sticky. The sun had come out and must be beating down on the roof hotter than anticipated for the end of April. This room, it was too stuffy. He stood and swayed on his feet. Could he make it down the stairs?

One step at a time. Though he must look like the walking dead.

At the top of the landing, he leaned against the rail, his chest rising and falling with short, rapid breaths. The narrow steps loomed close, then impossibly far away.

He ventured down one step, then another. With longer pauses than forward movement, he made it to the landing. From there, he could just peer into the hall below, but his head spun so badly he had to close his eyes. He'd performed surgeries under artillery bombardment and survived the horrors of Andersonville and the sinking *Sultana*. He would not let a spell of vertigo prove his undoing.

"Cade?"

His eyes flew open as Lily rushed toward him, dropping her armload of linens on the bottom step.

"What are you doing?" She mounted the steps until she reached his side, placing her hand under his left elbow. "Dr. Courtner said you shouldn't be out of bed, much less coming downstairs."

"Did you get my message?" His attempt to speak with authority came out in a raspy whisper.

"About the liniment? Yes, but it wasn't important."

His eyelids shot open at that. "*Nothing* is more important."

"Your health is, for one." She shook her head, the back of it encircled by her heavy blond braid. "Look at you—you're sweating. Do you have a fever?"

He pushed the hand she attempted to raise to his forehead away. "I'm fine. I need you to listen to me."

"No, you listen to me. You need to let me help you back upstairs. No one is doing dressings right now. I was helping Dr. Courtner identify and move the men most in need of hospital treatment."

Cade blinked at her. Obviously, the good doctor did not consider him among that number—what with the lack of Memphis surgeons able or willing to operate on his hand. But maybe those going across the river would receive the care they needed. He let out a deep breath, his shoulders sagging.

Lily's expression softened. "I'm sorry, Cade. He's already gone with them to the ferry."

Then he had a little time, at least, to assess the welfare of the remaining men. Cade grasped her forearm. "Take me to James. I need to see him."

Lily's lashes fluttered, and she withdrew almost imperceptibly. "I...I'm afraid that won't be possible."

"I can make it." He didn't wait for her to agree but started down the steps.

"No, Cade." Lily allowed him to pull away, though her tone pleaded with him to hear her out. "He was one of the men Dr. Courtner took. He feared the onset of pneumonia."

James was gone before Cade even got to check on him? Pneumonia coupled with his friend's severe burns could prove deadly. Anguish hit Cade with the force of a breaker. His face crumpling, he turned to look back at Lily. His foot slipped on the worn wooden tread. His legs went out from under him, and he came down hard on his back. Pain exploded through him with the force of a mortar shell. The scream that echoed in his ears couldn't be his own.

———————◆◆◆———————

"Sabotage."

The word slipped from Lily's lips without a conscious decision to speak it aloud. And with it, a crushing guilt compressed her chest. How could she for one moment blame Cade for his suspicions? He was here because of the worst possible kind of betrayal, and she had not stopped it when she'd had the chance.

At a moan from the man on the bed, she snapped the newspaper closed. She laid it on the table and leaned forward to remove the now-tepid cloth from Cade's forehead. "I'm sorry. I didn't mean to wake you." She pressed her fingers to his cheek and neck as his eyelashes fluttered open. He squinted in the evening light. Finally, his skin did not flame beneath her touch. "You seem cooler. How are you feeling?"

"Thirsty."

Lily rose and poured him some water, returning to help him drink. He drained the cup. "I think your fever has broken." Her relief almost dislodged the load of guilt about what she'd just read.

"Told you a fever could come and go after severe burns and that it didn't necessarily mean an infection." A touch of smugness in his statement teased a smile from her as she arranged the pillows for him to lie on his good side while propping his injured arm out flat.

"But if it had…" Her brows pulled down.

"It didn't."

"It still could." Lily couldn't let herself off so easily. If she hadn't allowed her hurt feelings to triumph over her Christian charity, he never would have wandered from his room in the first place.

Cade made the frustrated sound that usually meant he wanted to use his injured hand. Accompanying it, he rolled his eyes. "I don't know how long I've been in and out of it—"

"A little more than twenty-four hours."

"—but I do remember lots of ice and cold compresses. And maybe some more prayers?" A faint smile tugged his lips, and Lily averted her gaze. "You've taken the best care of me, Lily. Thank you. I don't know how the other patients are faring without you."

Did his gratitude mean he'd decided to trust her? Flushed by his praise, Lily busied herself rewetting and wringing out the cloth. "Our servants, Martha and Mika, are helping tend them. And Dr. Courtner, of course. He came back yesterday. Remember, he changed your dressings after you fell?" She glanced over her shoulder.

Cade's lips pulled to one side. "With carron oil, I think I recall."

"Yes. I made sure there was enough for all the dressing changes, so you can rest your mind about that. I'm just thankful you did not hurt your back worse...or your hand." She winced at the memory of him falling. Cade's bandages had protected his burns from further significant damage—except for pain that had to be excruciating.

He grunted. "Happened too fast to even try to brace myself."

"That's a mercy, then." Lily wiped her hands on her skirt. "Well, I suppose I should go. I can send Jacob up with supper in a bit. Is there anything I can get you first?"

Despite her reassurance to Cade, Martha and Mika were run off their feet, struggling to tend to the needs of the men and manage the kitchen as well. They'd seemed to understand she felt responsible for Cade's setback, but now that he'd improved, she shouldn't test their grace.

He tipped his head toward the newspaper. "You can tell me what you were reading in that. I'd ask you to hand it to me, but I couldn't turn the pages."

"Oh. Nothing important. Just passing the time while sitting with you." Lily lifted one shoulder in a half shrug while her other hand snuck out and tugged the newspaper behind her skirt.

Cade drew his mouth flat. "I deserve to know, Lily."

Her heart sinking, she rolled her lower lip between her teeth. "Don't you think it might be better to worry about all that once you're stronger?"

"The wondering is the worst thing. Go on. Tell me." He jerked his chin again. "What did you learn about the *Sultana*?"

"Well, um…" She unfolded the paper and pretended to scan it. Perhaps some news she'd heard earlier that day would distract him. "Dr. Courtner told me the first group of survivors would be leaving at five o'clock this evening on the *Belle St. Louis*. Over two hundred and fifty of them from Indiana, Ohio, and Michigan. I guess it will be a three-day journey to where they have to muster out?" She chanced a peek over the paper.

"At Camp Chase, Ohio. Yes." His eyes darkened and stared past her, unfocused. "I can't imagine how they had the courage to get on another steamer."

"Right, well…I heard some from Tennessee wanted to walk home instead. I don't understand why everyone can't be released in a less official way."

"That's the army for you. What of the death toll?"

Lily took a shaky breath. "They don't know yet. Bodies are still washing ashore." And steamers were firing their cannons over the top of the wreckage to try to dislodge more, though she'd not be mentioning that. "They do think there were over nine hundred and fifty survivors."

"More than I thought. But if my estimate of the number on board was anywhere near correct, that still means over half perished. Over a thousand." Cade's eyes briefly closed. "I don't think there's ever been a maritime disaster in our country on this scale before. Never. Not even at sea."

"And yet, with hundreds of thousands of lives lost in the war, and our president just assassinated, people are so weary of death and loss, they may prefer to turn away in denial." She didn't miss the way his attention flashed to her when she said *our president*.

"They cannot do that." The fire that lit behind his eyes provided a glimpse of the medical officer who'd given orders in the surgical tent. "These men had already sacrificed everything for their country. And then, when they were most vulnerable, someone's carelessness or greed exacted the ultimate price."

Lily's heart ached. She moved the paper aside. "I agree."

He puffed out a sigh. "Any speculation yet about what caused the explosion?"

Her shoulders tightened, but she attempted to keep her voice casual. "The Memphis papers say it was no one's fault. They only asked why other boats left Vicksburg without prisoners when the *Sultana* was overcrowded."

"And yet you're not holding a Memphis paper." He focused on the print of the circular facing him. "The *Cincinnati Commercial Tribune*?"

"All sorts of newspapers end up here in the inn."

"Sit down, Lily. Tell me what it says. Please." When she hesitated, he added, "I heard what you said as I was waking up. Sabotage?"

The word spoken out loud sent a tremor through her. Or maybe it was his piercing eyes. She lowered herself into the chair and turned a page with a shaking hand. "Apparently, a William Rowberry, the *Sultana*'s first mate, said the boat was running steady on little steam. He…mentioned a torpedo shaped like a lump of coal." She swallowed hard. The description corresponded to the plans she'd overheard a week or two before the explosion.

…leavin' the coal barge north of Memphis…

Once they shovel it in…

Cade's gaze held her hostage. Could he tell she was hiding something? Finally, he frowned. "That's awfully convenient."

"What do you mean?"

"Well, the first mate would be responsible for distributing the weight on board. We stopped in Memphis, and the captain paid some of the men to help unload over two hundred hogsheads of sugar from the hold. The hurricane deck was literally sagging under so many men, and yet, no one ever told any of them to move below."

So he wasn't upset about a possible coal torpedo? Lily cocked her head. "But what's convenient about it?"

"Sabotage would free Mr. Rowberry of responsibility."

"Oh." Her shoulders relaxed. "Well, I suppose the truth will come out soon."

Cade followed her movements as she folded the paper and stood up.

"Why do you say that?"

"The general in command at Memphis issued an order that forms a three-man team to investigate what happened."

And she could only pray Mr. Rowberry was lying.

Chapter Eight

After Lily left, Cade lay on his side and watched the light from the window turn from yellow to pink. For the first time since his arrival, peace settled over him. The article she'd read about potential sabotage didn't ruffle him... but it had her. Why? Could his sense of security be so important to her that she'd attempt to keep the report from him? What else could it be?

He'd thanked her for her care of him, but had he apologized for accusing her of drugging him? The notion seemed ludicrous now. He would laugh if it didn't shame him so much. But could he really have been so traumatized he'd imagined the effects of morphine? Regardless, it couldn't have been Lily. He could only throw himself upon her abundant grace.

Where did one get grace like that? Was it from her faith? The prayer she'd spoken over him when he'd first attempted to push her away because of their differing loyalties had not only shown him she was a true believer, but it had smashed the defensive wall he'd attempted to retreat behind. He'd never heard anyone pray like that, so heartfelt. No flowery words. Just sweet sincerity. How had he doubted her again after that? Even if she'd supported the Confederacy, their shared belief in God should bridge sectional allegiances.

Could her compassion also stem from understanding, as one who had also suffered? What had happened to her parents? When he'd asked about them before, she'd avoided answering.

After Jacob brought Cade's tray and left him to manage his soup the best he could, Cade found himself listening for her footsteps with increasing anticipation.

At last, she knocked and entered bearing a basin in one hand and a folded square of white cotton with a small tapestry box nestled in the other arm.

Cade lifted his head from the pillow. "What do you have there?"

"A peace offering, of sorts." A brief frown flitted over her face as she set everything on the table next to his supper tray.

"Looks like some sewing to me."

"It is." Lily puffed out a breath, then turned to him. "I've decided if I want you to trust me, I have to trust you."

Cade struggled to sit up and voice his apology. "Lily, I—"

"I take on sewing for Union officers."

His mouth dropped open. "I'm sorry…what?"

"I don't hate Northerners. In fact, I tried to convince my brother not to fight for the Confederacy."

Cade's mind spun. "Jacob?" He'd heard the Rebel armies were taking boys as young as twelve or thirteen in the last months of the war, but he couldn't imagine Lily's little brother shouldering a musket.

"No, silly. My twin, Hampton." She spoke evenly, though her stiff posture betrayed the effort her composure cost her. "But I failed, and he died at the Battle of Prairie Grove."

He had no idea where that was, but his heart went out to her. "I'm so sorry, Lily."

She inclined her head, then tucked stray hairs back into her braided and coiled bun. "Yes, well…. Do you have a brother?"

He offered a brief smile. "Only a sister—Amelia. And in these times, I've been thankful for that. She's married and helps her husband run his silk importing business, but the fact that she still lives near our parents gave me much comfort during the war."

Lily smoothed her neatly cinched bodice. What a small waist she had. "My uncle's family might have supported the Confederacy, but my parents didn't believe in slavery or secession. I don't think Hamp would've ever considered going off to fight for the South if Cecil hadn't—" She clamped her lips closed over the name, drawing Cade's immediate curiosity. But her redirect as she plopped onto the bedside chair prevented inquiry. "Anyway, they remained neutral as long as they could."

"But eventually...which side did they end up on?" That much, he had to ask.

"On the heavenly side." Lily pressed her lips together after she spoke, staring at him with the same reserve she'd used when speaking of her brother.

Compassion from suffering, then.

The war had threatened to take his humanity, and now, his livelihood, but she'd lost most of her family. He sat with his legs touching her skirt, close enough that he could finally use his good hand to cover hers. "Do you...want to tell me what happened?"

"Not really." She frowned at their joined hands, her striped bodice rising and falling with shallow breaths. "I hope that's enough for you to realize I'm not the enemy."

"I know you're not the enemy." He squeezed her hand. "Lily, I was a fool. I've seen the addictive effects of morphine on men before. My fear of that made me overreact. Can you forgive me?"

She met his gaze. "Under the circumstances, your caution is completely forgivable. And it's true that Aunt Susanna and Beth are Southern sympathizers. Uncle Thad—he tries to be moderate as my parents were, but his wife and daughter make it hard for him." Averting her eyes, she slid her hand from beneath his and made a show of smoothing her skirt. "I'm trying to save up enough money for me and Jacob to make it on our own, so it will help if I can get some sewing done while I'm sitting with you."

The fact that she wanted to sit with him left him speechless. Cade nodded.

"I think you said you needed to exercise your hand. You were too ill when Dr. Courtner examined it, but do you want to try now? I brought ice in that basin." She tipped her head toward the table.

Cade took a moment to catch up to her abrupt change of topic. "You remembered." As much as he appreciated that, he was loath to relinquish the discovery of Lily's background.

"Of course I remembered. May I?" She indicated the tied-off end of the wrapping at his forearm. When he nodded, she drew his injured limb onto her knee to begin the careful process of unwinding the strips that secured the board.

"What is your plan for you and Jacob?" he asked as she set to work unbinding the arm itself.

Lily flashed him a surprised look.

"I can't talk very well while you're doing that, but it would distract me if *you* did."

He didn't need to explain his nervousness. She offered him a gentle smile. "I have an old friend from Hopefield in Memphis. She has a seamstress shop. If I can get up enough money to see us settled in the city, I'm hoping she'll honor her previous offer of a job."

A good plan. Lily would find kindred spirits in Memphis. But… "Hopefield? Was that where you lived before coming here?"

She gave a brief nod, then straightened. "Perhaps you should sit at the table. It would give your arm more support."

"Good idea." With painful slowness, Cade pushed himself off the mattress. "Do you go to Memphis often?"

"Not often, but I need to make a trip soon. I haven't seen my friend for a while." She moved the tray and her sewing to the bed, then helped him to the chair.

He swallowed a groan as he settled on the hard seat. "When you go, do you think you might stop at the hospital and check on James Caldwell? Find out if he's recovering?"

"He's a good friend to you, isn't he?"

"The best." Cade forced the words past the constriction of his throat.

He wouldn't reveal to Lily the concern that nagged him. As good a man as James was, he might never have settled things with his Maker—and that was partly Cade's fault. Campaigns may have separated them early in the war, but in Andersonville, he should have been the one encouraging James, not the other way around. The truth was, being a prisoner of war might not have killed Cade, but it had very nearly killed his faith.

So why was it stirring now? Did Lily have something to do with that?

When she touched his shoulder, his heart leaped. "I'd be glad to check on him for you. Maybe Dr. Courtner knows which hospital the men from here were taken to."

"Thank you, Lily." He lowered his gaze after speaking her name. Funny how the river had swept away any formality between them from the moment they met, just as surely as it had almost swept them away as well.

With his arm laid across the solid surface, Lily completed the unwrapping. Only when she let out her breath did Cade realize he'd been holding his.

She grinned at him. "It's considerably less swollen."

True, but he tamped down premature hope. "Now my hand." When she drew closer, Cade shook his head. "I can do it."

Lily stood back and crossed her arms. "You like to be in control, don't you?"

A soft scoffing sound escaped him. "Guess that's a less-than-admirable trait the army, prison camp, and near death didn't yet purge me of." With his elbow propped on the desk, he carefully began unwrapping.

"Then I fear you may be incurable, Dr. Palmer."

His chuckle quickly died. He breathed more shallowly and moved more slowly as the security of the bindings fell away. His index finger was still wrapped and splinted separately, but even the faintest movement of the small bones in his palm shot pain and tingling through every finger. As his hand became visible, Cade's heart sank. "It looks the same."

Lily's touch on his shoulder was so light, he almost thought he imagined it. "It's only been two days. Maybe see if you can flex it a bit. Do I need to unwrap the index finger?"

"Not yet." He sat there holding up the hope of his future and fighting back tears. The idea of trying to clench his hand made his stomach ache. But Lily was right—he had to try.

"Well, you know what to do." As if sensing his need for space, she settled on the bed, reached into her sewing box, and focused on threading a needle. Silence descended while she set to work on a shirt cuff and he on his exercises.

By the time he finished only minutes later, sweat slicked his forehead. "I should ice it now." He panted out the statement.

"Let me help." Lily was by his side with a towel she slid under his arm. "Being a patient is a lot harder than being a doctor, huh?"

As she turned her face toward him, a wisp of her hair brushed his forehead. Both her smile and the tickling sensation made for helpful distractions. She placed chips of ice from the basin from his wrist to his upturned palm, causing him to suck in his breath. When the shock of the cold receded, he thanked her.

"You're welcome." She settled back onto his bed and took up her sewing again. "You said you were from Cincinnati. Did you have a practice there before you joined the army?"

"No. I'd just graduated when the war started. But a professor of mine promised a position with him."

"You must have really believed in the cause to enlist so quickly." Drawing her thread through the cotton, she gave him a quick glance.

"I did believe in the preservation of the Union and freedom for the slaves, yes, but if I'm being honest, those weren't my reasons. At least, not at first." Despite his tension, his shoulders sank a little with the admission.

"Then what?"

"I thought joining up would convince my parents of how committed I was to medicine. So I enlisted as an assistant surgeon with the 34th Ohio Volunteer Infantry in September of '61." Cade stared at the melting ice on his arm. "Like everyone else, when we entrained for the Kanawha River, we thought it would be a short war."

Lily straightened, and her gaze bore into him. "But you'd already gone to school to study medicine, right?"

"Against my parents' protests and prayers for my redirection all of the two years."

She cocked her head. "Surely nothing could be more honorable than becoming a doctor."

"Not when your father is the most renowned minister in Cincinnati."

Cade's fingers jerked involuntarily, and he grumbled under his breath at the pain that raced up his arm.

"He wanted you to follow in his footsteps. That's typical for a father. Understandable."

"I made it worse by telling him I would. Back when I was a boy."

Lily shrugged and snapped off her thread. "Children often change their minds."

"Exactly. How can you know for certain at that age what you're meant to do with your life?"

He pushed the memory of a very specific church service and the words he thought he'd heard from the Almighty from his mind. The way God had directed his path to medical school, complete with a sponsor and mentor, offered clear evidence to the contrary—that the call to preach he thought he'd heard that Sunday long ago had come from nothing but his overactive imagination.

"Well, I'm sure they're very proud of you now." Laying her sewing aside, she came to stand behind him. "Do you want to lift your arm for me to clean up the ice? Then I can help you rewrap your hand and arm."

"I'd appreciate that."

"I guess you still don't want Dr. Courtner's splint? He mentioned it again today."

"Not with that amount of swelling." What could he ask her that would turn the conversation away from his faltering career or his injury? Preferably, back toward her? If he dwelled on the condition of his hand, he'd not sleep a wink tonight.

Folding the wet towel and placing it on the tray, she posed another question before he could come up with one of his own. "How did you end up in Andersonville? I thought medical officers were sent back to their own lines."

"That might have been true early in the war, but by late 1864, the prisoner of war exchange had broken down. Besides, they didn't believe I was a doctor."

Lily fetched fresh bandages she'd left in his room. "How could that have been in question?"

Cade extended his arm to begin the rewrapping process. He waited until they'd worked together to secure his hand before answering. Exhaustion had set in. As tempting as it was to delay the topic until another time, he wanted to earn her trust more.

He sat back in his chair. "In June of last year, we attacked the Confederates at Lynchburg, Virginia. We could've held the town if the general let us occupy it overnight. But the Rebels got reinforcements, tons of them, and by the next morning, they started a fierce cannonade. We retreated under cover of night, but they dogged our rear. They found me when I was trying to mobilize the wounded. I wasn't wearing my coat, and it didn't help that a shell fragment had got me that afternoon, so I had my head wrapped."

"Really? You were wounded?"

"If you can call it that." Cade lifted the overlong swath of hair from his forehead to show her the thin scar.

Her eyes widened. "And they wouldn't listen to reason? I thought Andersonville was a prison for noncommissioned soldiers, anyway." She stood abruptly, snagged the damp towel, and took his chin in her hand. When he stiffened, his eyes going wide, she froze, then dropped her arm. "Sorry. I, uh…You worked up a sweat with those exercises. And no surprise." Her cheeks flushing, she practically shoved the towel into his good hand.

"Thank you." Cade wiped his face, then tossed the cloth onto the bed. "I had a fever."

"Again, already?" Lily pressed her hand to his forehead.

"Not now." He laughed and caught at her fingers, but she quickly tucked them away. He continued his explanation. "After the battle. I wasn't in much condition to argue with where they were taking me, and it seems Andersonville was the only place accepting prisoners at that time. Although, they shouldn't have been. . . ." A vision of the stockade, every inch packed with skeletal, sunburned men in rags, and Cade lowered his gaze and offered his arm again. Thankfully, she started wrapping.

"And James was with you through all that."

"Yes."

Lily caught her lower lip between her teeth, studying him for a moment, though he kept his head down. "I wish I had a friend like that," she said wistfully before applying herself to her task.

She was almost done—was, in fact, tying off the strip—and he'd allowed himself a moment to close his eyes and inhale the sweet scent of her hair so near when a voice called out, "Lily!" And feet stomped up the stairs.

Her head came up and panic slackened her features. She leaped up so suddenly that only a quick reaction from Cade saved her bumping his arm. As whoever it was crossed the landing, Lily bent over the bed, shoving the shirt she'd been sewing beneath his quilt. She'd barely whirled around when a woman Cade had yet to meet but who shared Beth's slender frame, pale skin, and black hair stopped in the threshold. Lily's aunt Susanna?

"There you are, *Miss* Lily. What made you think your duties were done for the evening?" Without sparing Cade so much as a glance, the woman mounted her fists on her hips.

"I know my duties are not done, Aunt. I'm rewrapping Ca—Lieutenant Palmer's arm." Lily's hand fluttered in his direction, but her aunt's gaze did not. Instead, she perused the rumpled bed.

"Are you, indeed?" Lily flushed, and Cade fumed at the woman's tone, laden with double meaning. "A duty which takes a whole hour while the rest of us kill ourselves trying to take care of all the other wounded men plus our guests and tavern customers."

Lily dipped her head. "I did not realize you still needed help. I'll be down as soon as I finish here."

"It would be easier and much more proper if this...*man* was downstairs with the others."

"Madam, that's quite enough." Cade used his good arm to push himself to standing and kept his expression schooled despite the pain shooting through his pelvis. "Besides being insulting to your own niece, your insinuations are, quite frankly, ridiculous."

Lily's aunt slowly blinked and turned her head toward him, as though he'd just materialized out of nowhere and she resented the intrusion. "Nevertheless, tomorrow, we can find you a room on the second floor."

"No, we cannot." The firm denial from Lily drew Cade's attention as well as her aunt's. Lily put her shoulders back. "This man has been fevered and may have a fractured hip. When he attempted the stairs only yesterday, he fell. He's not going anywhere."

"Watch yourself, young lady," Aunt Susanna practically hissed. "I don't know what gives you the right to show such cheek."

Lily's lashes fluttered, but she didn't otherwise move. "I speak on the doctor's orders."

The woman's gaze narrowed. "I will see you downstairs in five minutes. And hereafter, I will be keeping my eye on you."

As soon as her aunt vanished from the doorway, Lily's shoulders sagged.

Cade took a step in her direction. "She has no right to speak to you like that." No wonder Lily wanted to escape as soon as possible.

She turned to repack her sewing. "Jacob and I survive on her charity. I would say that gives her a right."

And I would say it's hardly charity. Cade bit back the thought before he could voice it. Lily's sudden reserve, her stiff movements, showed she would not welcome his judgments on her personal life. Or either she was dangerously close to tears. And what would he do about that? She'd only just made him privy to the smallest glimpse of her story.

And yet, Lily had stood up for him—despite the obviously demoralizing effect of her aunt. Strength undergirded her compassion. Strength... or something else? Cade stood frozen at the thought. Could it be that she wanted him to remain close to her?

Suddenly he was a lot less eager to leave.

Chapter Nine

Lily could only hope Cade's unexpected guest would bring him more joy than he'd brought Beth. The man had been quite adamant that he must see Cade when he'd learned they had men from Ohio recuperating at the inn. And Beth had been equally adamant that Lily, not herself, escort the gentleman caller upstairs. Beth had promptly disappeared to the storeroom.

Lily knocked on Cade's door. She reminded herself to use his proper name before she called out, "Lieutenant Palmer? You have a visitor."

"A visitor?" New levity warmed his voice. He must be feeling better today, the last day of April. Did he hope it was one of his fellow survivors? James, perhaps? "Well, come in."

He was lying on his side with Beth's copy of *Pilgrim's Progress* open before him. Jacob must have given it to him, though how Cade managed to turn the pages while propped on his good arm, Lily could only guess.

She clasped her hands in front of her. "Cade, this is Beth's beau. When he heard your name, he swore he knew your family in Cincinnati. I hope he's not mistaken."

As she stepped aside to admit the new arrival, Cade's face went blank, then—thank goodness—lit up. "Judge Hiram Winkler!"

Judge Winkler slid around Lily with the showmanship of a circus performer, top hat in one hand and silver-headed walking stick in the other. The gyrations of his tapestry vest from his exertion on the stairs distracted a bit from the athleticism of his flourish. But his expression displayed equal pleasure…until he had a moment to take in Cade's appearance. Then his face crumpled.

"Is it really you, my young friend?"

Cade's smile faltered. "It really is." Awareness—shame?—flared in his eyes.

Lily looked between the two men. Was Cade really that changed?

He attempted to leverage his weight on his good arm.

With a swish of skirts, Lily assisted Cade to a sitting position. "So you do know each other?" She infused cheer into the inquiry as she tied the sling Dr. Courtner had fashioned for use when Cade was out of bed around his neck.

"We've met briefly once or twice. Judge Winkler's brother, Henry, was our family physician." Cade tugged at the bandage encircling his chest.

"Would you like a shirt?" she asked in a low voice. She'd brought up one donated by the Sanitary Commission, but up until now, trying to don it had seemed foolish.

Cade gave a slight nod. "I'd also like you to stay," he whispered, "if you can."

The flush of pleasure took Lily quite off guard. "Of course I can." Beth had better cover for her with Aunt Susanna, as she'd covered for Beth with the judge. She whirled to the shelf where she'd left the shirt.

"Don't be fooled by Dr. Palmer's modesty." The sofa springs squeaked as Judge Winkler committed himself to their support. "He trained under Henry. My brother was so impressed by his apprentice that he arranged Cade's scholarship to The Cincinnati College of Medicine and Surgery. Said he'd never seen a more naturally gifted surgeon."

"Is that so?" Lily raised her brow at Judge Winkler. And that explained how Cade had gotten through medical school without his parents' support.

"It is so. In fact, he's still counting on you to join his practice." With a nod at Cade, the judge perched his hands atop his walking stick.

"Well, I owe him a debt I can never repay."

"Never fear, he will find a way for you to repay it." Winkler tittered.

Lily stopped halfway to the bed. She looked from the shirt in her hands to Cade. "Oh dear." The remark escaped under her breath.

He glanced at her. "What's the matter?"

"I'm so sorry." She held up the yoked front. "I forgot these don't unbutton all the way down." There was no way she could drape the one side around his bandaged arm as she might have one of her Garabaldi-style blouses.

"Please." Judge Winkler waved his hand. "His *dishabille* could never bother me. This man is a hero."

Tears misted Lily's eyes. "He certainly is."

Cade's smile was brief but reassuring. When she still hesitated, trying to come up with a miraculous solution, he waved her away. "Really…it's all right."

But she didn't miss his heightened color and the way he swiped at the hair on his chin—almost a full beard now. Lily's imagination filled in the ravages of time and deprivation. Last Cade had chatted with Judge Winkler, he'd have done so almost as an equal—a robust, polished, educated man, probably in his finest suit.

"I'll just get my sewing from the other room." Lily slunk away, shrinking inside that she'd made things more uncomfortable for him.

"My brother never gave up hope after you were captured that you'd make it." Winkler's gracious effort to resume his conversation with Cade followed her across the landing. "Nor did your parents."

"My parents?" Even from across the way, the catch in Cade's voice was audible. "You've seen them? Recently?"

Lily hurried to gather her latest project and supplies.

"Oh, yes. They are well," the judge said as she returned to the room. "Your sister and her husband too. They use the church as a base for charity work for widows, orphans, and those injured in service."

Cade had been attempting to sit upright, but he leaned forward now with his arms propped on his legs. A strangled laugh escaped him. "They have not changed, then."

"No, but they are so proud of you, Cade. You are all they speak about—their son, the Union surgeon."

"Truly?" He sat back up as Lily took her place on the nearby chair.

"Of course. When they saw your name on the list of Andersonville survivors—"

"What?" Shock glazed Cade's features.

Lily held the shirt she was stitching in her lap and frowned at Judge Winkler. "What list are you referring to, sir?"

"Well, the Union officers involved in the parole process sent a list of those headed for Camp Chase to the papers in St. Louis. They've been reprinted all over the region."

"So…my parents might have read about what happened to the *Sultana*, knowing I was aboard. And they might still be wondering if…" He balled his left hand.

Lily reached over and covered it.

Bracketed by his neatly trimmed goatee, Judge Winkler's full lips firmed. "I would say that it was quite possible, although I left Cincinnati before news of the disaster reached the city. I would also say it is no accident that you ended up here, in the inn of my intended's family."

Lily was starting to think the same thing herself…for very different reasons.

"I have to write them. Right away." Cade's widened gaze sought Lily's. "But with my left hand?"

She patted his arm. "I'll help you." Of course she would.

"Why not send a telegram?" Judge Winkler suggested. "It would be faster and more certain to get there. If you tell me what you want it to say, I'd be happy to wire one today. You can always follow up with a letter."

"That's a good idea." The lines on Cade's forehead relaxed. "Thank you, Judge."

The man lifted a dismissive finger. "It's the least I can do."

Cade suggested some basic language for the short message, then hesitated. "And you say…they seemed proud of my service?" The quaver in his voice twisted Lily's heart.

"Very much." The judge's countenance softened. "Henry told me how you thought God had called you into the ministry when you were a boy."

Lily refrained from intercepting Cade's quick, furtive glance, but she couldn't stop her eyes from widening. Wanting to be a minister and hearing God call you—those were two very different things.

The judge went on. "And I understand the decision you made as an adult. I believe they do too. Whatever your parents thought about you joining up, about your choice of career, they only want you home. And speaking of home…" He hefted his weight onto his cane and regained his feet. "I have much to do now that I am home myself—even before I can prepare my house in Marion for my bride." He winked at Lily.

She smiled. "We are all pleased for your return." If only that statement truly included Beth.

"Well, perhaps not all." Judge Winkler shuffled forward to shake Cade's hand in farewell. He sighed. "I've an appointment Tuesday morning at the provost office to swear my fealty. It helped speed things along that I spent the last couple of years with my brother's family in Ohio. But I still have to meet with some hard-nosed bureaucrats over in Memphis to ensure my proper subservience to their judiciary goals before they allow me to again run for office."

Lily rose, leaving her sewing in her chair. "You're going to Memphis in two days?"

"Indeed. I expect to find it much changed."

"You will. Might I accompany you?" When his bushy brows winged upward, she hurried to add, "Just on the ferry, and perhaps you might drop me by Gayoso Hospital. One of the lieutenant's friends he wanted me to check on is there, and, well, I have an errand nearby."

Cade nodded. "It would be safer than taking Jacob." As she'd told him she would do when she'd learned James' location from Dr. Courtner. "We would be indebted to you, Judge Winkler."

"Well, I'm happy to do it, if you don't mind lingering the balance of the afternoon, Miss Livingston."

"Not at all." Lily shared her smile with Cade. Hope rose in her heart. He'd just learned that the parents he'd been estranged from since the war anxiously prayed for his return. Perhaps after Lily went to Memphis, she'd have more good news for both of them.

———————— ◆◆◆ ————————

"I have a surprise for you. Close your eyes," Lily said the next morning after she knocked on Cade's door.

"I can't see anything, anyway." Between the lingering dark and the pillow in his face, he could barely make out her form and Jacob's as they tiptoed into his room. Why were they sneaking if he already knew they were there? And what kind of surprise required initiation under cover of darkness? Still, the excitement in her voice prompted him to begin the slow process of turning onto his side. He groaned when the ever-present crick in his neck clenched down—almost as bad as the pain in his back and hip.

The sound drew Lily's notice. "Don't look."

"Fine." Dutifully, he closed his eyes and suffered in silence.

Whispering, shuffling, and scraping ensued until Lily shushed her brother. "I told you, we can't drag it. Beth will hear." More footsteps, and then a cool breeze blew across Cade's face.

"Can I open my eyes now?"

"Yes." Jacob answered, his tone slightly impatient and still heavy from lack of sleep. "It's almost ready, but I can't light the lamp just yet."

"Well, can you help me sit up? And maybe bring me the basin for me to wash and brush my teeth?" Nothing was more demoralizing than facing a beautiful woman with crusty eyes and morning breath. When Jacob still didn't move, Cade added, "I owe you."

The boy had proven invaluable with tasks of a personal nature. And he only displayed ill temper when his sleep was interrupted. If only Cade had something to give him in return.

Jacob brought the items he requested. "No, sir, you don't owe me. I owe you."

The unexpectedly somber declaration drew Cade's head up. "Why is that?"

"Because you and the other men here fought for four years to keep our country together. I could give sponge baths and empty chamber pots for every bit as long and still be nowhere close to repaying you."

Hearing thanks for his service so nobly voiced—and by a twelve-year-old, of all people—watered a portion of Cade's soul he hadn't even been aware was parched. His throat clogged, and his hand holding his toothbrush dropped to his lap. He nearly choked on tears and baking soda before he could speak. "Jacob...there's no debt. We did what we did...willingly, so you'd have a better future. Just you remember that."

"Yes, sir."

The boy helped him into his sling and wet the washcloth, and by the time Lily returned, Cade had mostly gotten himself together, physically and emotionally. The lamp she brought in and set on his desk illuminated something else she carried—a wooden crutch.

Cade's eyes widened. "What's this?"

"Judge Winkler's walking stick made me realize a crutch might give you more independence, just until your hip and back heal better. And only the one, of course, since you couldn't hold on to the other." Lily brought it forward while Jacob gathered Cade's toiletries. "Why don't you try it out?"

"Thank you." Cade allowed her to help him up and position the crutch. It would be something of a trick without assistance, but he'd master it eventually.

With Lily at his side, they started for the door.

"Where are we going?" Not to the stairs, hopefully.

"You'll see."

The door to the third-story balcony stood open, admitting the cool breath of morning and the heart-lifting warble of an early bird. She escorted him to the threshold. The river still lay in inky darkness, but a line of golden light parted the horizon from the lightening sky.

"I thought the beginning of a new month would be the perfect time for you to see your first sunrise over the Mississippi." Lily swept her hand toward the green velvet sofa, which she and her brother had positioned in front of the railing, a quilt folded on one side. "Besides, you could use some fresh air and sunlight."

"Lily..." Once again, words failed him. How could the kindness of two people salve the wrath and cruelty of thousands?

She picked something up from one side of the seat, took Cade's crutch, and helped him lower himself onto the cushion. Lily tucked the blanket over him. "Well, I should go downstairs before I'm missed." As she turned from positioning his crutch nearby, he caught her hand.

"Sit with me. Please?" This moment wouldn't mean half as much if he couldn't share it with her. "Just for a bit."

She hesitated, then sank down beside him, her shoulders dropping. Cade adjusted the quilt to include her lap before he swiped up her hand again. Her furtive glance told of her shock, but Cade couldn't meet her eyes. Or explain that he needed human connection more than he ever had before. The feel of her hand in his anchored him from the nightmare he'd been drowning in—long before the *Sultana* ever exploded.

Lily breathed soft and shallow but held her silence as fingers of sun stretched from the eastern horizon. Its light touched the lacy white blooms on the pear tree below. A tugboat tooted on the river. Swallows winged their way heavenward through pink clouds.

"'The heavens declare the glory of God; and the firmament sheweth his handywork.'" Lily's quotation from Psalm 19:1 drew Cade's gaze. He drank in her softly glowing countenance before she peeked shyly at him. "I have something else for you."

"I can't imagine anything else I need." Except the healing of his back and the use of his hand. But even his injuries seemed far away right now, like something that must have happened to another person.

Releasing his hand, Lily placed the object she'd been holding on his lap. A heavy book. A Bible. "When I saw you trying to read *Pilgrim's Progress* yesterday, I thought this might be better."

Cade couldn't answer. He'd not held a Bible for almost a year. The solid weight of it brought a rush of memories and a shock of awareness. He did need this, as he'd unknowingly craved acknowledgment of his sacrifice. More.

"All right. Well." Lily planted both her hands on her knees. "I really had better go. I'll leave you to your devotions."

He couldn't find his voice until she was at the door. "Thank you." How rough and pitiful the words sounded. But they evoked a smile that nearly stopped his heart.

"You're welcome." She tapped the frame before whisking away.

When Cade raised the book's front cover, a breath rushed out of his chest. His chin lifted and eyes slid closed.

Oh, God, You sent me this girl…to save me from drowning in more than one way.

The Bible belonged to Lily. The pages opened to Romans 11, parted by force of habit thanks to a flattened clump of dried lavender. Did it mean something special to her? As Cade moved it, he read the verses beneath about God extending grace to others beyond His chosen people, the Jews. Grafting in branches of new Gentile believers.

"God hath not cast away his people which he foreknew…. Behold therefore the goodness and severity of God: on them which fell, severity; but toward thee, goodness, if thou continue in his goodness: otherwise thou also shalt be cut off."

Was he like the natural branch described, who had grown up a believer, but having turned his back on God, found himself in danger of being cut off?

"For the gifts and calling of God are without repentance."

Cade closed the Bible. He studied the traffic on the river to avoid thinking about what that meant. He could start by making peace with his family. Judge Winkler had given him hope for the future. So had Lily. God had not abandoned him, as he had so often feared in Andersonville.

He knew verse thirty-three by heart and said it aloud. "'O the depth of the riches both of the wisdom and knowledge of God! how unsearchable are his judgments, and his ways past finding out!'"

The morning seemed to ring with the truth of it. Something in his spirit stirred. The heavens *were* declaring the glory of God.

No…those were horse hooves and voices from somewhere down the lane. Cries, calls, weeping…*laughing*? Cade laid the Bible on the sofa and, with the help of the crutch, made it to his feet. Its use strained the skin on his back, but he could tolerate the discomfort long enough to learn what was going on.

A band of men mounted on thin horses rode down the main street. Citizens emerged from their houses and followed, growing louder in their welcome as they went. Such a motley band as those horsemen Cade had never seen. Full beards and dashing mustaches only partially concealed the gaunt, tanned faces beneath, their bodies lean but wiry with muscle. They wore wide-brimmed hats, knee-length black boots, and an odd assortment of civilian and military clothing. Pistols and sabers studded their sashes. Confederate partisans, then. They looked like specters of past glory, but something about their sudden appearance in the mists of morning defied deprivation, loss, and time. They would have made a perfect oil painting.

But they were very real, and they were stopping in front of River Rest. The man at the company's head dismounted and strode toward a knot of women who had gathered on the steps below. He swept off his plumed hat...and then he swept a blond woman into his arms.

Lily.

She stood stiffly as if stunned for a moment. And then she pulled his golden head against her shoulder.

Cade staggered back and closed his eyes. Was this the man whose name she'd been unable to speak? The giver of the flowers in her Bible? From all appearances, she'd given him much more—maybe even a promise to wait for his return.

Chapter Ten

Lily would have defied her aunt's summons to the porch had she known what awaited her. She wouldn't have avoided welcoming Cecil home, but neither would she have chosen to do so publicly. And she certainly would have taken a moment to fortify herself.

As it happened, she'd scarcely realized it was him before he'd pulled her into his arms. The sun dazzled her eyes, and a cheer went up at their reunion from the small crowd that had gathered. The lean man who held her smelled of horse and leather and sweat-damp wool.

Her knees went weak but not because of those things, and not because of joy or longing. It was the shock of that glimpse of his face—a face that had teased her through endless boyhood pranks and finally gone serious when he'd kissed her goodbye. A face she couldn't imagine seeing without also seeing her brother's. Even now, she almost looked for Hamp among the partisans dismounting in front of the inn. But he wasn't there, of course—just the man who'd vowed to come back for her, and who had, but oh, so changed.

The hat with its ragged plume, faded gray tunic, and worn-out cavalry boots held but a faint reflection of the derring-do with which he'd ridden out at the head of his newly formed troop in the summer of '62. He'd gone not to preserve slavery. He didn't own slaves. In fact, none of those in his company did. They were all plain farm boys, eager to prove their manhood and filled with the vision of an independent South. To make their own country with like-minded folk, to establish industry and trade. So they all said, refusing to acknowledge that their fight did indeed support the old regime, the state's southern plantation owners—many of whom paid for substitutes in the draft.

Cecil's shoulders slumped, and he inhaled a ragged breath that threatened the onset of tears. He returned not victorious but defeated. Lily's heart squeezed. She put aside thoughts of the staring faces and gave Cecil what he needed—compassion. She owed him that much. Not to mention, it was what her brother would have wanted.

Drawing Cecil's head against her shoulder, she smoothed his wavy locks, bleached a lighter gold by endless hours in the sun. "Welcome home, Cecil."

"Oh, Lily." He raised his head and cupped her face. "You're so beautiful. I can't believe it's been…"

"Since last summer." Before Timber Sutton told her Duke's Partisans had joined up with General Sterling Price for one last campaign.

As his green eyes searched hers, Lily swallowed. Was he going to kiss her? Here, in front of everyone? After all this time, he was a stranger. And in the space of the single last week, somehow, everything had changed. Things she had resigned herself to before no longer seemed inevitable.

Cecil seemed to read her reticence. A shadow passed over his expression, and he dropped his hands, though he took one of hers in his. "We couldn't do it, Lily." It was as if someone wrung the statement out of him.

"Win the war?"

"Take Missouri." He pulled her hand against him, squeezing her fingers, his expression haunted. "It was our last chance. Price had been their governor. He promised us the people would join us. It could've changed everything…should have…"

And yet, as Lily knew, the expected uprising had not occurred. Instead, Price's army had suffered a crushing defeat and then disintegrated, leaving roving bands of soldiers to fend for themselves. By December, Duke's Partisans had returned to Arkansas with the remains of the Trans-Mississippi forces—but with thirty-five hundred rather than twelve thousand, many unarmed.

"Cecil, it's time to let that go." She laid her hand on his forearm. "You're home now."

He ran his fingers over his face, smooth shaven but for a light goatee. "Yes, home to sign an oath of allegiance to the oppressors we've been fighting for three years." Bitterness rankled in his tone.

"Home to start a new life." She infused encouragement into the statement.

"You're right." Cecil kissed the back of her hand, his gaze holding hers captive with hidden meaning. Then he glanced at the reunions taking place all around them. He stepped closer, lowering his voice. "We have to go straight to the provost office, but when can I see you again? Privately. There is much we should discuss."

"You can come tonight." The answer came from Beth, not Lily, as the girl inserted herself with open arms between them.

A frown flickered over Cecil's face before he covered it with a smile, releasing Lily to embrace her cousin. "Dear Beth. Just the same, as always." He ruffled her hair, and when her lips turned down, he added, "Don't be mad. It's a comfort to know some things don't change."

That seemed to satisfy her. "Come tonight, and we'll tell you how much *has* changed. Our inn is filled with paroled Union prisoners of war."

Now Cecil's brows pulled down. "From the *Sultana*? I heard about that, but I thought the survivors were all in Memphis."

"Not all. A couple of groups have been sent north now, but there are still hundreds of them in private homes as well as the hospitals." Beth stepped back as Timber Sutton approached. The tall scout hugged both her and Lily.

"It's good to have you home, Timber." Lily patted his arm. "I didn't know you were still riding with Duke's Partisans." Judging from the way his thin shoulders bowed and dark circles and fine lines ringed his eyes, life on the run and in the saddle had taken its toll on the older man.

Timber doffed his wide-brimmed hat and smoothed his graying hair. "Yes, ma'am. I was the one who took the latest terms of surrender to Cecil."

Beth smiled at him. "You look as though you could use a good meal. You should come eat tonight too."

"I'd like that very much, Miss Beth." Timber nodded before replacing his hat.

As the scout excused himself to greet Aunt Susanna, Cecil frowned at Beth. "Is dinner such a good idea, with Yankees overflowin' the place?" He turned a questioning gaze on Lily. "Perhaps after I ride over and see what's left of my farm, I can take you out someplace."

Thanks to fear of the wrath of Cecil's raiders falling on any overzealous conscription agents, the Dukes had managed to survive on their property, once a fine spread. But Lily had occasionally glimpsed his parents and younger siblings in town. They were all so thin, a good yank could have snatched their clothes right off them. And the floods…had they encroached that far outside Hopefield? Should she say something to warn him?

While Lily debated with herself, Beth took a step forward. "No one will know you're here if you come to the private dining room. Six o'clock. We'll fix your favorite—pot roast."

"If you're certain…" Hesitation lingered in Cecil's voice.

"Of course. We *all* want to visit with you. We want to hear everything. And tell you all that has happened here. You can't imagine how awful it has been, nursing wounded Yankees. And feeding all of them!" Beth rolled her eyes, and Lily fought the urge to do the same. As though Beth had nursed a single one.

Lily did say, "The Sanitary Commission has helped."

"With the clothes and food, maybe. Not the nursing." She turned to Lily. "But you don't mind that so much, do you?" Her tone grew suggestive, and she arched her brow as she tossed Cecil a smug glance. "Lily is quite the little nurse."

What was her cousin about, goading Cecil minutes after his return?

He merely perused Lily with a tender smile. "She is nothing if not kind."

"Especially kind to the lieutenant she rescued herself. *Doctor* Palmer. Cade, is it? Swam out to get him in her unmentionables." Beth lifted her chin. "She can tell you all about it tonight."

When Cecil's gaze searched Lily's face, her stomach shrank up, but she smiled. She could never let him see the depth of her devotion to the Yankee upstairs—no matter how confusing her feelings for either man.

Cade had waited all he could. It was almost suppertime, and he hadn't seen Lily since his glimpse of her with the cavalryman. The troop had mounted back up shortly after and continued down the street, but who was he? And why had Lily welcomed him with such affection?

Not that it was any of his business. Nor should he be surprised if Lily had a Confederate sweetheart. She may have professed loyalty to the Union, but she came from a family of Southern sympathizers. Her brother had given his life for the Rebel cause. Could the man who'd returned be the one who'd convinced her twin to join up?

Maybe he'd also returned later today. He could have taken her out somewhere, and Cade would have no idea. Was she even safe with such an outlaw? Everyone knew partisans were notorious for taking what they wanted.

The possibility twisted his gut.

By the time Lily's light footfalls sounded on the steps, Cade's mental state matched his physical. He held his breath, but she went into her own room. Was she not even going to check on him? She thought a crutch fixed all? It was a mercy he'd made it back to bed with only its help, as exhausted as he'd been from sitting up so long. Or perhaps his trembling limbs had more to do with what he'd seen below.

Stop it.

His thoughts resembled a pouty child's. He closed the Bible he'd tried to read on and off all day. He couldn't pretend to concentrate anymore. He had to know if Lily was all right.

Somehow, he made it across his room and the landing. But he stopped and stared at her closed door. What should he say? While he was debating, the Bible he'd clutched between his good arm and the crutch slid from his grasp and landed on the floor with a thud. Its pages splayed, and the dried lavender spilled out.

"Drat it." How was he going to bend and pick it up?

Lily's door opened, and she stared at him, then at her Bible on the ground. It only took a moment for her to swoop it into her arms, pages smoothed, flower tucked away. "What are you doing, Cade?"

"Returning your Bible?"

She laughed lightly. "I never meant for you to bring it back to me. I would've gotten it from you soon."

"I'm sorry I dropped it." He was having trouble forming thoughts, much less sentences, for she wore a dress in a soft shade somewhere between blue and lavender, the scooped neck displaying her smooth skin. Little tucks of the shiny material and white gossamer ribbon alternated along the top of the bodice, the *V* at the bottom making her waist impossibly small. A hoop he'd never seen her wear before held out her skirt, which rustled as she moved. Taffeta?

"It's no matter. Did you enjoy reading it?"

She'd drawn her hair back in a cluster of ringlets that gleamed in the evening light. What had she just asked him? "Oh…yes. Very much. Thank you."

"I'll bring it back to you tomorrow. Right now, we're"—she held the door open wider to reveal Jacob in the room, performing his ablutions at the washbasin—"getting ready for supper."

"A very fancy supper, it seems."

"Cecil Duke is home!" The exclamation from her brother brought an instant flush to Lily's face.

"Cecil, yes…I believe you mentioned him before. I saw—" Cade wavered on the crutch, and Lily's hand shot out to secure it.

"There's a chair right here. Why don't you sit down a minute?" She helped him to the horsehair-cushioned, armless seat with a tufted, slightly frayed back. "Was there something else you needed?"

"Just to make sure you were all right. I was worried about you." Cade leaned his crutch against his leg. "But I suppose you were with…Cecil." Doggone it. What he'd intended to sound casual came out slightly petulant.

"Worried? I don't know why." A nervous giggle such as Cade had never heard from her escaped from Lily's lips. She turned toward a small walnut dresser, picked up a pair of pearl earbobs, and peeked into the mirror to slide them on. "You heard what Aunt Susanna said. She's making sure I pull my weight downstairs. I couldn't make it up here, but I knew Dr. Courtner called, and he told me you're doing better. That your hand was slightly less swollen?" She glanced around at him, one brow lifted.

"It was." The discovery had brought some hope to an otherwise miserable day. "Are you still going to Memphis tomorrow?"

"Yes. I plan to meet Judge Winkler at the provost office in the morning. I'm taking Mika with me so Jacob will be here to help you. Why?"

He'd already given her the message he wanted delivered to James—how he'd been praying for him and eagerly awaited news of his recovery. His hopes of traveling home together soon. He'd even told Lily that if occasion warranted, she might encourage his friend to seek a different kind of healing in God…the kind he was only beginning to realize he needed himself. "You don't happen to have another Bible lying around, do you?"

Lily picked a lace shawl up from the quilt on her bed. "I'll ask Uncle Thad. Maybe a New Testament. You want me to take it to James if we do?"

"That would be wonderful." The soldiers in the hospitals might have been given Testaments, but he'd rather not take a chance on it. Cade met her eyes, but the smile they shared was disrupted by Jacob, bumping into Lily as he whizzed by her.

"Hurry up, Lil. We don't wanna keep Lucky Cecil Duke waiting!" He darted through the doorway, snapping up his suspenders. His voice trailed him down the first flight of stairs. "He's gonna tell us how he's evaded the Yankees all this time."

Cade chuckled to dispel the instant discomfort on Lily's face. Because of what her brother just said or because he was leaving them alone together? That would be nothing new, but it *was* new that they were in her room… and strangely intimate. Then again, that was probably all in his head. "Lucky Cecil? Where did the man get such a name?"

"From making it through the whole war without getting shot once." Lily came to him and assisted him to his feet.

"Well, now, that *is* impressive. But he's luckier to be spending the evening with you, looking as lovely as you do." Had he just said that out loud? What had possessed him?

Still holding his arm, Lily swung her gaze up to his. "He was my brother's best friend. My friend, too, growing up."

He'd expected awkward thanks, not a serious explanation. Cade attempted lightness. "You must be awfully glad he's home."

"I'm glad for every man who comes home in one piece. But that doesn't mean he's not scarred." The soft furrowing of her forehead and pursing of her lips portrayed the sympathy he'd glimpsed before.

Now that was jealousy, plain and simple, ripping through him. How could Lily show the same compassion to him and to a Confederate guerilla? One had to be more genuine than the other. He didn't want to think about which.

Cade averted his face. "Scarred, maybe, but I daresay, special. Or his homecoming wouldn't be such an occasion." Instant conviction stayed his rebellious words, and he reached for and squeezed her hand. "I'm happy for you. If your brother couldn't come home, at least his best friend could."

She stared at him until he met her eyes. Her gaze pierced right through him. When she spoke, her voice was soft. "You saw, didn't you? This morning, from the balcony."

He cleared his throat. "I didn't mean to spy."

"There was hardly any need to, it was all so public. I wasn't prepared for…" She lowered her lashes, then tried again. "I lost Hamp just six months after he and Cecil left for the war. Cecil made my brother a promise before he died…to make sure I would be all right. A few months later, after both of my parents passed, Cecil wrote to me that he intended to honor that promise. Since then, everyone has assumed…"

Assumed Cecil would claim her. Cade kept his voice low. "Everyone, including you?"

"I can't stay here forever, you know. Back then, I didn't see any other options for after the war. But now, I do."

Cade's heart lurched and his breath caught. What did she mean?

"My sewing." Lily joggled his arm slightly. "Memphis?"

"Of course." He shook his head. Why had his chest tightened up like that?

"Anyway…" She stroked his arm as if placating a child. "I don't want you thinking I was hiding a Confederate fiancé from you, lying about my own allegiances. No such understanding has been reached."

And yet, Cecil intended to honor his promise. A man broken by war and starved for comfort would waste no time seeking solace in Lily's arms, especially looking as she did tonight. The notion soured Cade's stomach. As though he could outrun the sensation, he hobbled toward the exit. "It's no matter to me. If you love each other, you should do whatever is best for you."

"Who said anything about love?" She stepped around him, passing close as she reached for the door. "It's not something I've dared to even hope for…until now." The last words she uttered so softly, Cade questioned if he'd heard them right. Her gaze slid to the side, and she held the door open, but the faint smile on her lips sucked the breath from his lungs.

She couldn't be talking about a seamstress shop in Memphis this time. Could she possibly mean…?

His reflection in her dresser mirror stopped him mid-thought. He hadn't seen himself in almost a year. Could that gaunt, pale man, swathed in bandages, his face hidden in a ragged beard, actually be him? Andersonville had starved not just any fat but the muscles as well from his torso and arms, leaving him hollow eyed and sunken chested. He looked closer to forty-six than twenty-six.

What had made him think even for a minute that a woman like Lily might be attracted to him? Any woman, for that matter. No one could be attracted to that pitiful specter.

He should do himself a favor and stop imagining any sort of present or future connection with Lily Livingston. In another week or two, she'd resume her life with Lucky Cecil Duke. And he'd face the journey home on another steamer.

Chapter Eleven

"Where are you going?" Beth's demand, fired as she caught Lily and Mika slipping out the back door of the kitchen, brought Lily up short.

Her hand flew to the cloth that covered the contents of her basket—including the most recent shirt she'd repaired and a very telling Union military vest on which she'd replaced the buttons. Judge Winkler's visit to the provost marshal had offered not only the perfect opportunity to meet him outside the inn but also to deliver her latest completed projects. "Errands." Sometimes, the less said, the better.

Her cousin clunked a tray of dirty breakfast dishes on the counter, making Martha jump as she removed a pan of biscuits from the oven. "Land sakes."

The cook's glare bounced off Beth's back as she stalked across the room and put a hand on her hip. "And taking Mika? How do you expect us to manage?"

Maybe you'll actually have to take care of the men today.

Thankfully, Martha spoke up before Lily could voice her sassy thought. "Now, Miss Beth, you know Miss Lily can't be gallivantin' around town all on her own, what with the rough sort of men out there."

"Always worried about the lovely Lily, aren't we?" Despite the sarcastic gibe, Beth didn't spare Martha a glance as she approached Lily. "I don't think it's those men she's worried about. I think it's one she fears might show up again here."

"Beth, we really have to go." Her cousin was too close, both in body and assumption. Lily handed the basket to Mika, who stood in the alley.

"You hardly spoke to Cecil last night." Beth's eyes narrowed.

That was because he'd been bent on recounting the exploits of his partisans, lamenting lost opportunities and dead dreams. How did one talk to someone still living in the past? A part of the past she'd no wish to share. He may have returned in body, but judging by the depths of his despair, he was a long way from home in spirit. "I was letting him visit with all of you, as you wanted."

"And yet, all he wanted from you was a kind word. A little praise."

Lily bit her lip. Beth had served up plenty of that. Indeed, it had been the only thing to temporarily ignite a flare of life in Cecil's eyes.

Her cousin tilted her head. "Then you were so tired out by all that conversation that you had to flee to your room with a headache before he could beg a moment alone with you."

"I did have a headache." Said strain might have resulted from the incessant bouncing of her thoughts between the man in the dining room and the one in the room on the third story. Lily glanced away and tightened the silk bow of her bonnet ribbons. Had Cade actually been jealous of Cecil, or merely protective? It would be expected that he'd harbor suspicions of a Confederate partisan, so that was probably it. "We really have to go, Beth. We'll be back as soon as we can."

"Mm-hmm. And just how long will that be?"

She could hardly be gone all day with no explanation but local errands. Even if she'd managed to slip out undetected, she should have thought up a cover story to offer upon her return. But she was so terribly bad at lying. Lily sighed. She'd stick to part of the truth. "I'll be back by suppertime."

"Suppertime?" Beth squeaked.

"Fine." Lily flung her hand out. "The truth is I do need to get away from here. It's been a year since I've been to Memphis, and with all that's going on, I want to talk to my friend. You remember Sarah Goodson?"

Beth nodded. Though Sarah had been from Hopefield, their paths had crossed several times before the war—before Sarah had married Bob, a Memphis law clerk, and moved to the city, where she'd set up her seamstress shop.

"You know she's older than us." Only older than Beth by about a year, though Lily didn't point that out, age being a sore subject for her cousin. "And she's been married now for a while. So I figured she might be a good person to give me advice."

"Advice?"

"About…men. Marriage. You know." Lily didn't have to summon the blush that heated her face. "Cecil's been gone a long time. Naturally, I'm a little nervous when I think about…"

Beth's lips pressed tight, then she said, "You know any girl in Crittenden County would swoon to have him look her way."

Including Beth. Her adoration might be just what Cecil needed, though he'd never reciprocate any interest. Beth didn't fit Cecil's lofty and long-held ideals. "I know. I need to get the cotton out of my head. Cover for me?"

Her humble plea seemed to sway her cousin. Beth blew out a breath and flicked her hand toward the alley. "Go. But you owe me…big."

"Thanks, Beth." Grabbing Mika's arm, Lily hurried them away before her cousin could change her mind.

"I can't believe she's gone."

Lily stood on the sidewalk in front of the milliner's shop that now occupied the building where Sarah Goodson had conducted her seamstress enterprise. She'd been stunned to discover hats and bonnets in the window, a new name on the door, and new occupants running the business and living above. The middle-aged proprietress had told her Sarah had taken her three-year-old son and moved in with her husband's parents in Nashville after they received word he'd been killed in the battle for Atlanta.

While she and Sarah had never been close, Lily should have stayed in touch better. There was no reason for Sarah to have guessed Lily might finally take her up on an offer of employment made in early 1863. Before Mama passed, Aunt Susanna had been a lot nicer, and Lily had thought Jacob needed the stability of living with her and Uncle Thad.

How could she ever provide for herself and Jacob now? Remaining at the inn indefinitely was not an option. That left her but one.

Lily stared at the wagons and buggies rumbling by on the dirt street without any details of the hubbub registering. "Now what?"

"Now we go back to the hotel and see if we can visit your lieutenant's friend." Mika gazed earnestly at her from the shade of her straw bonnet, with little sprigs of black curls popping out beneath.

Did she have any idea Lily's question referred to her entire life trajectory and not just the next two hours until Judge Winkler picked them up? Addressing the girl's other misconception would be simpler. "He's not my lieutenant."

"Well, he's alive because of you, isn't he? I think that's very romantic." Mika released a sigh. "And he's a doctor."

"You're right." She flushed. "Not about the romance. About us going back to the hospital. There's nothing for me here." She had to put aside her personal quandary for later. "Hopefully, the receptionist will have verified James' location and prepared him for a visit."

They had been gone long enough to have given the staff the time they'd requested to make those arrangements. Maybe they would even offer a cup of tea for her parched throat. She had to be able to deliver Cade's message effectively, after all. Bringing good news back to him would assuage her own disappointment.

They passed between four-story buildings and the equally tall telegraph posts directly in front of them, their wires marring the blue sky and not a tree or familiar face in sight. The wonders of the city quickly lost their appeal in the dwarfing wave of aloneness swamping Lily.

"Nothing is more impressive than being a doctor." Completely unaware of Lily's personal predicament, Mika picked her previous thread of conversation right back up. "I haven't minded helping the wounded men. I've always wanted to be like Mother Bickerdyke. I was hoping to see her today, but I heard she moved to another post."

"Who?" Lily pulled her concentration back from the sense of despair that insisted on spiraling up.

"Mary Ann Bickerdyke, the most famous nurse of the war. She ran Gayoso Hospital for a while. And she hired escaped and former slaves to help her."

"She did?" The faraway look on Mika's face grabbed Lily's attention. She wasn't the only one with latent hopes and dreams.

Mika nodded, and her full lips slid into a smile. "They say one time, while Mrs. Bickerdyke was out on errands, the medical director sent all her colored helpers away. Well, she went straight to the general's head-quarters and got them back."

Lily laughed. "I wish I had that kind of backbone."

Mika's head swiveled her direction. "But you do, Miss Lily."

Another laugh, this one slightly bitter. "How?" She'd survived the war by keeping her head down and her opinions to herself. She'd not even had the courage to go to the provost with details of the conversation she'd overheard before the *Sultana* exploded.

"You take in sewing for the Union soldiers, don't you?"

"I do that for myself and Jacob." For self-centered, not altruistic reasons. And to what end now?

"Well, that helps me too. And we help the wounded soldiers. We finally get to do our part for the cause." Mika beamed—until a man in a shabby black frock coat and top hat stepped right in front of her, nearly knocking her off the sidewalk.

"Excuse you, sir!" The rebuke welled up with Lily's indignation. How dare he act as though Mika was not even there? As the buffoon strode away without a backward glance, the tails of his coat flapping, Lily slid her hand through Mika's arm. Maybe they'd fare better as a unit. "It would be nice to live someplace where people have manners."

"It's all right. I'm used to it, Miss Lily."

"It's not all right. Have you ever thought about going north?"

"By myself?" Mika's eyes bulged. "No. Mama and Papa will never leave here, not with them both having good jobs."

Lily patted her arm. "I suppose that makes sense, but would you leave if you could? Not that I want you to."

"Guess I wouldn't mind seein' more of this big country." Once again, she stared into the distance...or maybe she was taking in the four-story Gayoso Hotel across the way, with its massive, columned portico and the connected brick wing, which had been turned into a hospital.

They crossed the street with Lily's hoop tilting and a good bit of traffic dodging. The shade of the porch provided welcome relief from the brightness of the early-May afternoon. Reentering the foyer, Lily approached the desk and alerted the Sanitary Commission worker that they had returned to see James Caldwell from the *Sultana*.

"Yes, miss. A nurse will be right down."

Lily took a seat on the wooden bench by the wall. A copy of the *Memphis Daily Bulletin* lay on the table, and she snatched it up. "Maybe there's an update on the investigation." *Investigations* plural now. In addition to the Washburn Committee of three, Secretary of War Stanton had ordered an inquiry at Vicksburg, and General Grant had published a special order that dispatched a brevet colonel from Washington to begin interviews in the area.

Mika leaned closer. "About the *Sultana*? Folks are sayin' someone tried to blow it up."

Lily speared her with a glance. "Do you know anything about that? Did you hear anything, maybe at the inn?"

The girl's eyes widened, and she shook her head. "Not me, miss. I just hear folks talkin'. What about the paper?"

Lily didn't have to look far. Right on the front, a major article. She scanned it for a moment, her heart sinking.

"What's wrong, Miss Lily?" Mika whispered.

"It says some men who went to investigate the wreckage found a piece of a shell weighing nearly a pound." She swallowed. "Not only that, but a 'well-informed machinist' said there were three distinct explosions, and a witness told the committee he saw the doors to the furnace blown open just before the blast."

Lily lowered the paper. She hadn't time to process nor Mika to respond before Lily's gaze came to rest on a white-aproned nurse standing in front of her.

"Excuse me, miss. You are here to see James Caldwell?"

"Yes." Lily quickly folded the paper and laid it aside. She came to her feet and reached for her basket, which contained the New Testament she'd procured from Uncle Thad.

But the woman held out her hand, palm forward. "I'm sorry, but Private Caldwell is no longer with us. He succumbed to a fever from his severe burns and pneumonia of the lungs just last night."

———————◆•◆———————

"I'm sorry, Cade. I'm so sorry." Standing on the third-floor balcony of River Rest, Lily clutched the New Testament she'd intended to give to James.

Cade sat turned to one side on the sofa they'd left outdoors since the weather had been fair. While she'd been gone to Memphis, Jacob had attended Cade. But now she alone had to face him with the most awful news she could have brought. If only he would say something, react in some way. He just stared at her as though he didn't understand the language she was speaking.

"The nurse assured me everything was done for him. He had a better chance there than here. If it's any comfort, he passed in his sleep."

That provoked a response—but not the expected one. A wail rose from Cade's chest, and he bent forward, his forehead touching the curved back of the sofa. Hiding his face. But she didn't need to see his tears to know they were there—not with the way his shoulders shuddered.

Lily's heart wrenched, and she knelt next to him, her full skirts puffing out around her. She laid the Bible on the other side of Cade and touched his head, his soft, wavy hair. "I know it must hurt you that he was alone, that you couldn't be with him, but at least it was peaceful. They'd given him something for the pain—"

"No." His agonized face lifted. "You don't understand. If he died in his sleep, it means he had no time...no time to..."

"No time to what?" She searched his shimmering dark eyes.

"To make peace with God."

"You don't know that. It's been almost a week since the explosion. James would've had plenty of time to think and pray. I'm sure the chaplain visited him as well."

Cade shook his head. "James was stubborn. He always thought his optimism and good works would get him into heaven. He never seemed to realize there are no good people, just as my father used to say, only bad people who can either choose justice or grace."

She straightened as Cade rose up to swipe at his tears with his left hand. "I'm sure you told him that."

He moaned. "But I didn't. Oh, God, I didn't…" When sobs choked his voice, he covered his face.

His broken weeping grabbed and squeezed Lily's heart. What could she say to comfort him? All she could think to do was cup his neck with her hand and lower her temple to the top of his head.

Please, God, help him. I don't think this man can take much more loss.

"*There* they are!" The harsh voice coming from the doorway made Lily jerk upright. Beth stood in front of her mother, her face twisted in disgust. "And just look at them, practically lying on top of each other. I told you she'd been spending too much time up here."

Lily rose and Cade lifted his head and wiped his eyes as Aunt Susanna jerked the door wider and pushed past Beth with the singular focus of an ironclad ram. "Why am I not surprised? It would seem you've been consorting with the enemy in more ways than one."

Lily brushed at her own tears. "I just told this man his best friend died." She gestured to Cade. "Have you no pity?"

Aunt Susanna's chin lifted. "And how would you know such a thing?"

"Because I just called at Gayoso Hospital, where the men from here were taken."

Beth peeked around her mother. "I thought you went to see Sarah Goodson."

"I did. She'd moved away."

"Why don't you tell us where else you went?" Aunt Susanna crossed her arms.

"Where…I went…" Lily's brow knit. Everything since Memphis had become a blur, as though it had happened a month ago.

"The provost office?" Her aunt threw her arms down to her sides. "And don't bother to deny it. Beth followed you. She saw everything—you exchanging sewing projects for money with that private at the front desk—your go-between, I expect. How you made *her* beau a party to your secret doings."

"There's no crime in patching up soldiers' clothes!" The protest came out louder than Lily intended.

"There is if they're the enemy you've been expressly forbidden to interact with. Same as him." Aunt Susanna's glare swooped like a Mississippi kite in a feeding frenzy—down to pass judgment on Cade, then back to Lily. "Things are going to change around here. Beth, go into her room and find whatever else she's hiding." As her daughter went to oblige, Aunt Susanna severed the argument Lily sought to voice with a slice of her hand. "You will take in no more projects. You will go back to the kitchen and dining room, where you can earn your keep until Cecil Duke can take you off our hands."

Cade's back went stiff.

Lily spoke before he could. "Who will nurse the men in my place?"

"They'll be gone soon enough. Until then, if Mika and Jacob can't handle things, Beth can help them."

"Mama, no!" Beth hurried back to the doorway, clutching Lily's sewing basket. "I will not."

Her heart hammering, Lily stepped forward and reached for her basket. "Give me that."

But Aunt Susanna snagged the handle first. "I'll take it." She tossed aside the covering and pawed through the contents.

Beth followed her movements with a distracted frown, angling into her mother's view. "My regular customers want me, not her. And I won't tend to Yankees."

"You'll do as I say, as will your cousin. Aha!"

When her aunt held up the small velvet reticule that contained her payments from the past year, Lily's heart sank.

Aunt Susanna pulled the roll of greenbacks from inside. "Recompense for your secret labors, I presume?" She stuffed the bills back into the string purse without waiting for an answer. "I'll be confiscating this to help offset the cost of your and your brother's upkeep. Not to mention, these Yankees."

"No, ma'am." Cade fumbled for his crutch and attempted to slide it under his good arm. "You cannot take what does not belong to you. Lily earned that money fairly with her labor."

"*Lily*, is it?" Dropping the basket on the ground, Aunt Susanna turned for the landing. "You just go right ahead and stop me. Or you can stay and comfort each other, because this is the last you'll be spending any time together. Come, Beth. Let's leave the two lovebirds alone." With a cruel laugh, she whisked through the door.

"You *shall* be stopped, madam, one way or another! I promise you that." In Cade's haste to pursue, the bottom edge of his crutch caught on a rough board, and he fell back onto the sofa.

Lily held her hand out before he could attempt to rise again. "Let it go, Cade."

His straight dark brows slashed a cleft over his eyes. "How can you say that?"

She let out a sigh that seemed to leak her soul. "Because there was no seamstress shop in Memphis. That dream is already gone."

Chapter Twelve

"No seamstress shop? What happened?" As crushing as his own pain was, Cade's chest clenched for Lily. Despite the bravado of her words, her slumped posture and downcast expression told the enormity of her own loss.

She hefted another soft sigh. "It seems that when my friend lost her husband, she took their son and moved to be near his family in Nashville. Is there anyone not displaced by this war?" Lily ran her hand over her hair, little wisps drifting free in the river-scented breeze. She'd removed the flower-trimmed straw bonnet she'd worn that morning.

"I'm so sorry, Lily. Did you check to see if there was another place hiring?"

She shook her head. "We didn't really have time, what with..." What with her errand to the hospital. "It doesn't matter, anyway. The shops I did see were not familiar. I'd imagine they have new proprietors since the occupation, no one I'd know."

Yankees, she meant. Or at least, people in favor with the Union government. Cade ducked his head. "They might still need a skilled hand."

"Maybe." Lily shrugged one shoulder. "But it was different with Sarah. She could've helped me get connected, and having her husband there..." Once again, her lips pursed as she trailed off.

Of course. Cade grimaced. "He would've made it safer for you." How would a lovely young woman such as Lily fare in a city overflowing with Union soldiers with only a twelve-year-old to protect her? "I see the problem. But neither can you remain at the mercy of that awful woman." If he was able bodied, he'd whisk her and Jacob out of here so fast her head would spin.

Frankly, *his* head spun that he wanted to. Where could he take them? And why would she consent to go anywhere with him? And yet, the need to protect them persisted.

"I know." She scrubbed her eyes, then covered the side of her face. "She wasn't always like this. You know, folks have good reason to hate the Union as much as the Confederacy around here."

Even after her aunt insulted her, stole from her, and threatened to toss her onto the street, Lily excused the woman. Did she see the good—or at least, the possibility of redemption—in everyone? Where did that charity come from?

"Will you tell me what happened to your parents?" Cade patted the seat next to him, then moved aside the small Testament she'd placed there. Sight of it brought another lump to his throat, but he couldn't think of its meaning now. As long as she talked of her troubles, he could put his aside. Offering comfort or advice would be far preferable to examining his own failings—and his culpability for them.

She sighed again and sank down next to him. "When they were alive, we lived in Hopefield."

"You mentioned that. Is it near here?"

"You can't see it now. The river flooded what's left of it. But it lay directly across from Memphis and once had a lot of promise as a route for mail and then the start of the Memphis and Little Rock rail line. We had a post office, a depot, a school, a couple churches, a machine shop, and lots of restaurants and stores." A touch of pride lilted in her voice, along with a nostalgia that her distant gaze also reflected. "My father owned one of the mercantiles, and we lived above it."

Cade nodded, prompting her to continue. What had she meant by *what was left of it?*

"When the war started, the rail shops were converted to a Confederate armory, but it was abandoned when the Yankees took Memphis. Still, you remember I told you this was a sort of staging area for Confederate partisans?" Lily gained his assent with a glance. "In January of 1863, some regular Arkansas cavalry—fighting for the South, mind you—set about burning cotton they couldn't let the Yankees take and capturing a bunch of Union boats and the supplies they were carrying. Livestock, cash, medicine, ammunition—they took it all."

"I'd imagine that made the Yankees pretty mad." And Cade could guess part of what was coming.

"Right. So they sent some Indiana troops from Memphis, and they found out how Mound City, Marion, and Hopefield were supporting the guerillas. They came here to Mound City first. They arrested some people and burned some houses."

Cade's brows flew up.

"They were unoccupied."

"Thank goodness." The idea of his comrades exacting such harsh retribution upon the civilian population flushed him with shame.

"The next step was to send three companies of Illinois infantry to Hopefield. February nineteenth. I still remember it so clearly." Lily drew a tremulous breath, and Cade resisted the urge to take her hand. "They encircled the town and proceeded to inform us of their intentions. They gave us one hour to remove any personal belongings, then they fired every building in the place."

"Please tell me your family got out in time."

Her face twisted. "We would have...if Pa hadn't tried to load the wagon with the most valuable items from the store."

Cade did take her hand then. "Oh, Lily..."

"It wasn't the fire that killed him. It was his heart. There was a barn with a hidden cache of gunpowder that blew up when they set it ablaze. He heard that and knew they were close. He was like a crazy man, shouting, cursing, trying to carry things far too heavy for him to manage alone. Mama ran back to help him, but it was too late. He died right there in the street, clutching his chest."

Cade squeezed her fingers, the familiar frustration rising along with the ache of sympathy. If only he could wrap his other hand around hers as well. "That's terrible. And your mother? Did she get out?"

The corners of Lily's mouth lifted with a wistfulness that almost resembled a faint smile. "I'll never forget the sight of her driving the wagon away from the inferno, her face set like a mask, her hair blowing loose. But she was never the same. She got sick not long after we came here to Uncle Thad's. The news of Hampton's death finished her off."

Cade threw propriety to the wind and slid his arm around her. His heart surged when she gently lowered her head to his shoulder. "I can't imagine the pain you've been through."

"I have a sense you can," she whispered.

"As awful as it is…" He paused to fight back tears. "It can't be like losing both your parents…and your brother."

"Pain is pain. It just hurts." She lifted her face to him, her eyes glistening. "But it hurts a little less if you share it. I think this is the first I have."

Of course. She'd had to be strong for Jacob. "I'm thankful you felt you could." And that she had chosen him.

"Because you did the same." Shyly, she patted his knee.

Cade smiled until the reminder of his loss churned his memory like a piston turning a paddlewheel. He caught his breath. "I can't even visit his grave."

"You can, when you're strong enough. They're burying those from the *Sultana* at the Fort Pickering Cemetery."

Cade snorted, a sound that choked on the thickness of tears in his throat. "Nice of them." He'd heard that guards from the earthen fort two miles south of Memphis, at the end of the bluffs, had fired on survivors floating downriver with the wreckage, thinking they were part of some sort of enemy amphibious assault.

Lily redirected him by reaching up to place her hand over his on her shoulder. "It might help if you talk about him. Why was he so special to you? Can you tell me?"

Blinding loss swept over Cade, obscuring her beautiful face for a moment. He blinked it away. He could hardly refuse her the same transparency she'd just offered him. But he had to collect himself first.

Slowly, carefully, he moved his arm from around her back to his side, wincing as he did. He smoothed the bandage over his broken wrist without really looking at it. He found it easiest to start with stories of growing up in the same county, the same church, making her laugh at some of their boyhood pranks. How they'd signed up, both with the 34th. The early days of training and adjusting to military protocol. Cade skipped the blood and screams and sleeplessness and filth of field hospitals on campaign, but he could hardly circumvent the horrors of Andersonville—not and paint a picture that would do his friend justice.

"When we arrived at the end of last June, the place was at its fullest. I'd say somewhere over thirty thousand men."

Lily's mouth dropped open. "You're kidding."

"I wish I were. *Overcrowding* would be a compliment." Cade described the prison as best he could, the sentry boxes they called "pigeon roosts" and the deadline over which no prisoner could pass on threat of being shot. The shelters made of cloth or blankets dubbed "shebangs." He left out the lice and maggots, the raiders who attacked their fellow inmates for food and goods, and the excrement-clogged, eight-foot-wide branch of the ironically named Sweetwater Creek that offered the only source of water for both drinking and bathing. "I had a fever when I arrived, so I was put in the main stockade, not the officers' barracks. Not that I would have left James."

Lily cocked her head. "Is that why you wouldn't go to the hospital? Or didn't they have one?"

He gave a bitter laugh. "If you could call it that. They'd set up about five acres outside the camp with hospital tents and sheds, but we were told as emphatically as possible that we did not want to go there."

"Why not?"

"Well, the doctors examined about five hundred sick men every day and were only allowed to admit around two hundred. Keep in mind, there was a staff of fifteen. By August, it was down to twelve. Each surgeon had an assistant, usually a paroled prisoner. Men were dying in the hospital a hundred a day, not to mention those who didn't make it in camp."

"A...hundred?" Lily's fingers fluttered to her mouth. She swallowed hard. "So how did you get better? On your own?"

"No." Cade blew out a soft laugh. "I would've died in there if not for James, many times over. That was the first. A new acting assistant surgeon had just arrived, Dr. Howell, and was making his tour of the whole facility. James couldn't get close to him, but he stood up and shouted that I was a surgeon who should be treated immediately."

"Oh my. I'm sure Dr. Howell saw the value in that."

"He did, but I wouldn't go unless he agreed to take James with me. He took care of me, and then he stayed on as *my* assistant."

A gentle smile lit Lily's face. "It sounds as though you saved each other."

He didn't deserve the admiration in her eyes. "Maybe then. But after that, James saved me every day. He kept me from losing my mind. You don't know what it's like to struggle to treat men without proper supplies and equipment. We tried everything."

"I'm sure you did."

"No, Lily, you don't understand." Now that he'd opened the gate on the angst he'd long corralled, it was all stampeding out. He could no more stop it than a cowboy could a runaway herd. "By the droves, they died of disease, scurvy, and dysentery. The tiniest scratch or bite could turn into gangrene. We helped those poor fellows along with amputations. Some were in such misery, they would shorten their suffering by taking their own lives. Their bodies were carried to the Dead House in a wagon, piled in with their limbs sticking out in full view of the stockade, and buried in a mass grave." Just as suddenly as the deluge of details started, they dried up.

Lily stared at him in silence, her face stricken.

Cade dragged in a breath. "That's what James saved me from... from thinking that was all there'd ever be and the rest of life had been a dream. In all that time, he never despaired. He always put others first. And he reminded me that I'd one day be free to make people healthy and whole again."

"And that's why you have to. That's why the use of your hand is so important." She took hold of his good one.

A tear slipped down his cheek, but of course, he couldn't brush it away—not without releasing the lifeline of Lily's hand. She did it for him, and then she pulled his head onto *her* shoulder.

"Do you see why it was so important for me to talk to him about God?" A whisper was all Cade could manage.

She nodded. Her fingers worked out the tightness of the muscles at the base of his skull. How long since he'd experienced a tender touch like that? His whole body melted. His spirit too.

Cade suppressed a groan. "When my faith should have been our anchor, I let James take on that burden."

"And from what you just told me about him, and from how much he already knew of God from your father's sermons alone, we have to trust that James had some important conversations with his Maker before he went to meet Him. Don't you think?"

A ragged breath caught in his throat. He couldn't agree to something he had no confidence about. At least not yet. He had much to work out in thought and prayer. Instead, he said, "Thank you, Lily." He lifted his head. The evening light shed a pink glow on her features, fresh and flushed like a girl waiting for her beau at a ball. "For being so kind to me. Far kinder than you had to."

She shook her head. "Please, don't thank me, Cade." Her lips pinched together.

He wasn't going to make the mistake of again withholding praise where it was due. And truth. "No, I don't think I could have made it through this without you. You give me hope—"

"Cade, stop." She put her hand on his chest. Tears had flooded her eyes. "I'm not as good as you think I am."

"What are you talking about? You've been a godsend."

"I'm not a godsend." She leaped to her feet, her fists clenching at her sides. Her fitted bodice rose and fell rapidly. "I'm far closer to the enemy you thought I was when you got here."

She ran into the inn before he could respond, her withdrawal adding a fresh layer of anguish to the pain she'd just sought to alleviate.

The hope wrought by the apparent healing of Cade's hand shriveled like paper on fire at the overwhelming sorrow of the loss of James. What was he going to tell the Caldwells? How could he explain to them that their son had survived four years of battle and prison only to perish in a tragedy such as this?

Newspaper reports gave apparent credence to rumors of sabotage. Cade prayed the investigations would disprove the early witness statements, although the alternative—greed or carelessness on the part of Union officials—might be worse. At least if the explosion was the work of Confederate saboteurs, they could comfort themselves that the loss of so many men had been an act of war. Part of the rebellion.

Then there was the personal piece of the disaster. How Cade, the physician and friend the Caldwells had trusted, had not been by James' side in the end. Nor could he offer comfort or reassurance about those final hours. Not only had Cade failed to keep James healthy in body but in spirit as well. And that guilt pierced far deeper.

Only the magnitude of his internal struggle kept his mind from Lily's strange, hurtfully abrupt departure, though he circled back to it often enough, plugging in the gaps of suffering with further uncertainties. Especially when he was finally about to drift off to sleep that night. At last, Cade gave up, clumped over to the desk to turn up the oil lamp Jacob had left burning low, and opened what was supposed to be James' Testament. Within its covers he found solace—a shoring up of broken-down places that allowed him repose at last.

A knock on the door woke him. Birds sang outside, and faint, golden light spilled through the lace curtain. *Lily!* Cade wiped his face and propped himself up. "Come in."

Beth opened the door and entered with a tray. She paused just inside the threshold, taking in the dismay he didn't attempt to hide. Her lower lip pulled up. "Sorry. I know I'm not who you were expecting, but Mama made good on her threats. I'm to start my nursing duties with you."

"Lily is in the kitchen?" Cade struggled to a sitting position. He'd give Lily's bitter cousin no reason to touch him if he could help it.

"Yes." Beth rested the tray on the chair and slid it over in front of him, like a small table.

"And Jacob?"

"I asked to bring your breakfast instead." Beth spoke with her face averted, the morning sun highlighting the slight craters on her cheeks and forehead. She wore her straight, dark hair in a severe bun that did her no further favors.

Cade blinked at her. "Why would you do that?"

"I never got the chance to apologize."

A ragged laugh barked out of him. "For your auspicious welcome? Or for your witch hunt last night?"

"For all of it." Beth uncovered a plate of biscuits and gravy and handed Cade a cup of chicory coffee, speaking without meeting his eyes. "I'm sure Lily has told you why we despise Yankees, but it was never meant personally. Not even the other thing I came to confess."

"Which is?" Cade took a tentative sip of the lukewarm brew. If only it possessed the stimulant to actually revive him.

"That first night, putting morphine in your broth."

He spluttered and almost dropped the tin cup.

Beth was at his side, steadying his hand. "There's nothing in your coffee."

He withdrew from her touch. "I believe that about as much as I believe this is coffee."

"Point taken." One corner of her thin mouth lifted. "In full transparency, I only did it the once. And that broth went to all the wounded men. I thought it would be an easy way to administer the morphine."

Cade raised his brows. "Let me guess. You didn't want our moaning to keep you up all night."

"Well, yes, that did occur to me, and I hoped it might ease the suffering. I've never seen such terrible injuries. I'm not completely heartless, you know." Her mouth flattened as she gazed at him, still holding the cup in his lap. "Do you want me to take a sip to prove it's safe?"

"No." Nothing could have gotten the drink to his lips faster. Cade took two gulps of the brew—bitter but not abnormally so—and handed the cup back to her. "Why are you telling me this now?"

She set the coffee on the tray. "As I said, I'm not completely heartless. I had no idea my mother would behave as she did."

"Didn't you? What did you *think* she would do?" Like mother, like daughter. He didn't trust this show of concession, so he made no effort to soften the edge in his tone.

Beth bent to cut the biscuits into bites he could easily fork. "Make Lily shoulder more of the work and stop doing business with Yankees. But not take her money, and certainly not make me take her place serving the enemy." Her gaze flashed up to Cade's. "Yes, I still consider you my enemy. That will never change. But Mama said things that shouldn't have been said."

"On that much, we agree."

"I saw the way you looked at Lily." Beth tilted her head. "You care for her, don't you?"

Cade's fingers tightened on the edge of the mattress. "I'm protective of her, yes. Probably because of the debt I owe her. One I can never repay."

"Is that all?" Lily's cousin held his eyes a moment. "There's no need to be ashamed. It's normal for a patient to develop feelings for his nurse." She positioned his fork with the first bite within easy reach.

Cade gave a scoffing laugh. "What else can there be? I'm going home soon, and her sweetheart just returned from the war." And didn't Lily's absence this morning confirm that she'd heed the wishes of her family?

"You saw that, did you?" Beth straightened, brushing off her skirt. "If you feel what I think you do for her, all the more reason to let her know. And waste no time about it."

Chapter Thirteen

Lily's guilt mounted with each step of the poor nag pulling the buggy. As they turned onto Main Street, she leaned forward to peer at Cecil past her brother, who sat between them on the narrow seat with his elbows in and knees drawn up and a decided downward quirk to his mouth. "Do you think she's going to make it?"

"She'll make it." As he gave her the side eye, Cecil cocked up one corner of his lips—not exactly a smile. "Seein' as how you made me walk her the whole six miles."

Here, there, *and* back. And only after she'd failed to talk him out of the three of them walking home from his family's place. "Can you blame me, given the sad shape she's in?"

"Maybe I should stable her with Joss long enough for a good feedin'… and me some of Martha's apple pie." Cecil sent her a wink, and she couldn't resist a small smile. Sweet as his words were, his deep voice with its honeyed accent wasn't a trial either. Unlike the horse, Cecil appeared more than equal to the occasion in a brown suit and sage-green brocade vest from pre-war days. She could almost believe the past four years hadn't even happened. Until she looked into Cecil's haunted eyes.

"I still don't see why we didn't hitch up your stallion," Jacob grumbled.

"A fine warhorse like that?" Cecil's one eyebrow lifted. "He already had to surrender to the Yankees. Let's leave Blitz a shred of dignity, young man." He elbowed her brother—which required very little movement.

Jacob rolled his eyes. "Longest buggy ride I ever took."

"All the more time we get to spend together." Cecil smiled over at Lily.

His cheerful bravado tugged at her heart. He'd certainly put in more effort today than at supper night before last—probably trying to make up for the lost opportunity. Cecil said he'd been surprised she'd agreed to his invitation for a buggy ride this morning. How could she refuse when he'd already driven his old mare all the way into town? And when he relayed how much his family yearned to see her again?

Of course, his shocked countenance when she'd appeared with bonnet and gloves on and Jacob at her side had betrayed his dismay at the unexpected chaperone. He'd quickly hidden it, though, and gone to teasing her brother out of his own case of the mopes at being roped into such an uninteresting assignment.

"Besides," Cecil resumed, "not as though we have a lot of choices for fine equestrians left. Don't know how I'm goin' to get the corn planted. It's late already."

What did he expect after four years of war? A war in which he'd rebelled against the government and lost. She gathered her striped cotton skirt in her gloved hand. "I hear the Union officials can help with that."

The glance he shot her made her bite her tongue. For his heartache, she could lay no blame. The state of the farm had been hard to take in without betraying her pity. Cecil's father had done what he could to keep the place going, but the flare-up of an old injury made him rely on his children who were too young for heavy manual labor. Fences were falling down, paint was peeling, the roof leaked, and fields sat fallow—some of them too marshy and muddy to plant. Lily had hesitated to take tea and cake with Mrs. Duke lest the sacrifice of the refreshments prove a hardship.

Of their welcome there had been no doubt. Cecil's parents spent most of their visit recounting her old adventures with their son and Hamp and hinting at plans for the future. Their eyes had followed Cecil as though his mere presence put everything to rights again. But the man was in no position to work miracles—even if he would eventually see sense and accept a handout from the government. How could he possibly provide for his own family of six, much less her and Jacob?

Marrying Cecil might not be an option, after all. At least, not soon enough to satisfy Aunt Susanna. Lily fought down panic, followed by a sickening swirl of self-loathing. There she was again, looking out for herself. But if she didn't do so, who would? And her brother—she wouldn't allow him to stop attending school to work endless hours in some factory, just another type of casualty of the war.

Under the circumstances, would Aunt Susanna grant her a long engagement? Lily could talk to Uncle Thad, get him to intercede for them. Maybe he'd even convince his wife to not make their lives miserable until Cecil could "take them off their hands."

Immediately, Lily's thoughts swung to Cade, and she braced herself with one hand on the armrest and the other on her stomach as the buggy came to a stop. The panic intensified. She stole a glance at the third-floor balcony. She didn't see him, but he could be sitting on the sofa. She leaned forward. "Pull on down the alley to the livery."

"Absolutely not." Cecil drew back as though she'd suggested he walk down the street in his long underwear. "I'll deliver you to the front door, as any gentleman should. Although…I will take that as an invitation for pie. And accept."

"Very well." Lily offered a weak smile. While Cecil rounded the buggy, Jacob clambered over her legs and leaped to the ground.

"*Finally.*" He ran toward the inn without looking back.

Lily took Cecil's hand and stepped onto the running board. "I'm afraid Uncle Thad's usually too busy to give him the training in manners he lacks."

"An oversight which needs correctin' right away." Cecil encased her waist in a firm grip, lifting her to the ground before she could protest. He held her in place, his face inches from hers as she raised her chin in a startled reflex. His green eyes glowed, feral and catlike. "I'm up to the challenge, but you'll need to be closer." His fingers tightened suggestively. "Much closer."

Lily attempted to free herself but only succeeded in gaining a few inches. Cecil's arms remained looped around her waist. Another peek at the balcony without the cover of the buggy top revealed what she feared most. Cade stood back from the railing, but he watched them, nevertheless.

She'd told herself she couldn't avoid Cecil forever, especially since he might be her only chance to secure a home for herself and Jacob. But had she really just been running away from her feelings for the man on the balcony? A man who would despise her if he knew her silence had cost countless lives, including that of his best friend—and maybe his own ability to practice medicine.

Her pulse raced, and she turned her face away from Cecil. "You have more than enough laid to your charge already. I won't add to your burden."

"You're not a burden, Lily. Never. You're the reason I made it through this war in one piece, and I want nothing more than to—"

"Cecil?"

Lily's sigh of relief mingled with Cecil's sigh of frustration as he looked toward her brother leaning over the bottom porch rail. "Yes, Jacob?" he replied with carefully measured patience.

"There's a man in the alley says he needs to speak with ya." Jacob pointed toward the livery, then darted inside. The door slammed behind him.

"I'm sorry. Can I meet you in the kitchen?" Cecil offered her his arm.

She took it for him to escort her to the steps. "Of course."

As he raised her hand and dropped a kiss atop her light-gray glove, a soft whistling from the edge of the porch stole her notice. The tune instantly evoked the accompanying words. "Oh, I'm a good old Rebel, now that's just what I am..."

The man who was waiting for Cecil. Lily's heart almost stopped. The gambler hat couldn't hide that long, greasy black hair or the sly expression of the suspected saboteur who'd manhandled her in the back room of River Rest...Frenchie.

It was quite a quandary—invent an excuse to keep Jacob with them to delay being alone with Cecil or send her brother on his way so Lily could ask Cecil about Frenchie. As Cecil outlined the improvements he meant to make on his farm, her assessment swung back and forth between her brother and her suitor while they ate their pie in the private dining room. Memory of the scene in this very location when she'd overheard the saboteur plotting—and endured his groping hands—made up her mind. She had no need to hurry Jacob along, though. He'd inhaled his dessert before she'd taken two bites of hers.

"Bye." Leaving his dirty plate on the table, he bolted up from his chair, apparently having had his fill of their company as well as the pie. The gleam in Cecil's eye said he felt similarly.

Lily raised her index finger. "Plate!" When he turned back around, she nodded toward the door. "Take it to the kitchen."

Jacob returned to do as bid—thankfully, without a sigh this time.

When the door swung shut behind him, Cecil sat up straight, pushing his own plate away. He reached across the table to take her hand. "Finally... the moment I've been waitin' for. To be alone with you."

A protective shield clamped down on her chest—a response to not only his words but the gleam in his eyes. There was a new hunger there, a desperation. But she wanted him to state his intentions, didn't she? No, not *wanted*. Needed. So she didn't remove her hand from his.

"You do realize, all the things I'm talkin' about, the future I'm envisionin'...I can't see it without you."

"Cecil...you know what you've always meant to me. But a lot has changed." It wouldn't be fair to either of them to pretend she worshipped his wartime exploits as Beth did. "We might need some time...both of us."

"What has changed? If you feel the same..."

"I don't know how I feel. I'm still fond of you, of course. Always will be." They had too much shared history for that to not be true. Cecil would always be a golden memory of her girlhood, no matter what the future held. "But I haven't supported the same things you have. You hate all the Yankees stand for, and I agree that some of the soldiers have done awful things to our people here. But I can see where the military government has tried to help us retain order and justice and set up farming communities so we wouldn't starve. And they've done a lot for the black people."

"I don't care if the slaves are free. They aren't takin' my job, and I never relied on any to work my land. We took care of ourselves before the war, and we will again." Cecil spoke with the conviction of the independent man he was. It was that spirit that had kept the South fighting so long, against inconceivable odds.

"And I appreciate that about you, but there's more." Lily slid her hand back across the table. "Aunt Susanna…she just threatened me for taking in sewing from Union officers." Why was she telling him this? To lay a foundation of honesty, or to push him away?

He planted his hands on the table. "She threatened you?"

Well, that wasn't the reaction she expected. A shoot of admiration popped through her defenses. "And took the money I'd earned for the last year."

"How dare she?" Cecil's brow bunched, and a storm brewed in his eyes. "But what did you need money for? Isn't your uncle takin' care of you?"

"Thad is good to us, but you know how tight times have been. I've used the extra cash for a nest egg and the little things we needed here and there. Thankfully, Aunt Susanna hasn't noticed—until now. She forbade me from continuing. I'm afraid Jacob and I have overstayed our welcome."

"All the more reason to not dillydally. Lily, I need you. I don't blame you for sewin' for Yankees if that's what gave you security. But I'm here now. And you need me too." Cecil pushed back his chair and came around the table. He held out his hand to her, his face tender. "Let me hold you. Please. I've waited so long."

With her legs trembling, she rose and stepped into his open arms. He wrapped her against his chest, and at the beat of his heart—steady, not elevated—she relaxed a little. To have a strong man to protect her, to not have to face hardships alone…wouldn't that be a relief? So why didn't she stop making excuses and just do what had been expected of her all along?

And yet another one slipped past her lips. "Without that money, Cecil, I have nothing. And you have six mouths to feed already, including yourself."

"I don't care if you have nothing. To me, you bring everything. With your help, I can make it work." He stroked her back. Perhaps she'd been wrong to be wary of him. He'd always been so patient with her, acting more than anything like a surrogate older brother ever since she lost hers. No, before that…ever since…

Pushing the memory that never failed to erect her guard aside, she lifted her face. "But where will you put me?"

The skin at the corners of his eyes crinkled into laugh lines. "In my room."

Heat swept up from her neck, and she dipped her chin. So much for being an older brother. "And Jacob?"

"In with mine. Samuel is only a year younger. They'll get on like a house afire." He chuckled. "And as they grow, we'll have more hands for the work."

Was that what she wanted for Jacob? To become a farmer? To be tied to this land forever? Land that was wasted and its people embittered by war? Even if she could hold firm in her convictions and embrace unity, living among disillusioned Rebels would surely affect one as young as her brother.

Lily lowered her lashes. "Cecil, who was that man you were talking to in the alley?"

At her abrupt change of topic, he dropped his arms. "No one important. Why?"

A chill swept over her, and not from the removal of his embrace. "I've seen him before. In here, early last month. He was talking with Timber Sutton and another man about interfering with shipping. It sounded…" Slowly, she raised her eyes. "It sounded as though they were planning to blow up a boat."

"The *Sultana*?" The name left him in a rush of breath. "Do you really think…"

"I don't know. I didn't hear any names or dates, just fragments of conversation. But the timing has haunted me."

"And you've told no one of this?"

Lily shook her head. "Only Beth knows. She was in there with them."

Cecil averted his gaze, rapid blinking veiling the thoughts that churned behind his eyes. Then he looked back at her and said with a conviction that stiffened her spine, "Don't."

"Why not?"

"Because Alex LeFleur is a dangerous man, Lily. If he were to find out you pointed a finger at him for the *Sultana*…"

"Alex LeFleur? Is that his real name?" She pressed her hands against her corset stays. Their pressure had suddenly grown intolerable.

Cecil nodded abruptly. "At least, that's what he goes by in St. Louis, where he's from. But you'd do well to forget it. Forget you ever saw him."

"Why?"

"Not only did he run messages for Charlie Dale, a known Confederate agent and saboteur who worked with both General Price's regulars and the bushwhackers, but before the war, he was a steamboat captain infamous for gamblin' and prostitution. Good women are *not* safe around him." He emphasized his point by wrapping his fingers around Lily's arms.

"Then what is his business with you?"

He hesitated before answering. "He's recruitin' former rangers to continue to harass Union shipping."

"He's what?" Her voice rose higher than intended, and she stepped back.

"Don't worry, I told him no. Not my men. I trained them to act honorably during the war. That's how we survived so long. The last thing I'm going to do is get them killed now."

"Cecil, this man has to be stopped." And now she had a name to go with the face.

"Lily…" He recaptured her elbow.

Before he could finish his statement, the door to the kitchen swung open, and Beth stood there, scowling as she looked between them. "If it's not too much trouble, Martha could use some help preparing supper. I've got to distribute clean linens to the men and collect the laundry for Mika."

Pray tell, what was Lily's aunt doing? "I'll be there in just a minute, Beth." She spoke in a firm but soft tone, though her effort at conciliation failed to dissipate the tension.

Beth's face twisted. "Certainly. What's another minute with your sweetheart when you were gone all day yesterday, again this morning, and half the afternoon?" Her sarcastic words trailed behind her as she pivoted and marched away.

Cecil gave Lily a sympathetic smile. "I see your aunt isn't the only one out of temper with you lately."

"You have no idea." Lily heaved a sigh, but she couldn't let the previous topic go. Nor the threat it represented. Not this time. "Listen. I have to go to the provost marshal with the information about Alex LeFleur. I won't have another potential explosion on my hands."

"Lily, you can't do that. It's not safe."

"Safe for me? Or for the hundreds or thousands of people he might kill next?" She searched Cecil's face for the truth. Was he protecting her, Frenchie…or himself? He could be concerned that taking her tale to the officials could bring his own activities into question. She'd do her best to keep his name out of it, but…"If you care about me as you say, you won't try to stop me."

Chapter Fourteen

All day, the darkness had loomed over Cade, threatening to pull him into a vortex of loss and self-recrimination. Reading the New Testament Lily had brought him helped…until he glimpsed her returning from some sort of outing with that former partisan, who possessed the dress and manners of a popinjay. He handled her as if he owned rights to her and then charmed away his presumption with a kiss to her hand.

It was bad enough that Lily was avoiding him. Now Cade knew she'd spent the morning with her former suitor. Not so former. Was this what she'd meant by being his enemy? She intended to follow through with her courtship and marry Cecil Duke, even though she'd hinted she did not love him?

And why wouldn't she marry him? The possibility of providing for herself had been snatched from her, and time was running out. But now Beth, as well as Lily herself, had implied that Cade might provide her another option.

The idea was crazy. Ludicrous. They barely knew each other. Many would consider them on opposite sides of the national struggle, which the surrender terms by no means ended. And in no way could Cade compete with Lily's dashing ex-Confederate. Not only had Cade lost the stature and health he'd once enjoyed, he also faced an uncertain future—a rift in his family and the unanswered question of how he would earn his own living.

And yet Lily must care about him. Why would she have tended him with such devotion, said the things she did, and taken him into her confidence otherwise? By her own admission, she shared his ideals, and more importantly, his faith. Both of them clung to their spiritual heritage despite all they'd been through, and somehow, they strengthened each other in it. Believed for each other where they no longer could do so for themselves. It was a beautiful thing. As beautiful as the love taking root with the determination of a sapling shoot breaking through dry ground.

But was it love? Or was it, as he'd said to Beth, the traumatic circumstances of their meeting? Gratefulness on his part and pity on hers?

Could Lily ever love him?

There was one way to find out. He had to take a risk.

If Lily would not come to him, and he couldn't go to her, he'd do what he'd almost forgotten how to—call on the Word of God. Or in this case, send it out. He sat down with the Testament and turned to Proverbs, where he quickly found the verse he remembered in chapter thirty-one. Then he took a pencil and a scrap of paper Beth had left in the room and painstakingly wrote out the words with his left hand.

"Who can find a virtuous woman? For her price is far above rubies."

It looked like child's scrawl, but maybe the obvious effort would convince Lily of his sincerity. It was all he had to give her—the message of his heart. Would she consider the rest of the passage, even though he daren't write it?

"The heart of her husband doth safely trust in her…"

Husband? He'd surely lost his mind.

Cade quickly closed the Bible and carried the paper across the landing before he could talk himself out of this. He knocked on Lily's door even though he was sure no one was in the room. He didn't feel right about entering without permission, so he dropped the message on the floorboards and did a little dance until he got it to slide under the door. There. No taking it back.

An immediate fear seized him. What if Lily had even this morning accepted a proposal from Cecil? What a fool Cade would look.

No. He couldn't dwell on it. He had to stay active, not just to take his mind off his vulnerable state, but to push his body to resume function. His hip pained him considerably less, and nothing was wrong with his legs, so he headed for the stairs.

On a sudden internal urging, he stopped and returned to his room, picking up the Testament. He slid the small book beneath the top of the bandages that passed over his chest.

One step at a time, relying on the rail and his crutch, he made his way down to the second floor—an area he'd barely glimpsed until now. Long halls extended from either side. Beth's room lay beneath his, so he took a chance that the family would want to separate themselves and guests from *Sultana* survivors and hobbled down the hall to his right. He got lucky, for the first door he came to stood open, and a man with a splinted leg and bandages covering half his face lay in the bed. The scruffy-chinned soldier looked over and greeted him with a smile.

Half an hour later, Cade emerged, his equilibrium and focus restored. He hadn't been able to do much for the young private short of confirming the slow progress of his healing, but they'd exchanged stories and news. The paper the soldier was reading revealed that a fourth investigation into the *Sultana* explosion had begun in Vicksburg, but the small piece had been buried on an interior page while lead articles described President Lincoln's funeral train inching its way from Washington, DC, to his home state of Illinois. All along the route, thousands of people, black and white, turned out at the depots and beside the tracks to mourn their fallen leader. Meanwhile, officials from Memphis had taken a steamer to attend the funeral that would be held the next day in Springfield.

The heaviness that hung in the room after reading about the nation in mourning called for words of hope. While Cade read the Beatitudes and accounts of Jesus' healing the multitudes, the private had leaned his head back and closed his eyes. A soft smile had curved his lips.

It was the same in every room Cade visited for the next two hours—check the wounds, exchange the stories, and read the Bible. By the last couple of visits, Cade found the courage to pray for the men. They actually accepted…and seemed comforted by his fumbling words. Words he might not be able to pray for himself but which came with surprising ease for others.

He was clumping his way to his last call for the day when a figure in a rose-colored day dress with burgundy trim, those full sleeves called pagoda style, and white undersleeves stopped on the landing, coming up from below.

"Cade?" Lily hurried toward him.

He braced himself against the wall, as weak-kneed at sight of her as he was weary from his endeavors. Dressed like that, she must have been with the partisan all day. What was it, suppertime? His rumbling stomach said it must be so, but his mind fixated on the flush on her cheeks, no doubt wrought by the spring sunshine. Or the flattering attentions of her beau.

A show of jealousy would only diminish him in her eyes. He put on a smile. "Did you have a good ride?"

"Oh." She stopped, her skirt swaying. "That was this morning. I've been back since…well, never mind. I just used an apron to assist Martha with dinner, but before I deal with dishes, I figured I'd change. But what are you doing down here? Did Jacob help you?"

"I helped myself." He flashed a grin. "Got to get moving if I'm ever to get out of this place."

That did not come out as intended. Her lips parted, and her lashes fluttered, but he could hardly set things right by saying he was even more motivated to regain mobility so he could leave with her rather than without her.

"Of course." Her mouth pursed, she avoided his gaze.

He tried again. "The—uh—fresh air seems to have done you good." Cade waved his arm draped over his crutch toward her face.

"Oh, am I sunburned?" She raised her fingers to her cheek. "I did wear a bonnet, I promise, but I was out longer than I'd intended. Everything is so beautiful. The azaleas and roses are starting to bloom. People are putting in their gardens. There's new life everywhere."

And had she been envisioning *her* new life? With Cecil? "Wish I could see it." The outdoors, of course, not her future with another man.

"I wish you could have come with me."

Lily's soft admission snapped Cade's gaze back to her face. She meant that? His heart surged. "Me too. Maybe soon. Thus, the walking." His gesture indicated the hall.

"Right." She gave her head a quick shake, but her brow remained knit. "What are you doing, making medical calls on all these men?"

"Mainly just visiting. And reading to them some." When Cade tapped the top edge of the Testament secured against his chest, Lily's eyes widened. A good moment for a bit of levity, before she could question him about that. "Although I admit, I may have been checking up on Dr. Courtner's work a little."

"Just a little?" A dimple appeared in Lily's cheek. "And what is your professional assessment, Dr. Palmer?"

The title drew a smile from Cade. Was she flirting with him? He'd be safer to take her literally. "It's not bad, though the man across the hall could use his dressings changed as soon as possible, and the one at the end in number nine is showing signs of pyemia."

"Signs of what?"

"Sepsis. Blood poisoning. Did Dr. Courtner leave any silver nitrate?" Cade shifted his weight on his crutch.

"I—I don't know. I can check. Why?"

"The French found it highly effective against infection. You might apply some honey in the meantime. Is Dr. Courtner coming today?"

"He should be here tonight. I'll be sure to tell him—as soon as I can escape from the dirty dishwater, that is." Lily released a sigh.

"Maybe if he requests your assistance with his patients, your aunt would have to agree. Something tells me you make a much better nurse than your cousin." Cade winked at her.

"Oh no." Lily clasped her hands beneath her chin. "She wasn't too awful this morning, was she? Jacob told me she took up your tray."

"We managed to come to an understanding of sorts." Cade rubbed his beard, then grimaced. "Although she did admit to putting morphine in the beef broth."

"No!" Lily's arms fell to her sides. "Oh, Cade, I'm so sorry. I had no idea."

"I know that. And in her misguided way, I think she actually believed she was helping not only me but all the men. But maybe if you tell Dr. Courtner what she did, you'll get put back on bedside duty. And then I can see you again." He allowed his mouth to lift in a smile—hopefully one that looked more charming than needy.

"I would like that, but I might not be here in the morning, anyway."

Cade's stomach bottomed out. "You won't?" Was she going out again with Cecil?

"No. I have an important errand to run. Listen, I…" Lily's face contorted, and she turned away from him, then back to him just as quickly. "I want to apologize for last evening. I don't know what I was saying. I promise, I'm not normally so confusing."

"*Life* is confusing right now."

She nodded, her expression relaxing some. "It's true that you don't know everything about me. I mean, we don't know everything about each other. How could we, so soon? But I do consider you a true friend. Definitely not an enemy. So maybe you can just forget what I said when both of our emotions were running high and forgive me?"

Cade mentally stumbled past that phrase, *true friend*, and forced himself to move his suddenly stiff lips. "There's nothing to forgive."

Her forehead pulled tight again. "But there is. Now of all times, I should not have added to your grief. I feel awful about that. Are you doing all right? Truly?" She peered at him.

She meant regarding James. Cade straightened his shoulders, as much as he could while leaning on the crutch. "Talking with the men helped." Some.

"I'm so glad. I want to be there for you too. And I want you to know, I'm working on the things about myself I'm ashamed of. I'm going to fix them, to do the right thing from here on out. I guess I want to be more like you in that." The admiring smile she beamed Cade's way penetrated the cobwebs of confusion in his brain.

He cocked his head. "What do you mean about doing the right thing?" Was she referring to their relationship or something else? Maybe something to do with her mysterious errand?

"It's nothing. Nothing you need to worry about." Lily pressed her fingers to his arm. "Can I help you back upstairs while I'm headed that direction?"

"Uh, no. I've got one more stop before I call it a night. I'll make it on my own."

"Well, be careful." Concern laced her tone. "I wouldn't want to see you get hurt again." She hovered there a moment, still touching him, then suddenly, she rose up on her toes and brushed his temple with her lips. Before he could react, she scampered away.

She called him a friend and then kissed him? Did she not know that even that brief, chaste gesture was like manna to a starving man?

Chapter Fifteen

Rain tapped against the windowpanes of the provost marshal's office, competing with the irregular dot-dash patterns of the telegraph machine in the next room. The private who served as clerk to Provost Marshal Liam O'Henry had been at it—sending and receiving communications—since he'd unlocked the front door to admit Lily when they opened fifteen minutes ago. She'd slipped out the inn's kitchen door right after plating breakfast, telling only Martha where she was headed. And without explanation. The fewer people who knew about Alex LaFleur, the better.

When she'd arrived, Private Watson had looked for her basket, for a major had dropped off a coat in urgent want of repair. It had pained her to say she couldn't accept any sewing for the time being. And pained her more to stammer out the gist of her reason for being here.

O'Henry had taken in her story so calmly that Lily's own anxiety grew. He now sat surveying her, cocked back in his slatted swivel chair, portly and dignified in his Union blues, clutching a smoking cigar between two fat fingers. She'd told him everything she knew short of how she'd learned LaFleur was recruiting men, though, of course, a little sleuthing would quickly bring her association to Cecil to light. She couldn't worry about that now. A lot of lives could once again be at stake.

"Let me get this straight." The chair creaked as the man finally leaned forward and banked his cigar. "You think this Alex LaFleur was behind the sinking of the *Sultana.*"

Lily took a deep breath and almost choked on the smoke. "I didn't say that. I said it was a possibility. Determining the truth of it is up to you." Now that she'd shed her knowledge, she wanted nothing more than to leave it in the hands of law and justice and run out the door. Her personal life was complicated enough without adding spies and saboteurs.

"Why didn't you come forward when you first heard this conversation?"

Lily fiddled with the wavy-braid trim on her elbow-length wool cloak. "I was told this Frenchie was merely a braggart. I couldn't believe he would go through with it." And she hadn't wanted Aunt Susanna to learn Lily had gone to the authorities about Southern sympathizers meeting in the inn and throw her out—something that could still happen if she didn't hightail it back before her absence was discovered. Martha had agreed to cover for her, to say if questioned that she'd sent Lily on some sort of kitchen business, but that would only hold off Susanna's suspicions for so long. "Only recently did I learn of his association with the saboteur, Charlie Dale."

"I'd still like to know the name of the person who told you about him, and that LaFleur was recruiting former partisans."

Lily held his gaze. "He's a former Confederate himself. That's all I'll tell you." She made a quick assessment of the stacks of papers on his desk. More jutted from square pigeonholes in a stacking filing shelf behind him. "Don't you want to take some notes while I tell you what this Frenchie looks like? I can't draw very well, but unless you or Private Watson can, I can provide fairly accurate details. I've seen him up close." Far too close. She shivered. Was Cecil correct that the man might come after her should he learn she'd ratted on him?

"I can do better than that." Swiveling abruptly, O'Henry pulled a printed circular from one of the slots behind him and slapped a pencil sketch on the desk in front of her. "Is this the man?"

She stared into the menacing dark eyes of Alex LaFleur. Lily swallowed. "That's him."

"I thought as much. He's already in our sights, but he never stays in one place long enough for our agents to nab him. I'll put it out to the Memphis Pinkertons that he's in the area, and they'll make a thorough sweep. Hopefully, we'll get the jump on him this time."

"And you can arrest him then?"

"We can bring him in for questioning."

"That's it?" Lily's shoulders dropped.

O'Henry shrugged. "Unfortunately, we don't have hard evidence to tie him to any particular crimes—just a lot of hearsay. He lets others do his dirty work. But if we can find where he's staying, we stand a chance of uncovering something indicting." The provost marshal spun his sketch around and slipped it back into its pigeonhole.

"So he might be back out on the streets after that?" Madder than a spurned spinster and aware that someone at River Rest had acted the spy.

"Miss Livingston, if it comes to that, I will personally let you know and assign undercover guards at your uncle's inn. The last thing we'd want would be reprisals against the Union boys still recuperating there."

Her eyes went wide. Once again, she could put Cade in danger. "I should have come to you earlier, in April, even though I was uncertain. But I didn't want to get involved. It was selfish of me. I see that now, but I also have a little brother to protect. And my aunt, she…" Tears filled her eyes, but she couldn't bring herself to slander her family members to a stranger, especially one with the authority to punish Southern sympathizers. Hadn't there been enough of that?

The provost marshal's florid face softened, and he leaned forward. "We're aware of your circumstances, Miss Lily. We know perfectly well who in this county is friend and foe. Even if your suspicions about LaFleur prove true, the blame for this doesn't rest on you."

"Doesn't it?" Lily blinked the moisture away. It clung to her lashes, framing the officer before her in a film of regret.

He pressed his lips together briefly. "Well. You've done the right thing now. If it's any comfort, I'm hearing the evidence in the interviews is turning away from sabotage."

"Really?" Lily threaded the strings of her reticule over her wrist. She rose, though her hope didn't. "My cook just said she heard the captain of the *Sultana's* brother-in-law and another man, part owner of the steamer, are visiting the wreckage today, hoping to find evidence that will support their innocence."

O'Henry flapped his beefy hand. "Even if that is true, they won't find anything."

"Others already have, it seems." With a practiced motion, she lifted her lower hoop rungs and the back of her dress from her chair, then allowed them to fall free.

"Pieces of a shell? Is that what you're talking about?"

Lily smoothed her skirt as she glanced toward the door. She really must be going. "Yes, that is what the latest report said was found."

He shook his head. "Miss Lily, a coal torpedo doesn't look like a shell. It's specifically designed to resemble anything but."

"What do you mean?"

"Well, it's all in the construction. First, the engineers take a piece of coal the right size." O'Henry gave an estimate with his fingers. "Then they fill it with explosive, put a plug in, and dip the thing in a mixture of boiling coal tar, beeswax, and coal dust. Finally, they immerse it in ice water. That coats it, but when the surface gloss is scraped off, the torpedo resembles a lump of coal in weight, smell, and appearance. So I don't believe the latest fragments that were found at Hen's Island were from a coal torpedo."

"Oh..." Lily released the soft exclamation on a relieved breath. If he was correct—and this was the first thing that had given her true hope—she might not have to keep carrying this awful weight of responsibility. "Thank you for telling me that."

O'Henry smiled. "I'm glad that gives you some relief. Nevertheless, we will follow up on LaFleur. Even if he didn't sink the *Sultana*, he's wanted in connection with countless other crimes. And we will do all we can to ensure he does not commit another. Leave it with the officials, Miss Lily."

"Yes, sir. Thank you, sir." Lily bobbed a curtsy of sorts before turning for the door.

Private Watson didn't even look up from his decoding as she let herself out onto the street—probably more occupied than usual with messages pertaining to President Lincoln's funeral. The newspapers said he was being buried today in his hometown of Springfield, Illinois.

Lily pulled the wide rim of her black bonnet forward as far as possible to create a shield from the rain. It had been light enough when she set out to not bother with an umbrella, but now she wished she had. She kept to porches and awnings as much as possible as she made her way down the street, the mud of which was churned by horse hooves and wagon wheels. The bottom bone of her hoop clicked in a rapid cadence every time her square-toed boots hit the front. The chill of the damp morning penetrated her dress and cape.

Well, she'd be warm soon enough, laboring over the stove and running meals to the patrons. While Dr. Courtner had indeed requested her assistance last night, Aunt Susanna had delayed telling her until she'd finished the dishes. By the time Lily located him, the physician had already sent Beth away and worked himself into a considerably grumpy humor. It had made for a very long and late evening. And her aunt had made it clear Lily was to return to the kitchen this morning.

Still, she'd been able to assist Dr. Courtner when he changed Cade's dressings and oversaw his exercises. Cade had definitely gained more flexibility and strength, but he hadn't seemed as happy about it as Lily would have expected. He'd tracked her movements with a certain quiet speculation but made no attempt to detain her when she followed the elderly physician from the room. Only when she'd returned to hers had she found the shaky-handed note that he must have written and slipped under her door. Its contents had kept her awake even later, as she weighed its implications against her fresh suspicions about Cecil.

Was Cade merely complimenting her attributes, seeking to reassure her that he didn't hold a grudge over her inconsistent behavior? Or something more? Surely, on so brief an acquaintance, he could offer her no assurances. She'd only fallen asleep after praying over the matter, but she possessed no greater clarity this morning.

By the time Lily reached the inn, rain pelted down hard from the heavy skies. She pushed the kitchen door open and almost ran straight into Beth, who must have been standing just on the other side, preparing to look out.

Her cousin's demand as Lily shook water from her skirts confirmed it.

"Where have you been? I've got to go out, but I couldn't leave until you were back. Martha needs someone to make the johnnycakes."

Lily untied the bow of her bonnet. "What's so urgent?"

"I could ask you the same thing—if I had time." Beth scowled at her. "Before he left last night, Dr. Courtner ordered honey compresses for two of the men, those in danger of infection."

Lily removed her bonnet and hung it on the peg nearest the door. "Yes, until he can replenish his stock of silver nitrate." The fact that the doctor had taken Cade's recommendations and was even using his secondary suggestion as a preventative measure brought a swell of pride for Cade.

"What are you smiling about? Do you know how much honey that will take? We've run through our stores faster than a mouse at a grain mill, and now I have to go to the mercantile. In this downpour. Have you seen my cloak anywhere?"

Lily riffled through the selection of aprons and capes hanging on the pegs. "No." She glanced at Martha, who held her biggest pottery bowl on her hip as she whipped batter. The cook offered a quick shake of her head along with a warning lift of her eyebrows. She must have already been the recipient of Beth's ire. "I'm sorry. Would you like to borrow my cape?"

"Fine. Dr. Courtner wanted that honey applied first thing. And Judge Winkler is calling at noon."

As she unhooked the crocheted clasp of the outer garment at her throat, something nudged Lily to take closer notice of the faint wobble of her cousin's lower lip rather than her impatiently outstretched hand. "Beth…" Lily slipped out of her cape and pressed it into her cousin's grip, but she pinned her fingers there a moment. "Is that what has you in a tizzy? The judge's visit?"

Beth took a tremulous breath. "You're so lucky. A man like Cecil wants you. I think Hiram is going to propose—if not today, very soon. But I don't know how I can say yes, Lily."

The unaccustomed plea for understanding in the use of her name lassoed Lily's heart. She touched her cousin's arm and looked into her eyes. "Then you shouldn't."

"What else am I to do?" A bitter laugh tumbled out. "Stay here forever, working my hands raw serving sweaty men?"

Lily had never considered that Beth might feel just as trapped as she did, even with her own family. "You should wait for the right one."

"And what if he never comes?" Beth took the cape and shrugged into it. "Not everyone has your options."

It was Lily's turn to give a wry laugh. She reached up to fasten the frog clasp beneath Beth's chin. "*Do* I have options?"

"Yes. You do." Beth's abrupt response stilled Lily's fingers. "You have two men in love with you. I'd give anything…"

Beth thought Cade was in love with Lily? The idea so stunned her, she almost let her cousin pass without attempting to assuage her pain. Just in time, she focused and grabbed Beth's elbow. "Hiram does love you, Beth. You should see his face when he speaks of you. He'll treat you like a queen."

Beth stared at her a moment, then her mouth twisted. "I don't want to be his queen."

Banging out the door, she left Lily standing there with her chest aching. Beth's bitterness sprang from a deep personal well of rejection and inferiority. Now she was judging her suitor with the same harsh measure that had been used on her.

Why had Lily not tried harder to reach Beth with the love of Christ, the only love that could heal and fulfill her? Guilt rose like the floodwaters of the Mississippi. She'd been so focused on her own struggles, she'd missed another opportunity to do the right thing. Now it might be too late.

Chapter Sixteen

Lily had just returned from delivering a tray of chicken potpies—more of a potato pie in chicken broth, thanks to the continued shortages—to a table of Sanitary Commission workers when her aunt swept into the kitchen, imperious in her severe navy dress. As she consulted notes on the pad where she kept her daily but ever-expanding list of duties, everyone stopped what they were doing to watch her with unveiled dread.

Aunt Susanna didn't even notice. In fact, had she even assessed who was actually in the room before she started firing off orders? "Mika, the upstairs linen closet is low on hand towels. Lily, take the midday meal to the railroad man in room five. And while you're up there, room six is ready for a change of sheets. The family staying there just checked out. And I…I will take tea to the rich spinster sisters in the private dining room." Crossing to the small, ornate Chinese chest where they stored tea, coffee, and sugar, she opened it with a key from her silver chatelaine.

Mika spoke up from the sink. "The towels are in the storeroom. I washed them last night but put them on the dryin' rack in there since it was raining."

"I can collect them and take them upstairs when I go," Lily said as she transferred a golden-crusted pie from the counter to a clean tray. No need for Mika to make an extra trip.

The girl shot her an appreciative glance. "Thank you, Miss Lily. And Miss Beth? I also cleaned your cloak. It's hangin' in there as well."

Beth paused in serving up Martha's bread pudding into a series of small bowls she'd lined up on the counter. She whirled on Mika with her mouth hanging open. "You took my cloak without telling me? I never asked you to wash it."

Mika blinked her round eyes. "The hem was muddy. I thought you might want it freshened up in case the weather stayed cool for your outing with the judge today."

"You're never to touch my things without asking first." Beth pointed her goopy spoon at the servant girl. Lily, who had approached for a serving of bread pudding, ducked out of the way. "Never. Do you hear?"

Lily frowned and placed her hand on her cousin's wrist, slowly lowering it with the utensil that shook in her grip. "Beth." She spoke the name with soft emphasis. "Mika only meant to be helpful. You should be thanking her instead of scolding her."

Beth slanted a glare at her. "And you should stop telling me what to do."

"You're overreacting." And they both knew why.

"I'm not overreacting. These *servants* keep forgetting their place these days."

Lily shook her head as she scooped up a bowl of bread pudding. Thanks to her mother's upbringing and example, Beth was as bad as a petulant plantation belle. "You know she did nothing wrong. It's your own frustration talking." She wanted to say more, even to offer to pray with Beth before she met with Judge Winkler, but she could hardly do so with her aunt there.

Indeed, the woman diverted their attention almost immediately, speaking while she poured hot water from the kettle into a dainty china teapot. "Your cousin is right this time, Beth. You should compose yourself. Judge Winkler has already arrived."

"He has?" Beth gasped. "He's early."

Aunt Susanna placed the lid back on the teapot. "Try not to sound so pleased. He went up for a brief visit to that lieutenant, apparently a friend of his. He's probably already waiting for you in the foyer." Beth paled, her wide eyes meeting her mother's even gaze as Aunt Susanna returned the kettle to the stovetop. "You should have worn your blue silk dress, not that old cotton rag. Take off your apron, at least. And fix your hair. It looks like a rat's nest."

Beth pivoted away from Lily's sympathetic expression, snatching off her apron, balling it up, and throwing it onto the counter. Hopefully, her cousin would find a way to navigate her relational quandary with reason rather than emotion. If only Lily could find a way to do the same. She'd been playing the *what if* game with herself all morning. She suppressed a sigh and went to fetch coffee for her guest's tray.

After folding a small stack of hand towels from the storeroom, Lily balanced them in one arm and secured the tray in the other. As she pulled the storeroom door closed, the stack toppled, and the top two towels fell off.

"Ugh." She slid the tray onto the bench that sat against the stairwell—thankfully, empty—and knelt to collect the linens. As she swept up the one that had landed partly beneath the bench, she spied a tiny slip of folded paper. Was it a note someone had dropped? Lily reached for it and opened it.

She stared at a series of four-letter…well, she couldn't rightly call them *words*. For while they were arranged like words, they made no sense. They were just random combinations of letters.

But *were* they random?

Lily squinted. What was she looking at? Some kind of code?

"Oh, Miss Lily, let me help you with that." Dressed in a black frock coat, charcoal-colored pants, and a striped silk vest, Judge Winkler peered over the stair rail. He tapped his way down the steps with his walking stick.

Lily slid the paper between the two towels and put them back atop her stack. Before he could attempt to squat next to her, she waved him off. "Thank you, Judge Winkler, but there's no need. I have it." Even if he had gotten down, she'd have to help *him* back up, not the other way around. She rose and tucked the towels under her arm. "But if you don't mind handing me that tray…"

"Of course, Miss Lily." He picked it up and held it out with a solicitous smile. "I've just been up to see Dr. Palmer. He's looking much improved. And he has a small surprise for you." He offered her a wink as jaunty as the ruby stickpin that glinted from the folds of his dove-gray cravat.

"A surprise for me?" Lily touched her chest before she took hold of the tray.

Whatever was Cade up to? Another scripture, perhaps? Or maybe he'd found a flowery poem among Beth's volumes. The idea made her flush. But at least it meant he wasn't upset she'd sent Jacob to check on him this morning instead of going herself, since she'd had to leave for the provost office so early.

As it seemed, he was getting more and more independent, anyway. Soon, he'd be able to accomplish most tasks for himself. No…soon, he'd be leaving. And that twisted her stomach into a knot.

"Yes. Before we know it, he'll be reunited with his family." Judge Winkler's words, pronounced so joyfully, only served to emphasize the reality Lily dreaded. He removed his hat and smoothed his graying hair into place. "I delivered his parents' reply to the telegram I sent."

"What did it say?" Lily asked breathlessly.

"That they praised God for their son's deliverance and awaited news of his return." Judge Winkler replaced his top hat. "I assured him we will let them know as soon as he is cleared for transport. I hear they're scheduling several steamers to take the remaining men north next week."

"So soon." Lily's throat worked to subdue the obstruction that suddenly lodged there. "It's already Thursday."

Judge Winkler peered at her with his head tilted. "My dear girl, your compassion does you credit. Yes, I was also taken by surprise at how quickly the government is moving these men, including those wounded so grievously. I shouldn't wonder if the journey doesn't finish some of them off."

Lily gasped.

The judge reassured her with a hand to her arm. "Not the men you've cared for here, surely. Cade tells me they are recovering nicely. Well, with a couple exceptions, perhaps."

Indeed. And Cade would take it upon himself to try to oversee those on the voyage north. She had to see him today, even if she had to sneak some time. If she hurried with the linen change, she could fit in a quick visit to the third floor before returning to the kitchen. Even as she thought it, an undeniable awareness rose. A quick visit was not enough. She needed much more time with him than she had.

Lily edged toward the steps. "If you'll excuse me, Judge Winkler, I need to take this upstairs."

"My apologies. I've kept you standing with that heavy tray." Once again, Judge Winkler lifted his hat.

"Pray, don't worry, Judge. And I'm sure Beth will be right out."

Her chest squeezed as she mounted the steps. Poor man. Whatever his age or appearance, his kind heart made him deserving of a woman who would return his adoration. But if Beth found the courage to turn him down, he might very soon suffer a *broken* heart.

Lily knocked on the door of number five. When the guest inside rumbled a reply, she announced, "Your dinner, sir." But she didn't wait for him to open the door. She'd learned the hard way about presenting herself with meal trays or deliveries at the rooms of certain types of men. And one could rarely identify such types in advance. Instead, she placed the tray on the floor and whisked into room six. There she set the towels on the bureau, drawing from between the top two that strange note she'd found in the entry hall.

Lily frowned at the three lines of print. Block letters, all in groups of four. What could it mean?

"There you are!" The booming voice behind her startled her down to her toes.

She didn't even have to think about the instinct to tuck the paper between two hooks of her bodice. It was that compelling. She simply obeyed. By the time she whirled to face Cecil, the message nestled between her bodice and her corset cover, near her heart...which betrayed her. For it did not leap with the thrill one would expect. Instead, it gave a dull thud that vaguely resembled another name. *Cade*. Her disappointment that Cecil's arrival would delay if not supplant her visit to Cade was too strong to be denied.

"Cecil." She spoke the name of the man before her and summoned a warm smile.

"They told me I'd find you somewhere up here, but makin' up a room?" His gaze traveled from the dresser, scattered with whiskey bottles and a plate holding half a gnawed chicken, to the rope bed with the blue-and-white-striped ticking peeking from beneath the rumpled covers. "That's maid's work."

"Which is why I'm doing it." Lily grabbed a couple of hand towels and carried them over to the washstand, where she hung one each over the thin rails on the sides. Avoiding inspection of the dirty water in the basin, she bent to collect the soiled linens, picking them up with the tips of her fingers.

"You're not a maid."

She tossed the towels onto the cotton sheets, shooting him a look. "I'm not a *servant*. Though I'm awfully close. What did you think I do here, Cecil?"

He advanced into the room a few steps. "Cookin'? Servin' some food, maybe?" With a gingerly grasp, he plucked the corner of the sheet from under the mattress and helped her begin to fold it. His assistance softened her.

"And taking little old ladies tea on trays with fresh flowers, no doubt." Indeed, that was her aunt's job. Lily gave an unladylike snort. She grabbed a pillow, its feather contents packed tight, and started shaking it loose of its case. "No, with the extra men here, we've all had to step up and do whatever needs done."

"That's right. Beth said you were helpin' nurse the Yankees." Cecil straightened and stared at her. "One in particular. You never told me about him."

That was because she'd been terrified either her little brother or her own face would somehow betray her feelings on the matter. She shrugged, dropped the pillowcase onto the pile of linens, and reached for the other pillow. "Nothing to tell. He'll be leaving soon enough."

"*Not* soon enough."

Cecil's mumbled comment made Lily stop shaking the pillow. But his countenance had hardened rather than twisted. Hatred, not jealousy, then. Ought she to be relieved or dismayed? She wrested the pillowcase free. "What brings you to town again so soon?"

He looked up, incredulous lines making a *V* in his forehead. "You really have to ask? After the way we left things last night?"

"I wasn't upset with you, Cecil."

"No, you just didn't believe a word I said."

"I—I don't know what to believe." Especially now, with that strange message tucked into her bodice. Could it have something to do with the saboteurs who'd frequented River Rest? The possibility momentarily stole her breath.

"Did you go to the provost marshal?"

His question snagged her attention. "Yes. I had to. I couldn't keep a secret like that again. But I made sure to keep your name out of it."

Cecil leaned his fists on the ticking, somehow seemingly oblivious to the suspicious stains there. "Lily, that's not what I'm worried about. I thought I made that clear. If that man learns you informed on him, you're not safe here."

She bit her lower lip, her resolve wavering. Perhaps Cecil's only concern truly had been her welfare. Should she show him the coded message? If spies like Charlie Dale had sent communications to guerillas during the war, Cecil might know how to decipher it.

"You need to let me protect you."

That threw up her walls faster than the Rebs had entrenched Vicksburg. She'd keep the message to herself for now. Maybe show it to Cade.

In a show of nonchalance, Lily shrugged and rolled the dirty linens into a ball. "They're looking for him already...although maybe you already knew that." She cut him a glance.

Straightening to his considerable height, Cecil released a gusty sigh. "Look, I'm not keepin' anything from you, Lily. I'd never talked with Frenchie—LaFleur—whoever he is—before yesterday. And I told him to pike off. All I want is to rebuild a respectable life in the county where I grew up. To protect my family and raise one of my own. And I can't picture doin' that without you."

"Cecil…"

As if his name she spoke so wistfully summoned rather than placated him, he circled the bed, his gaze pinning her in place.

What was she going to do? She was as cornered as Beth. Only, just as surely as she now stood between the wall and Cecil, she stood between two men, and she didn't know if the one she wanted felt the same about her. Even if he did, if it did come to light that her silence had enabled the saboteurs to fire the *Sultana*, his disgust for her would surely extinguish any reservations he held about jumping on the next steamer north.

But she couldn't leave Cecil hanging. To do so after all this time would be nothing but cruel.

He stopped a few inches from her. "I didn't get to say what I wanted to last night. So when I had to come into town for supplies this morning, why wouldn't I come by?"

Indeed, he wore the clothing of a farmer today—old wool pants, a striped cotton shirt, and a nubby linen vest. Floppy hat and square-toed work boots. The garb made him no less commanding as he loomed over her, smelling of hay and leather. And countless childhood days fishing by the creek and berry picking. Not memories she could easily let go.

Maybe the nostalgia reflected on her face, for Cecil's expression softened too. He brushed the side of her cheek with the tips of his long fingers. "Remember the dance at my place the night before Hamp and I left for the war?"

She dipped her head. "How can I forget?" She could still envision the bonfire and hear the lilt of the fiddle as long lines of figures spun and sashayed through the Virginia reel, the bonfire behind them shooting sparks up to the twinkling stars. The intoxication of independence and adventure and glory had been so strong upon them all that it had moved even her.

"'The Last Rose of Summer'…remember?"

"Of course." Her breath stalled as his hand slid behind her neck. He'd kissed her at the end of their last waltz together, and she'd felt safe enough to let him. Not just because it was her brother's best friend and her protector taking the liberty but because they hadn't been alone and he'd been leaving the next day. But now, they *were* alone, and he wasn't leaving. And he was lowering his mouth to hers.

"Cecil…" She planted her palms on his chest and turned her face to the side.

He wrapped one hand around her waist and angled her chin back to him with the other. "What are you doin', Lily? Are you playin' games with me? Well, I don't need games. I've waited long enough for you to be mine."

"I know, but Cecil—"

"I need your devotion and your affection, and by heaven, I will have them."

"Stop—wait!" Her arms flailed in an attempt to push him back, but Cecil fought her hands down and crushed her against him, slanting his mouth over hers. She broke loose long enough to get out a "no!"

But it wasn't her protest that stopped him. It was a voice from the doorway, low with anger and shaking with threat. "Take your hands off her. The lady said no."

The moment Cecil's hold slackened, Lily ducked free.

Cecil gaped at her rescuer, who now stood just inside the room. "Who the blazes are you?"

Lily could ask the same thing, for she barely recognized the freshly shaven man who confronted Cecil, his white shirt rolled up at the elbows. At least, she might not have, had it not been for the sling around his arm and the crutch raised in his left hand, as if he prepared to beat Cecil off her. From the look on Cade's face, the danger of reinjuring himself wouldn't stop him.

Chapter Seventeen

"Cade?"

When Lily spoke his name, Cade spared her but the briefest of glances, keeping his focus on the tall ex-Confederate who was himself barely visible through the red haze of Cade's anger. His legs tingled, and his heart beat out of his chest, but his heightened emotions obscured any pain. How dare the man force his affections on Lily? She barely reached his chin. If someone hadn't come to her rescue…

But thank God he'd been hobbling down the hall when she cried out. "Come over here, Lily."

She did, but to support him, not get behind him. She pressed on the end of the crutch he held almost horizontal in a white-knuckled grip. "Put that down. You're going to reinjure yourself."

He shot her an incredulous glance. She wouldn't even allow him to pose a semi-convincing threat? Truth be told, he would have rammed the former partisan using his crutch like a spear if he'd had to. Wrestled him to the floor even if it ripped the bandages from his own back and shattered his hand. Didn't she know that? He settled for an assurance passed through tight lips. "I'll handle this."

Lucky Cecil had reclaimed his composure. He came around the bed, his eyes narrowed. "Cade, is it? You're the one Lily rescued." Sarcasm dripped from a voice already laden with a heavy Southern accent.

"Well, I guess I just returned the favor." Cade spat the quip out like a green crab apple.

"And I guess I just saw the problem." Cecil stared at Lily as though she'd fallen in a latrine. "Now I know what changed."

"Cecil, you don't know what you're talking about. He just wanted to make sure I was all right. Cade, you should sit down." She tried to take his arm, but he shook her free, angling to keep himself between her and Cecil.

"Just wanted to make sure you were all right, hmm? Is that all? Then why is he lookin' at me as though he wants to take my head off? As if he could." Cecil's top lip curled up in something between a mocking smile and a snarl.

Cade scoffed in return. "Nothing personal. I'd look at any scoundrel the same way."

"A scoundrel, am I?" Cecil's fair brows flew up.

"Please, both of you, stop." Lily attempted to step between them, her hand raised.

Cade nudged her back with his crutch, never taking his eyes off Cecil. "Yes, a scoundrel. What else? A gentleman doesn't force himself on a lady."

"What do you know of that, you bag of bones?" Cecil stepped closer, puffing his chest out. He glared down at Cade. "I'd fight you…if you were still a man. We may have lost this war, but you're the one who's whipped."

Heat rushed up Cade's neck into his face. He wanted nothing more than the use of his right hand—this time not to heal but to throttle. He could almost feel the Rebel's throat under his fingers. Maybe, in this moment, his injury was a good thing. He blew out a disgusted breath. "You're not worth it. Get out of here."

"You can't send me away."

"No, but I can." Lily spoke firmly, though she kept her head lowered. "Please, Cecil, you should go. We'll talk again when you've calmed down."

"Would that make any difference?" The former partisan searched her face.

Cade's breath hitched as he also turned to read what was written there.

Lily's lips trembled, and she blinked rapidly. With uncertainty? But then she attempted to meet Cecil's eyes and failed. "I don't know."

But she did. Cecil had seen it just as surely as Cade had—sorrow. The warm rush of amazement that swept through Cade nearly made his knees buckle.

Lily's former beau shook his head, his features twisting. "How could you, Lily? After all I did to protect you. You'd throw yourself away on the enemy?"

"He is not my enemy." She whispered the words, soft but clear. When Lily slipped her hand around Cade's elbow, he gaped at her. She didn't turn her face from Cecil. "I'm sorry, Cecil. Now please go."

The ex-ranger stared at her a moment as if he couldn't believe his ears. Finally, he spoke, his tone gravelly. "You will regret this." Then he pivoted and stalked from the room.

Cade and Lily stood there unmoving, Cecil's retreating steps and their own breathing the only sounds. When the footfalls faded into silence, Cade let the crutch drop from his hand as he turned to wrap his arm around Lily. His fingers shoved up into her hair, and he drew her head to him, pressing a kiss on her forehead.

"Oh, Cade." Her quavering cry was muffled in his shirt, which he'd gotten on for the first time with a good deal of trouble and a little help from Jacob. Was she weeping? "What have I done?"

Gratitude he expected, but regret? Did she fear she'd made a mistake with her old beau? Cade pulled back to peer at her. "I assume you just sent away a man you didn't love. One who was trying to take advantage of you."

She lifted her face. Tears indeed streaked it. "Maybe he was, but it was the first time he's ever pressed me like that. And I haven't made it easy for him."

"That doesn't excuse his behavior." But what did she mean, she hadn't made it easy? At the rapid play of imaginings behind his eyes, Cade's brows tugged down.

"Don't frown at me like that." Lily cupped his cheek with one of her hands. His skin, newly exposed by the razor, tingled where her fingers touched and where her gaze swept over it, her thorough perusal not missing an inch. "You shaved. I hardly recognized you."

He rubbed the close-trimmed remnant of his goatee. "I had some help." And he sported a nick or two to prove it. Jacob would need a lot of practice with a razor before a beard of his own started sprouting out.

"Well, it looks nice." The fullness of her tone and her suddenly averted eyes indicated she might find it a bit more than nice. "And I can't bear to have you mad at me too."

Cade's shoulders relaxed. He could hardly remain tense enough to punch through a wall when she looked at him like that. "I'm not mad. I'm concerned."

At his obvious understatement, she choked back what might have been a laugh. "You deserve an explanation. But first, let's sit down. Please. Before you fall down."

She tugged at him, and he slanted a sideways look at her. "Concern gives a man a tremendous amount of energy." In fact, his veins still pulsed and burned. He hated to think what else might pulse and burn after the provocation wore off.

Lily's laugh, so sudden, free, and clear, went a long way toward restoring his peace. Cade allowed her to lead him to the bed, where he collapsed to a sitting position, his crutch Lily plucked from the floor propped at one side and her at the other. She nestled under his good arm. It did him good to imagine she might at least draw comfort from his nearness.

He filled his lungs with air, then released it slowly. "I remember what you said about Cecil having made a promise to your brother before he died. Is that what you're talking about? What you think I don't understand?"

"That's part of it." She kept her lashes lowered.

Cade prompted her. "He mentioned that he protected you."

"Not only me, but our family. Everyone in the county knew if they messed with us, they'd have not only Cecil but his band of raiders to deal with."

"I see. I imagine that was quite invaluable here in no-man's-land." He rubbed Lily's shoulder gently, softly, while staring out the open door. "And also that he would take it as an insult that now that the need for that is gone, you rebuffed him."

"Yes." Lily sniffled and swiped at her nose. "I reckon he's entitled to feel led on. Used. And that's why I need an opportunity to tell him, if he'll ever hear me out, how much I treasure his generosity and kindness… and want to remain his friend. Because we were friends long before we were anything else."

Cade stilled at her words. "So you did love him once?" He had to ask, though the question hurt even being voiced.

She gave a light laugh, but without humor. "Adored. Admired. Appreciated. But loved? I'm not sure that I ever did."

He did all he could to disguise his relief. "Apparently, he didn't know that."

Her shoulders sagged. "That's what I meant when I said I didn't make it easy for him. For those years apart, I let him think I was waiting for him to come back. It wasn't all a ruse. At first, it was more of a girlhood dream." Lily lifted her chin and sighed, as if images from the past played out before her eyes. "Cecil was dashing and handsome, and all the girls envied me. I guess I loved him as much as a naive young woman could. And it wasn't all selfish, either, because after my parents died, marrying him offered my only way out of here, for both me and Jacob."

"And still would have," Cade said flatly. Until she'd squandered that chance minutes earlier. For him?

Lily didn't seem to have heard. She concluded her explanation in a soft voice, looking straight ahead. "Not to mention, I owed him. I was bound to him even before he made that promise to Hamp."

Something closed around Cade's chest. "In what way *bound to him*?" Just repeating the words left a sour taste in his mouth.

Lily covered her face. For a moment, she breathed loudly, unsteadily. Then she dropped her hand. "I've never told anybody else. Only Hamp and Cecil know."

"Know what?" He tried to turn her to face him, but she squared her shoulders, insisting on looking forward rather than at him.

"How Cecil rescued me from another boy when I was sixteen. Much as you rescued me today, only worse. Much worse."

Cade went perfectly still. A black hole opened before his eyes. Was she saying what he thought she was saying?

She flashed the briefest glance at him, then quickly looked away. "No, he didn't have his way with me, but it was bad enough. Humiliating. My honor was ruined. And Cecil found me in that compromised position. He beat the boy within an inch of his life and threatened to finish the job if he ever came near me again. From that day on, Cecil became my shadow. My protector. And he never told anyone except for Hamp. People just assumed Cecil was courting me, and I reckon that's how it started. Even when the other boy eventually moved away, Cecil was always there."

Cade blinked and shook his head, struggling to process what she'd just told him. He tightened his arm around Lily and drew her closer. "I'm so sorry you went through that. And after hearing it, I'm grateful to—and even sorry for—Cecil." Under different circumstances, he probably could have liked the fellow.

"Then you can see why this is so hard for him. I was afraid of men for a long time—I still am sometimes—but not Cecil. He never pushed me for affection, not until today."

"Affection that's forced is not really affection."

"You're right," Lily murmured the soft admission. "Of course it isn't."

Cade drew a deep breath. With Lily nestled in his arms—well, *arm*—he could afford to be generous. "But you spoke the truth when you said this war leaves men with unseen scars. And under those, I believe Cecil has a good heart."

"Yes, he does, and it means a lot to hear you say that." Lily wiped another tear away. "But we are not of the same mind and spirit, him and me." She raised her head from Cade's shoulder. "Not like…"

"Like you and I?" Cade held his breath.

And she nodded. "I can only give my heart to someone who shares my beliefs."

He did, that. This was his cue to kiss her if ever there was one. But he could hardly swoop in where Cecil had just failed. Not without asking. And not in an awkward side hug. He lowered his arm and angled toward her before doubt slammed into him with the force of a locomotive.

Would she even welcome an advance? He'd begun to fill out, if only incrementally, and the ability to shave and don a shirt had made him feel human again. Yet sharing the same mind and spirit hardly guaranteed attraction. Perhaps the connection on her part more resembled the bond of deep friendship. Even if something more potent stirred, what future could he offer her when ambiguity blanketed his own?

And yet…he'd never forgive himself if he didn't try. He reached for her hand. "Lily…"

"Oh!" The hand he sought bounced up to her bodice. "That made me remember. Something very important."

What could be more important than a declaration of their feelings? But as she unfastened one of her bodice hooks and her fingers quested under her cotton dress, his eyes widened. This he hadn't been prepared for.

From beneath her bodice, she withdrew a small paper, unfolded it, and handed it to him. "Do you know what this is?"

Cade did his best to focus on the writing before him, but he must not be doing too good of a job, for the words made no sense. Then he sucked in a breath and glanced up at her. "Where did you find this?"

"From beneath the bench in the entry hallway, where I guess someone dropped it. I think it's a code. Is it?"

Cade smoothed the paper on his leg. "Yes. It seems to be a type of cipher. Vignère, if I'm not mistaken."

"What's that?"

"A polyalphabetic substitution cipher that evolved from Caesar cipher."

"What?" Lily gave her head a quick shake.

"Caesar cipher encrypts a message by shifting each letter in the plain text message up or down a certain number of places in the alphabet. So if the message was right-shifted by a preset amount—say, four spaces—*A* would become *E*, and so forth." Cade's limited ability to gesture wasn't helping matters, as Lily gave him a blank stare.

"How do you know all this?"

"There was a guy in prison who'd acted as a courier who was always talking about such things."

"All right." She swiped her hand over one side of her face as if clearing her thoughts. "If this is Vignère or whatever you called it, how does that work? Can you read this?" She pointed to the message.

"Not without a corresponding chart or wheel. Military officials and spies use one or the other when decoding. And we'd have to know the key word or phrase the sender used."

"So there's no way we can figure out what the person who dropped this intended."

"With no more than the coded message? No." He frowned. "Do you have reason to believe someone meant to deliver it here? Or pass it through someone at the inn?"

Lily's eyes widened, and then she grabbed up the paper. She refolded it and tucked it back inside her bodice. As evasive as General Sherman on his way to Atlanta.

"Lily?" Cade turned her chin toward him, his heart beating an irregular rhythm. "What do you know?"

Chapter Eighteen

Lily's racing pulse created a rushing in her ears that almost drowned out Cade's question. She would have read the suspicion in his gaze even if she hadn't heard it in his voice. This was it—her moment to share the burden she'd been carrying. She'd just sent away the man who had been her security for five years, but she could no more hope for a future with Cade when she kept secrets from him than she could keep Cecil hanging when her heart longed for another. But this secret…it could take away that hope before it even had a chance to blossom.

She wet her lips. "I don't know anything for certain, but it's possible spies and saboteurs loyal to the South have frequented River Rest."

"Why do you believe that?" Cade's brows were so straight it only took a slight frown to make them appear to hinge on the inside corners of his eyes. Not to mention, with his beard gone, the prominence of his strong jaw and high cheekbones that she'd just found so appealing now seemed intimidating.

Lily swallowed. "A week or two before the explosion on the *Sultana*, I overheard a conversation in the private dining room."

For the second time that day, she recounted what had been said by

Frenchie and the other men and how afterward Beth had minimized the seriousness of the threat. But the right words evaded her, and Lily stumbled and stammered even as she attempted to keep the telling impersonal. It *was* personal. Profoundly—as Cade's expression showed, reflecting a procession from concern to alarm and then finally to shock when Lily related Cecil's conversation with Frenchie…Alex LaFleur, associate of Charlie Dale, a known Confederate saboteur.

"As soon as I realized who he was, I had to go to the authorities. First thing this morning, I called on the provost marshal and told him everything." Lily twisted her fingers in her skirt, chancing a peek at Cade.

His face had gone blank. "You told him everything—but after the fact. After LaFleur killed over a thousand men." *Including James.* He didn't say it, but Lily could pinpoint the moment the thought crossed his mind. Sorrow washed over him in an almost visible wave, leaving his eyes clouded and his head and shoulders weighted.

"We don't know that." Lily reached for his hand, but he slid his back. "There is no evidence. In fact, though the provost marshal said LaFleur was wanted in connection with a number of crimes, they have no direct evidence against him in any of them. And the shell fragments most recently found at the wreck of the *Sultana* do not match the appearance of a coal torpedo."

Cade darted a glance at her. "That's not what the first mate said."

"But you told me he could've been lying to protect himself. O'Henry said the more recent testimonies discount sabotage. Didn't you say the boiler had just been repaired? If it hadn't been tested and the boat was so overcrowded, isn't a mechanical malfunction the more likely cause?"

He searched her eyes, then shook his head. "For your sake, I hope so, Lily."

Her chest caved inward with the heaviness of his implication. "You've lost faith in me, and before we even know the truth."

"The truth is you were privy to information that held hundreds of lives in the balance, and you chose to ignore it. That choice is not dependent on the outcome."

"I know. And I hate myself for it." Lily took a shuddering breath and buried her face in her hands. "But I was so afraid."

"Of what?"

"If Aunt Susanna or Beth found out I'd reported men they considered friends to the authorities, they could be angry enough to throw me and Jacob out…and I didn't have another place for us to go."

"So you put your comfort above all those lives."

Certainly, that was a minimization, but guilt still stabbed her like the sharpest bayonet. "Yes. Although 'comfort' makes it sound so warm and cozy. It wasn't just comfort. It was survival. You don't understand what it was like around here." Dropping her hands, she shook her head briskly. Tears overflowed and ran down her cheeks. "The only way to survive has been silence. That and loyalty to family. If you spoke out against one side or the other, you could expect reprisals—and family members turning against each other often exacted the harshest. That's why I've kept my convictions to myself. That…and learning the hard way."

"What do you mean?" His question came out dry, but at least he was still talking to her.

Lily pressed her hand to her thudding heart. "I mean my brother. Hamp. The morning he left, I asked him not to go." She'd awakened from the previous night of revelry with cold clarity—and bone-numbing fear. Almost like a premonition. Somehow, she'd known if Hampton left, he wouldn't come back. "I told him I knew he didn't believe in many of the things the South was fighting for, and he was only going because Cecil had talked him into it with that silver tongue of his. I begged him to stay, be true to his moral convictions, and keep us safe. But nothing I said would convince him. I only succeeded in making him mad."

Cade adjusted the sling around his right arm. "Did you see him again? Get to set it right?"

"No. And he didn't write either. He died thinking his twin sister was his enemy."

"I'm certain he didn't think that."

When Cade's hand moved over hers, she almost blubbered out loud. "But I'll never know this side of heaven, will I?" Abruptly, she wiped her face with her free hand.

"No, but *he'll* know. He knows now."

With a groan, Lily pulled free, angling to face him. She didn't deserve his comfort, even as she pleaded for his understanding. "But don't you see? I've never stopped regretting it. Ever since Hamp and my parents died, I've gotten along by going along—with the community, our relatives who took us in, even Cecil's plan to come back for me. I did it for my remaining brother. I couldn't lose him too."

Cade tilted his head. "That's why it was so hard for you to let Cecil go."

"Yes!" Lily threw her hands open. "I made two huge decisions today that went against everything I've known and done for the past four years. And I made them without having a safety net." Especially if Cade rejected her.

He reached for his crutch. "Thank you for explaining."

"That's it?" And stated so coldly, while looking at the floor.

He tucked his bottom lip and offered the barest glance. "I know that took courage."

"*That* took courage?" The question practically wailed out of her. "Telling *you* took courage!" Lily popped up and started pacing before him, her hands clasped to her chest. "I've been carrying this around with me, Cade, and I couldn't bring myself to tell you because I was so afraid of what you'd think of me. That you wouldn't be able to forgive me. And I can't blame you. That I could have even potentially contributed to your suffering and the suffering…the deaths…of all these men, men who deserved such a fate the least of anyone…I can hardly live with myself."

Cade struggled to his feet, securing the crutch under his arm. "Even if LaFleur is guilty of firing the *Sultana*, Lily, he did it. Not you." His words might absolve her of responsibility, yet his tone did anything but.

She stopped and stared at him. "I know I might have prevented it. I know silence was the wrong decision, Cade. I'm never going to fail to speak up for what's right and true again, even if it costs me." She swallowed and spoke almost in a whisper. "Even if it costs me everything." As it well might right now. Lily pleaded with her eyes and words. "Can you ever forgive me?"

She needed this more than she'd ever needed anything. Cade leaving her and never seeing him again would be hard enough. His doing so with this gulf between them would be more than she could live with.

He'd left Lily hanging. Cade knew he had, but he couldn't bring himself to do otherwise. Just as he'd not only come to trust her but acknowledged his feelings for her, she'd dealt a blow he'd never seen coming. His walls had gone back up in an instant. When she'd begged for his forgiveness, he hadn't been able to extend it beyond that wall. Not yet.

He'd told her he needed time. He'd left her standing in the guest room on the second floor and returned to his own, where he'd been ever since. Never had it felt more like a prison, the walls closing in along with the descending darkness. Cade sat on his bed and read his Bible and prayed, but nothing was assuaging the anger that now mingled with his grief. Not to mention the doubt.

His whole life had been about putting others before himself. Lily's sense of self-preservation may well have compromised the safety of two thousand innocent people. But the thing that hurt worse was that she'd kept it from him. They'd discussed the possible sabotage of the *Sultana* on more than one occasion, and officials had interviewed witnesses all week, giving Lily ample opportunity to confess her suspicions either to Cade or to the investigating committees. If she'd come forward even then, even after fear held her silent the first time… But only when the same culprit had approached her beau had she been willing to shed her silence. Out of concern for another attack—or more for Cecil and his comrades?

As Lily had spoken of the early days of the war this afternoon, Cade had not missed the gleam in her eye. Regardless of what she said about going along to get along, like so many, she'd romanticized the Confederacy. Had her silence protected those Rebel ghosts as much as herself?

First the sabotage, then her understanding with Cecil and the reason for it, a reason that bound her to him more tightly than Cade had guessed… What else might she be keeping from him? And why did the girl he'd been falling in love with have to be the one whose negligence could have caused this whole tragedy? Why had God allowed him to be such a fool?

There it was, the root of his angst—anger. Not at Lily but at God. Even his frustration with his parents hadn't really pointed at them. He'd been so certain the opportunity to go to medical school had been divinely ordained that he couldn't fathom why they didn't see it. But really, he'd wondered why God wouldn't *let* them see it. Wouldn't change their hearts. Wouldn't change His own mind.

"For the gifts and calling of God are without repentance."

Deep down, Cade knew even better than his parents that the voice he'd heard in church that Sunday had indeed been his Creator's. Cade had cloaked his decision to pursue medicine in the noblest of language, but underneath it all, becoming a physician had seemed so much more admirable than being a preacher. Admirable in the eyes of men.

And that was selfishness, just as ugly as his reason for anger at Lily. But his was worse, for at its root lay rebellion. He'd been mad at God when God had every right to be mad at him.

Cade grabbed his crutch and hefted himself to his feet. The oil lamp flickered on the desk as he paced by it, to the end of the room, and back to the bed. Judge Winkler's words returned to him, that it was no accident Cade had been taken here, to the Livingstons' inn. If that was true, maybe it hadn't been simply so that the judge could put him in touch with his parents. God had known Lily would care for him. And he would care for her.

But that also meant God had allowed his capture, the wasting of his body and his medical talents in Andersonville, the explosion on the *Sultana*, the death of James. The seemingly senseless deaths of over a thousand men. Why?

Cade's father had preached more than once on the nature of evil, how Adam and Eve let it into the world when they chose to eat the forbidden fruit pointed out to them by that age-old serpent, Satan. Since that time, *"man is born unto trouble, as the sparks fly upward."* Cade could picture his father quoting that scripture, index finger swirling up toward heaven. He'd talked about how God allowed people a choice, and many in every generation chose evil. Because serving oneself was, in reality, serving evil instead of God.

Just as Cade had done in choosing medicine—for even something that looked good and might be good for someone else was not good when it was outside God's will for him. He'd always been taught that only in God's perfect will lay the fullness of peace and joy.

Had God allowed him to come to the end of himself in order to get his attention? But how could good ever come of this—not only for him, but for all the men involved, the men lost, and their families?

His spirit cried out for justice. Wasn't God a God of justice?

Cade stopped pacing on the far side of the room and listened for that quiet inner voice he'd blocked out for years. Nothing. But he turned to the Bible on the bed, shuffled over, and flipped the pages to an almost-forgotten story in Genesis—that of Joseph, sold into slavery by his jealous brothers, falsely accused and imprisoned, yet eventually raised to rule in a foreign land. He read, *"Ye thought evil against me; but God meant it unto good, to bring to pass, as it is this day, to save much people alive."*

Hadn't Cade seen even in James' death that saving someone spiritually was even more important than saving someone physically?

Stop fighting.

The voice inside brought Cade's head up. Had he imagined it? It had been so long since God had spoken to him. And yet, he'd heard the words in his spirit as clear as a steamboat's bell. And along with them, an inner warmth so intense it buckled his knees.

God was not mad at him. He was not punishing him. He was calling him home.

Cade leaned the crutch on the side of the bed and used the edge of the mattress to lower himself to his knees. He couldn't fold his hands, but he laid the left over the right and bowed his head. His heart thudded—not with fear but with the solemn resignation of a man who realizes he's been fighting the wrong war.

He prayed in a whisper. "Lord, I'm sorry for running from Your calling all these years. If You still want me to preach Your Word, show me the way. I don't want to fight You anymore, but I've loved being a doctor. Is there any way…I could do both?" His flesh wrestled with his spirit, trying to find a way to hold on. "I'll need You to give me back the fire to help save men's souls. And please, show me how Lily fits into this. I believe

You are a God of truth and justice. So let the truth come out and justice be served. Use us to be part of that, if it be Thy will. Amen."

He'd taken a step in the right direction, but so many questions remained. Could he really give up medicine and devote himself solely to ministry? The process would not be easy, practically or emotionally. But Cade's willingness to consider it opened the door to a measure of peace. Now he could anticipate the reunion with his earthly father as well. And with Lily. He had much to tell her.

He reached for his crutch. As he put his weight on it, it skidded to one side, and he thudded back onto his knees. A breath whooshed out of him. *Thank You, God.* He'd cushioned his arm, and his pelvis only gave a brief twinge of pain. His hip must be healing too.

The point of the crutch had loosened a section of the floorboard. It now sat at an angle, laid against the one next to it. Cade leaned over to right it, but as he did, his fingers brushed the edge of something in the shallow cavity beneath the floor. He pulled a small velvet bag into the light. The object inside was hard and round. He removed it and stared at a wooden cipher wheel with the letters *CSA* engraved in the center. Confederate States of America.

Chapter Nineteen

Friday's dawn had barely grayed the edges of the curtains when a soft knock on the door disturbed Lily's slumber—what little of it she'd had. Tears that had cost her far more than sleeplessness puffed her eyelids shut even now, and with a draft of alertness, the terrible ache in her heart returned. She didn't want to remember what it was. She moaned and pulled the quilt over her head.

Jacob tugged back on his side of the covers and also ignored the summons.

"Lily, please." The voice came not from her brother but from the other side of the door, low and plaintive. Earnest.

Cade.

Lily's heartbeat took off like a colt out of a stall, jolting her awake. He'd left her standing there yesterday after baring her heart—all her secrets save her feelings for him—and now he expected her to answer his summons before daybreak?

Another spate of tapping. "I have to talk to you. Please, it's urgent."

Had he injured himself? Someone had to make certain it wasn't so... but not her. She nudged her brother and whispered, "Jacob, you go."

He groaned and threw his arm over his head.

Cade knocked and Lily gently shook Jacob. "Please? Make sure he's all right, then you can come back to bed."

With a gusty sigh, Jacob tossed back the quilt. His feet thudded onto the floorboards, then his steps shuffled across the room. Lily kept her back turned, though it was all she could do not to peek as her brother cracked the door open.

Light spilled in from the landing, along with Cade's persuasive tones. "Jacob, is Lily awake? I must talk to her right away."

"What for? So's you can make her cry again?" At Jacob's question, twangy with irritability, Lily slapped her hand over her eyes. He wasn't done. "I had to listen to her snifflin' half the night. For the second time in a week. I'm thinkin' it's best if you leave her alone."

As hot as her face had become, Lily almost smiled. Her little brother was becoming a man, after all. She'd never heard him stand up for her like that.

"I'm sorry I hurt her, and that's part of why I have to talk to her, but the other part is even timelier." Cade's tone dipped low with urgency. "Did she tell you about that strange message we found?"

Lily lowered the covers and turned her head toward the door.

"Yeah." Jacob scratched his ear. "What of it?"

"I found something else."

Another message? Lily sat up in bed and raised her voice. "Give me a minute to dress. I'll be right there."

"Thank you, Lily." The closing door cut off Cade's sigh of relief.

Jacob returned to bed, but rather than climbing back in as Lily slid out, he sat frowning at her as she gathered her dress and undergarments. "Cecil never made you cry."

That's because I'm not in love with Cecil.

The immediate answer that popped into Lily's head froze her hands and feet. She couldn't be thinking straight. The emotion of the evening— the need to convince Cade she was on his side, to seek his approval—had overcome her senses. To expunge her guilt, a need that he'd denied. Even if he forgave her now, the best she could hope for on such short acquaintance was to part ways amicably. Maybe to satisfy herself that he fared well in an exchange of letters.

Never mind. If he'd found something that might shed light on that cryptic message, that's what she needed to focus on. Lily headed for the partition to Jacob's former side of the room, which they now used for changing. She paused with her hand on the curtain. "There are things you don't understand, Jacob. Things it's best if I don't tell you."

"What things? What you do affects my future too, Lily."

"I know that. And haven't I always taken care of you?"

As Lily exchanged her nightgown for her pantalets and chemise, Jacob's strident plumping of his feather pillow reached her ears. "Why do you treat me like a kid? If I'm old enough to help take care of these men here, I'm old enough to understand. Why don't you like Cecil anymore?"

Lily sighed. She'd shared enough with Jacob to impart the value of keeping one nation under God—a nation without the curse of slavery—but like most every boy in Crittenden County, the exploits of Duke's Partisans awed him. "I will always care for Cecil." The few times during the night that her mind had strayed from her own predicament, it had circled back to her former beau. It shouldn't have taken Cecil demanding her affection for her to realize it had already settled on someone else. "But you know he and I have different views. I should never have led him on." She bent to pull up her cotton stocking and roll it over her garter.

"Does that mean you're going to marry Cade instead?"

Lily almost tripped trying to get her second stocking on. "I've not even known him two weeks. Why would you ask such a thing?"

The bed frame creaked as Jacob settled in. "Dunno. You *are* on the same side. And lotsa folks got married quick during the war."

"Folks who already knew each other. Besides, the war's over. Go back to sleep."

As Jacob gave a sigh and smacked his lips, Lily finished dressing, but her brother's suggestion wouldn't leave her head. Was it so ludicrous? Weren't marriages of convenience made all the time, for all sorts of reasons? And this was much more than convenience. So much more. Her heart had leaped at the mere suggestion of a life with Cade.

She shook her head. Even if they stayed in touch after Cade mustered out, it was not as if she'd ever have a reason to visit Cincinnati, and he even less to return to Mound City, the site of the worst tragedy he'd faced during the war. Surely he'd get out of here as fast as he could and never look back. Why would he want her, the biggest possible reminder of that tragedy, to play any part in his future? When he faced so many unknowns, she could hardly hope to saddle him with not only herself but also Jacob.

Lily swiped the message she'd hidden in her dresser before leaving her room. She found Cade's door standing open, the light burning. He leaned over his desk, pencil in his left hand, writing something with painstaking exactness on a piece of paper, his brow knit in either concentration or frustration. He'd removed his sling, presumably for ease of movement. Dr. Courtner had also left off the board that acted as a splint when he'd last rewrapped Cade's wrist, but Cade kept his bandaged right arm propped on the desk.

As the threshold squeaked beneath Lily's stockinged feet, his head jerked up.

She spoke abruptly. "I brought the message." Now that she was here, she wanted to leave. Why had she hurried over? She should have made him wait.

"Shh." The unexpected shushing and the finger to his lips only added to her shame. But when he gestured her over, she came.

"Pull the door to."

Lily blinked at him, for they'd always left the door open for propriety's sake. She stepped back over to push it shut—mostly. She might trust him, but she did not trust her aunt or cousin. If they caught her alone with Cade again, especially with the door closed, she might find herself begging on the streets for her ticket fare north.

"What are you doing?" Returning to his side, she peered over his shoulder at unsteady rows of letters, both sensible and not.

He laid down his pencil and reached for the slip of paper she held loosely between her fingers, placing it atop the desk as well. "I'm trying to remember how Vignère cipher works. But first things first." Before she could take a step back, he grabbed her hand. Cade looked up into her face. "Lily, can you forgive me for hurting you yesterday? I shouldn't have left you like that, but in the moment, I didn't know what else to do."

She dipped her chin. "I understand why you needed time. But...does this mean you forgive *me*?"

When he laughed, she had to stop from gaping at him, so foreign was the sound. Had he laughed much, before the war? Had she? Lily could hardly remember. She could only pray to God that one day, they'd be able to shake off this heavy darkness from their souls.

"To say the least." He squeezed her hand. "God gave me a talking-to last night, about that and other things. Suffice it to say, if He were handing out medals for selfishness, I'd have more than earned mine."

"I don't understand." She shook her head. "You? Selfish? I've always thought your ability to put others before yourself is one of your most admirable qualities."

The unreserved smile that crinkled his laugh lines and brought light to his eyes made her catch her breath. "And selfishly, I'd love to hear you list the others." He winked. When she flushed, he chuckled again. "You see?"

"It's hardly a crime to want others to think well of you."

He dropped her hand and lowered his gaze. "Not until you want it so much you put that above what God thinks."

Lily made a face. "When did you ever do that?"

"When I chose to become a doctor rather than a minister." As she stood unmoving, he glanced up at her, his features once again tight. "Yes, you heard Judge Winkler right. I saw your face the day he visited, when he mentioned that I thought I'd been called to ministry. When I was a boy, I did hear the call of God on my life. As I grew older, I talked myself out of it. Put my own wishes ahead of God's. But recent events have shown me I have to get my priorities in order."

Her heart bottomed out. "What does that mean?" She should be happy Cade had heard from God, and she couldn't deny the new peace in his demeanor. But something in the way he said that...it made her think again of him leaving. Closing up a house the way a refugee would before fleeing an invading army.

"It means putting the spiritual ahead of the physical."

Lily swallowed. "All right…" But it wasn't, really. If he had a new purpose that had nothing to do with whether his hand healed, she was already about as helpful to him as the discarded paper wrappings she used with her hair-curling tongs. But did that mean he would never practice medicine again? How could he give it up so suddenly?

Her questions must have reflected on her face, for his softened into a tender smile. "I want to tell you all about it, and there's so much I need to say to you. But I'm still working it out myself, to be honest." He took her hand again, and this time, he brought her knuckles to his lips. Her breath had scarcely left her chest before he was turning back to the desk. "And I'm afraid this might be even more pressing."

Surely, nothing could be more pressing than their futures. But blinking away a ridiculous sheen of tears, Lily forced herself to focus on what Cade wanted to show her. He was pulling something from behind the paper on which he'd been writing. She gasped. "Is that…?"

"Yes." Amber flecks highlighted by the oil lamp danced in his dark eyes as he lifted them toward her again. "A Confederate cipher disk."

She asked him the same question he'd asked her the day prior. "Where did you find this?"

He jerked his thumb toward the far corner of the room. "On the other side of the bed, in a space under a loose floorboard."

Lily's eyes went wide. "It must be Beth's."

"Perhaps."

"Who else's? She's the one who was always up here before you came."

Cade nodded, lining up the *A*s on the inner and outer wheels of the disk. "It would help to explain why she was so upset when you suggested putting me up here. But it could also be your aunt, could it not?"

"I suppose it could."

"And who else is involved? Whoever hid this disk is not acting on her own."

Lily blinked at the memory of Beth sitting practically in Frenchie's lap. "You think one of them could be passing messages for the saboteurs?"

"Or for someone else they're close to."

The harsh lines around his mouth gave her a clue. "Cecil?" She laid her hand over her heart. "He couldn't be involved. He told me that was the first he'd ever seen LaFleur, and that he'd ordered him to go away."

Cade tilted his head. "Did you hear the conversation?"

"Well, no…" Lily straightened her spine, running her hands down her bodice as she let out a deep breath. "Oh, Cade, it can't be." She'd been living in a hotbed of spies, and she'd had no idea. She was even more culpable than she'd imagined.

He touched her arm. "That doesn't matter right now. It would be foolish to let on to anyone that we know about this, much less confront someone. At the moment, we need to concentrate on decoding this message. It might give us some important information."

Lily nodded and bent closer as she said, "All right, but how?"

Cade smoothed the coded message out flat. "If this is Caesar cipher and we don't know how many places to shift right or left by, we could mess around for days and get nowhere. So I'm going with my hunch that this is Vignère, especially since it's been most commonly used during the war."

She straightened. "But didn't you also say we'd have to know a code word or phrase to break a Vignère cipher?"

A smile flashed over his face. "So I did. I happen to remember a couple my courier friend told me the Confederates liked to use. *Complete victory* was the last one he knew about before he was captured. Can you write that here?" He pointed to the blank area at the bottom of the larger page. "Only, break it up into sections of four, not how it's naturally written."

As Lily leaned around Cade to print the phrase in block letters, a whiff of his shaving soap sent tingles through her. Her upper arm pressed against his. Her hair, which she'd not taken the time to braid last night or bind this morning, fell like a golden waterfall between them. When she glanced back at him, searching for his approval, Cade reached up to brush a strand of her locks behind her shoulder. The intensity of his gaze made her hasten to stand up straight. "Um, perhaps I should run get my own chair."

"Of course." Was that a blush on his cheeks? He certainly averted his gaze quickly. "I should have thought of that. Months of being an invalid has dried up all my manners."

"Not at all. I'll be right back." Lily welcomed the momentary escape, though she told herself the fluttering in her chest had to do with excitement about the message rather than the man. Before she left with the chair, she interrupted Jacob's snoring with a shake to his arm, reminding him to head downstairs soon and requesting that he tell anyone who asked about her that she'd had some urgent personal business to attend to. Let them wonder what that was.

When she returned, Cade had continued where she'd left off, printing *complete victory* in groupings of four letters all the way to the right margin. As she placed her chair next to his—far enough apart that they wouldn't be touching—he slid the paper over to her.

He tapped the space below the line he'd just completed. "Right here, can you print what is written on the paper you found in the hall? The encoded message?"

"Break it up the same way, in fours?" She took the pencil he offered her.

Cade nodded, and she did as he said.

"Now what?"

"Now we use the cipher disk." He placed it between them. "Let me show you an example. This *N* on the encoded message—we know the key is a *D* since it sits under the *D* in the code word line, so we'll align the *A* on the inner wheel to a *D* on the outer wheel."

"Why are we doing that? Where did an *A* come from?" Lily shook her head.

"The *A* is our pointer. Now we'll find the *N* on the outer wheel matches a *K* on the inner wheel. So a *K* is what we would write down as the letter in the plain text message the sender intended." The matter-of-fact look he gave her indicated he'd just explained something as simple as two plus two.

Lily slapped her hand to her cheek. "I have no idea what you just said."

"All right. Scoot closer." He put down the cipher wheel to tug on her chair, leaving her no choice but to do as he requested. "Now let's transcribe one for real. I'll talk you through every step, and you write down the letter we come up with."

"Very well." She dutifully took up her pencil, watching while Cade followed the same steps for the first two letters in the message.

By the third, he gave a sigh of frustration. "That's not it."

"Because we have three consonants in a row?" She grinned. Even she could see that something wasn't working. "Maybe we got a step wrong."

He gave her a sideways glare. "We didn't get a step wrong."

"Okay, then, did your courier friend tell you another common phrase?"

Cade rubbed his chin, where the growing light showed what had appeared to be shadows around his goatee was actually an overnight growth of beard. Maybe she'd ask if he needed her help shaving this time. Lily almost choked on the notion. What was she thinking? She couldn't follow a cipher that a child could decode when sitting next to the man, much less perform so intimate a task as shaving him.

"Are you all right?" He'd cocked his head again and was frowning at her.

Lily fanned her face. "I'm fine. What about that phrase?"

He drummed his fingers on the desk. "Well, he said they sometimes used *Confederate*, but I'm willing to bet there was another phrase in use this year that he didn't know about. Apparently, they changed the favored phrase often, and he'd been in Andersonville longer than I had."

"Well, let's try it." Anything to detract from the blush burning up her cheeks. Lily printed and then reprinted the new word above *complete victory*.

For the next fifteen minutes or so, they went through the same process with the same result—nonsense.

Lily surveyed Cade, whose shoulders had sagged. "What now?"

"I have no idea."

"We can't just give up, not when we're so close. What if this message has something to do with LaFleur and the *Sultana*? It could be the evidence O'Henry needs to arrest him."

"You tell me." Cade threw his hand up. Then he closed his eyes and took a deep breath. "No. Now we pray."

"What?"

He looked over at her. "That's what I was doing earlier, kneeling by the bed and praying for truth and justice, when I found the cipher wheel. None of this is an accident, Lily. I think God wants the culprits caught as much as we do. So let's ask Him."

Lily blinked rapidly. She'd long since given up on asking God for provision or direction. Long ago taken matters into her own hands. Her dreams had crumbled under her repeated losses, along with any belief in the Almighty's good plan. But Cade's firm confidence buoyed her doubt. If he wanted to pray, she certainly wouldn't stop him. "Fine, then."

He opened his palm on the desk, and she placed her hand in his. A sense of security so unexpected and potent came over her that she hardly heard the words he uttered asking God to help them. *Home.* This was the sense of it that she'd been missing since her parents died. Cade at her side, even when he was injured and weak, made her stronger and safer than she'd ever been before. Could that have anything to do with his new reliance on God?

"Lily?"

She opened her eyes. Oh dear. He'd quit praying and was staring at her again. She had to ask him not to leave her. If he knew how she felt about him…

"Cade, I—" Lily's mouth fell open in mid-sentence, for a phrase dropped into her mind, overshadowing all else. "'Free Arkansas.'"

"What?"

"'Free Arkansas.' That's the password Frenchie—LaFleur—used to get into the meeting that night. I heard him at the back door when I was throwing out the dishwater." But where had the memory come from? She hadn't even thought about that strange moment since.

Cade's eyes flashed open wide. "We'll try it." Eagerness heightened his agreement.

As Lily seized the pencil, somewhere close outside the room, the floor squeaked. She froze. She and Cade exchanged a glance. Lily lowered her pencil. "I'll go see," she whispered.

Cade reached for his crutch as she crept across the floor. Her heart hammered. Was someone eavesdropping through the partially open door? And if they were, was she really ready to find out who?

Chapter Twenty

A sense of unreality swept Cade as he stared at the message they'd just decoded. His heart surged back to the rate it had when he and Lily thought they heard someone outside the room. After a thorough check, she'd assured him no one was there and it must have been Jacob going down to work, for her brother had left their room.

It had taken them over half an hour to decode the cipher using the *Free Arkansas* code. At first, when the letters *S*, *T*, and *L* had emerged from the disk, he'd almost given up. But Lily had urged him to press on. The next three letters had clearly spelled *MAY*. And the three after that, *SIX*. Then *NOON*. And finally, *LADY JANE*.

The full message read *STL MAY SIX NOON LADY JANE.*

Cade stared at Lily. "Something is happening on May sixth at noon. But what does *STL* stand for? And who is Jane?"

She tapped her finger on the paper. "I don't think *Jane* is a person. Why would the sender waste letters to identify her as a lady? I think it's a boat, the *Lady Jane.*"

"Of course." Why hadn't he thought of that? And why did that name sound familiar? Cade rubbed his chin a moment, then suddenly plunked his hand down on the desk. "Lily…that steamer…it's the same one that took officials from Memphis to Lincoln's funeral."

Her eyes rounded. "What? How do you know?"

"I read it in the paper Wednesday, when I visited the other men."

Lily's fingers fluttered to her lips. "May sixth is tomorrow. Could they be returning then?"

"Very likely. And *STL*…" Cade pointed to the letters. "Could that refer to St. Louis?"

She released a soft breath. "They would stop there on the way home. Oh, Cade, what if this is a plan to plant another coal torpedo, or arrange some other sort of attack? Who better for Southern sympathizers to target than the highest government officials and military officers from Memphis?"

Cade's heart dropped. "And all in one place at one time." Not only could the tragedy rival the *Sultana*'s, but such an act of aggression could trigger riots and reprisals on either side of the river—and grip the government's iron fist of control tight enough to squeeze the last bit of life from this region. He reached for his crutch. "We have to get this to the provost marshal, and without delay."

Lily caught hold of his arm. "What are you doing?"

"I'm going with you." Cade got to his feet.

Pushing her chair back as she also stood, Lily made a scoffing sound. "Are you jesting? You can barely get around the inn. The provost office is two blocks away."

"I'll make it. I'm hardly letting you go alone, not with LaFleur in town."

"And what are you going to do to stop him?" Lily flung her hand out. "Beat him with your crutch? He's far more of a threat than Cecil ever was."

As the reality of his helpless state hit him once again, Cade let out a soft growl. He tapped his crutch on the floor while he considered his options. Finally, he asked, "Does your uncle have a sidearm?"

The way Lily pressed her lips together told him she'd rejected the notion before she did so aloud. "I don't know where he keeps it, and I wouldn't dare go looking. He or Aunt Susanna would probably still be in their room. But it's a moot point. I can't let you risk getting hurt again, not when you've come so far."

Cade balled his hand. If only he could rip the bandages off the other one, its use magically restored. "If you won't let me go with you, at least take someone else."

She glanced at him as she stacked the papers and the cipher wheel on the desk. "Who? Jacob? Mika? They're children. I won't involve them in this, and I can't trust anyone else."

She was right. Someone in her household had hidden that cipher wheel, which put her in as much danger within as without. "Lily, if the person who was to pass or receive that coded message is aware it's missing…"

Lily shook her head. "How could they know for sure? Besides, I can avoid my family until after I deliver the information to the provost. If I slip out the kitchen door, no one will even know I'm gone. I'll be back before anyone misses me."

"I don't like this at all." Cade propped his crutch against the desk. He slid a strand of her glorious hair behind her shoulder, which he clasped and squeezed gently. "If anything happened to you…"

She blinked up at him, a glow of what resembled wonder igniting behind her eyes. Did she not realize what she meant to him? How remarkable she was? He allowed himself the pleasure of cupping her cheek, though he didn't dare hope for more than that.

But then she took a step toward him. "I feel the same about you."

Cade moved his hand to the back of her head, releasing a soft breath at the sensation of her hair flowing through his fingers, wafting its sweet fragrance. His heart thrummed as everything in him strained toward her. He lowered his head until her breath fanned his face. If only he could taste her sweet lips just once—but he veered away the second before making the contact he craved.

"I'm sorry, Lily," he whispered.

She pulled back a fraction to stare at him with impossibly large brown eyes. "What are you sorry for?"

He let out a shaky laugh. "I wouldn't ever assume you'd think of me in that way. I know what I am now—"

"Do you?" A challenging light ignited behind her assessing gaze.

"And after what you said about how you didn't trust—"

He didn't get to finish that sentence, either, for in one swift move, Lily stepped around his bandaged arm, wrapped her own arms around his neck, and pulled his face down to hers. The lips he'd imagined to be soft and yielding met his firmly, seeking, almost demanding a response.

A shock of awareness bolted through him, and a low moan gathered in his throat as he dropped his arm to pull her closer. Her soft form against his brought a rush of pleasure so foreign after so much pain that it stole his breath. He deepened the kiss, answering her unasked question. Yes. He wanted her. And even more alarming, these feelings he'd been seeking to explain any other way would no longer be explained away. He was falling in love with her.

Lily pulled back, though she still caressed his hair as he struggled to catch his breath. Her mischievous smile melted his heart. "Does that tell you what I think of you, Lieutenant Palmer?"

It did. It also told him that whatever her plan, he couldn't let her go to the provost alone.

———————◦❦◦———————

After the way Cade kissed her, Lily had no trouble sneaking down the stairs. She practically floated, her basket on her arm containing the message for Provost Marshal O'Henry. While Cade hadn't declared his feelings outright, the tender passion of his response certainly had. And he'd made her promise they'd talk about their future as soon as she returned.

She smiled. The hesitation she'd sensed in him had stemmed from insecurity, and from respect for her, rather than doubts about her as she'd first feared.

Only when Lily insisted that delivering the coded message to the authorities was something she must do herself to assuage her guilt had Cade relented about accompanying her. At last, he'd agreed to remain behind. He'd be praying. He bid her be careful before dropping another soft kiss on her lips, then closed his door behind her.

Lily had made it through the inn without encountering anyone and was tying on her bonnet at the back door when approaching voices made her whirl.

Martha followed Mika into the kitchen, both carrying overflowing baskets of rumpled linens. "It's just for today, Mika. After she settles things with the judge—" Martha stopped, clamping her lips together when she caught sight of Lily.

"Are you leavin' too?" Mika asked her, more of a cry than a question. Her round face crumpled.

"Whatever is the matter?" Lily rushed forward, placing a hand on the girl's arm before the tears filling her eyes could overflow.

"I'm sorry, Miss Lily." Mika gave her head with its coiled and braided hair a brisk shake, though her mouth still wobbled. "It's nothin'."

"Clearly, it's not nothing. What has happened?"

Martha spoke up as she slid her basket onto a nearby table. "Silly child was just frettin' about how she's gonna get her duties done, what with Miss Beth being gone...and now you too." Was that the slightest hint of rebuke in the phrase?

"Beth is gone?" Lily glanced down the hallway. That would make things easier for her.

Mika nodded. She plunked her own basket at her feet and jerked her sleeve across her eyes. "To see the reverend's wife. She told me I'd have to take the medicine to the men, but when I said I couldn't because the missus expects me to do laundry every Friday, she told me not to back talk her. Then she slapped me." She rubbed her cheek.

Lily gasped and braced the girl's chin. Indeed, a dark splotch remained on the side of Mika's face. "Why would she do such a thing?" She could maybe imagine Aunt Susanna losing control to such a degree, but Beth? The only force Lily had known her to use resided in her sharp tongue.

"I don't know, but I can't take it anymore. I can't stand it here." A tear rolled from beneath Mika's downcast fringe of lashes, and her chest shuddered as she sucked in an unsteady breath.

Drawing her lower lip up, Lily rubbed the girl's arm. "I'm so sorry, Mika." She certainly understood the sense of being trapped.

"That's enough whining." Martha picked up her daughter's laundry basket, placing it back in her arms and giving her a little shove. "Go on, now." Then to Lily, she added, "Miss Beth is not herself. Things went poorly with Judge Winkler yesterday."

"Oh." Lily's eyes widened. "She refused him?"

"She tried to, but he left in such a fury that the missus found out, and she fairly boxed Miss Beth's ears. She told her she had to go to him and take it back. I reckon Miss Beth went to the reverend's wife for advice, though it be awful early to be makin' a social call. Even in a spiritual crisis."

Lily covered her face and moaned. "This is my fault. I should have checked on Beth last night." Instead, she'd closeted herself in her room, crying when Cade had withheld his forgiveness. She faced Mika, who was dolefully gathering her scrub board and lye soap from the cabinet near the sink. "I promise, Mika, I'll make certain that never happens again, but right now, I really do have urgent business to attend to."

Mika gaped at her. "Who's gonna help Mama in the kitchen? I can't do it all."

"Hush up, girl." Martha's gaze and tone rivaled a slap. She turned back to Lily with a placating look. "Never mind her. I can manage one breakfast by myself."

"It's all right, Martha." Lily had never known Mika to complain, even though she did shoulder far too heavy a load for a girl her age. Beth must have been fiercer than a cornered opossum this morning. "Where is Jacob?"

Martha tipped her red-turbaned head toward the door. "He's outside, gettin' the laundry fire going." They boiled the guests' linens in a big black cauldron over a fire in the courtyard.

"Very good. Instruct him in dispensing the medicine this morning, Mika." Lily edged toward the door. Every minute she remained increased her risk of being caught by Aunt Susanna, who would demand to know her destination. "Hopefully, I will be back in time to help serve breakfast."

Martha nodded, but Mika avoided Lily's gaze. Lily slipped out the door with a heaviness on her chest. She'd worried about her own future, but how much more must someone like Mika? The girl deserved the chance to make something of herself. Even if the new government provided such opportunities, Aunt Susanna and Beth would never allow her to explore them. She'd be stuck behind a washboard her whole life. Mika might not be Lily's responsibility, but surely there was something she could do.

Yes. She could talk to Cade about it.

Lily's concern lifted, and she hastened down the street with a lighter heart. She was no longer alone. Together, they had so many more options. The sun rose on a beautiful new day. Lily hesitated to leave its warmth for the alley to her left that remained in shadow, but by taking it, she could cut off a few minutes on her trip to the provost. She pressed her basket and skirts close against her body to avoid the trash lining the brick buildings on either side as she hurried toward the end of the lane.

When Lily was inches from the light, a tall form stepped around the side of the building. A cloth smothered her face. Lily flung her arm out, and her feet scrambled for purchase as the man jerked her back into the alley. When she attempted to drag in a breath to cry out, a sweet, pungent scent filled her nostrils. The swing of her basket backward at the man's head terminated as her body went limp and she slumped in his arms.

Cade lost sight of Lily when she turned into the alley. He increased his pace, though his hip ached and his crutch did more to hinder than help. The sling he'd put back on did little to protect his injured arm from the impact of every swinging step. Traffic picked up on the street leading away from the docks, timber drays and wagons of grain. Union soldiers on horseback. Cade's awkward progress drew more than one curious or pitying glance, but he didn't allow it to slow him. He had to keep Lily in view, even as he did so without letting her know he followed. He would wait outside the provost office and then deal with her ire after he insisted on escorting her home.

But when he paused at the corner to catch his breath and peer down the alley, he could see all the way to the end. How had Lily gotten so far ahead of him? She would have had to practically sprint.

He'd need to almost do the same, or he'd lose her. Cade's chest tightened. His breath labored and his crutch thumped as he hobbled along. He had no idea where the provost office was. It had been a mercy that he'd passed the livery stable in time to see Lily hurry down the alley behind it and the inn, then turn onto the side street. And now, she'd apparently vanished from this alley that connected to a street running parallel behind the inn.

Cade reached the end and looked both ways. No figure in a checked dress with a basket at her side. In fact, no one in view. Only a stray dog who paused his foraging as Cade bellowed Lily's name. When no one answered, Cade tossed his crutch to the ground.

The painful thudding of his heart warned him he couldn't have simply lost her. Someone must have taken her. But where? Had he overlooked a door in the alley? He took a step back and turned—right into a solid form.

The man's beefy hands shot out and grasped Cade's forearms.

Chapter Twenty-One

Why had he thrown down his crutch when it was the only weapon he possessed? Cade jerked free of the big man's clutches quick enough to take him off guard, enabling Cade to pivot for the crutch. But he stumbled, and once again, his assailant grabbed him, this time by his good arm.

"Whoa there, buddy."

It took Cade a moment to realize the guy was attempting to steady him, not accost him. As he slowly straightened to peer into a heavyset face as flushed as his own must be, the middle-aged man held up his hands.

"I'm not here to hurt you. I saw you leave the inn and thought you might need some help."

"You followed me from the inn?" Cade peered at him. Flashes of memory struggled to piece themselves into a bigger picture. "Wait…are you…"

"Thaddeus Livingston. I'm the one who brought you up from the river, though I'd hardly blame you if you don't remember."

The face, the voice, the argument on the street with Beth all came back to Cade. "You're Lily's uncle."

"That's right." Thad let his arms drop to his sides and offered a conciliatory smile.

Cade's desperation overtook his manners. "I have to go. I was following her, and I'd just lost sight of her."

"Following who? Lily?" Her uncle perused both sides of the street, then his bushy head swiveled back to Cade, and his brows lowered. "Why?"

"She was going to the—" Cade couldn't reveal Lily's destination without being pressed to explain her mission. He bought himself a moment by stooping again for his crutch, which Thad helped him regain and position beneath his arm. The man's frown had softened from suspicion to concern.

Cade needed help. He couldn't search the area quickly enough on his own. Lily had described her uncle as a moderate, but one who was influenced by his Rebel-loving wife and daughter. In Cade's experience, women, even those who were far less direct than Susanna and Beth Livingston, wielded the real power in most households. And yet, Thad didn't seem like a pushover. He'd more than stood up to his daughter the day Cade arrived.

But if helping Lily meant betraying Susanna and Beth, could he trust Lily's uncle that far? Was it fair to even ask that of him?

Cade had no choice. He took a deep breath and let it out with a silent prayer. *God, let this man be a true patriot.*

"I need you to listen to me." He addressed Thad straight on, eyes locked, in the tone he'd used when he had to tell a man that only an amputation might save his life. "Lily may be in danger. She was going to the provost marshal with an important message."

Thad's glare had returned to menacing. "What kind of message?"

Cade puffed out a breath. "Sir, I can't go into that right now. I was following her to keep an eye on her, but after she turned down this alley, she disappeared. Will you help me search for her? I can explain more later." At that point, if Lily's family turned on her, he could take her away.

"Very well." Thad glanced around—seemingly ruling out, as Cade had planned to do, any doors in the alley. There were none. "I'll be faster checking up and down the street and inside any buildings open nearby. You go on to the provost and see if she's showed up. I'll meet you there in fifteen minutes."

Cade nodded. "A sound plan." As much as the blood thrumming

through his veins fired every nerve to leap into action, it made more sense for him to take the straight route to the provost. He turned, then swiveled back to Thad. "Which way?"

Thad pointed to the right. "Down the street half a block." He ran along the boardwalk the opposite way, trying a nearby door while Cade headed in the direction he'd indicated.

He peered inside stores as he passed. Most still displayed CLOSED signs, which helped him refrain from attempting entry. All along, he prayed Lily would step from around a corner or call to him from behind. But he reached the one-story brick provost office without sight of her.

Inside, a young private looked up from transcribing a telegraph message. "May I help you, sir?"

Cade leaned his crutch and his good arm on the counter. "Yes, I'm looking for a young woman, early twenties, blonde, petite." The description came out with short puffs of breath. But...if Lily had sewed for Union soldiers, this man might be acquainted with her. "Lily Livingston?"

"Oh." The soldier's brows winged upward. His look of recognition surged hope through Cade that faded when he spoke. "No, I'm afraid Miss Livingston has not been by today."

"So you know her? She's come in here before?" He had to make sure they were talking about the same person.

"Why, yes. Just yesterday—"

"What's this about Miss Livingston?" A stalwart older man boomed the question from the doorway of an inner office. He wore a tidy Union uniform, his ginger hair carefully combed over a balding head. His expression relaxed, then firmed into respect when he took in Cade's crutch, bandaged arm, and loose shirt sans vest or coat. "You must be one of the boys from the *Sultana*. I'm the provost marshal here in Mound City. Liam O'Henry."

"Lieutenant Cade Palmer, sir." Though he so lacked the strength to salute in this moment that he practically hung from the counter. "You haven't seen Miss Livingston today?"

"No, although we just got here. Why?" Chin tucked, the man folded his arms over his thick chest.

Finally, Cade was among people he could trust. His explanation poured out. "Lily—Miss Livingston—was bringing you a coded message we found at River Rest. We believe it was being passed between saboteurs."

Both O'Henry's head and the private's jerked up at the same time. The provost marshal's arms fell to his sides. "If it was coded, how did you know that?"

"I found a Confederate cipher wheel hidden in my room."

"You *what?*" The man took a step forward.

There was no time to go into those details. Cade pressed forward with the most pertinent information. "We were able to break the code."

"How? Were you some sort of spy?"

Cade gave an impatient shake of his head. "Just familiar with Vignère cipher. The key was a phrase Lily had once heard as a password for a meeting there at the inn." He rushed his explanation before her uncle could show up. "The message gave a date and time, tomorrow at noon, as well as a location, St. Louis."

"For what?"

"We don't know for certain, but we believe it may represent a threat on another steamer, the one also mentioned—the *Lady Jane*."

O'Henry's jaw dropped. "God preserve us." The door burst open, and when Thad stormed in, the provost marshal rounded on him. "Thad, did you know about this?"

He and Lily's uncle were on a first-name basis? Odd as that was, Cade had to warn the provost marshal before he could say too much.

Thad's broad chest heaved. "Know about what?"

Cade leaned forward on his crutch and made a rapid slicing motion by his inside hip, but the officer paid him no heed. "Your niece and the lieutenant here finding a coded message. Miss Lily came to me this week after she sighted a suspected saboteur in town. After her visit, I got the Pinkertons right on it. Two of them went yesterday evening to investigate a hideout of his they learned about west of here, near Crowley's Ridge. And now this guest of yours tells me he and Miss Lily found evidence of a new plot afoot, right there at River Rest."

"No. I had no idea." Thad's glittering gaze swept to Cade. "But I wish you had come to me sooner. I can't find Lily anywhere."

———————◆◆———————

Lily swam back to consciousness through a spinning whirlpool of nausea. She'd barely opened her eyes before the need to retch overwhelmed her. Rising from her recumbent position, she managed to lean to the side before emptying the contents of her stomach.

"Whoa, whoa, little lady!" A woman's exclamation broke into her heaving, and a metal container of some sort slid across the floor and stopped beneath her. "Glad I was prepared. Ether will do that to you."

Ether? What had happened to her? She hadn't had an operation, not since that specialist in Memphis had pulled her bad tooth at the start of the war. Last Lily remembered, she'd been walking down an alley…

Fabric scraped across her lips as the speaker haloed in the glow of an oil lamp wiped Lily's mouth. Was it nighttime? Closing her eyes against the light, Lily fell back onto a lumpy mattress. Her limp arm and hand flopped well over the edge. A cot, then. A lingering scent of sweat and cheap cologne clung to the bedding. Her mouth might as well be stuffed with cotton. And that awful taste… "Water," she rasped.

Footsteps crossed a hardwood floor, a pitcher clanked against a glass, and the woman returned to Lily's side. A hand cradled the back of her head. Lily accepted the assistance in rising to drink a couple of swallows of tepid water, but when her stomach immediately rebelled, she turned her face away and sank back down.

"That's right. Not too much at first." The glass thunked on a nearby piece of furniture, and a chair scraped.

"Who are you?" Lily peeked at her seated companion from beneath her arm.

"You can call me Madam Tilly."

"Madam?" The stranger's voice had been firm though not unkind, but the hard lines of her face made Lily look away. This woman had not lived gently, though powder and rouge sought to conceal her middle age. She wore her unnaturally ink-black hair in the ringlet style of a younger woman bound for a party. And her vibrant green silk dress with its square-necked, low-cut tea bodice would be out of place anywhere except…except a brothel. Lily's queasy stomach knotted. "Where am I?"

"That's not for me to explain."

Why not? Lily craned her neck and took in a small room with sparse furniture apart from the cot on which she lay, two brick walls, two frame walls, and no windows before the rising drowsiness tugged her head and eyelids down again.

The woman's voice tethered her to consciousness. "You're not even supposed to be awake yet. I'm just to watch you until the captain comes back."

The captain? Lily's attempt to chase that thought ended in a mental wall. She grasped on to another. Where had she been going in that alley? Oh, yes…the provost. She had a message that must be delivered. Lives were at stake. She pushed herself up on her elbows. "My basket…I need…I must go…"

The madam gave her a light push, and Lily fell back onto the mattress. "You're not going anywhere, my sweet. Not until Alex says you are."

That name produced a chill, but why?

She was so tired. Lily could no longer battle the fatigue that rose like an internal fog, carrying her once again to oblivion.

———— ⚬•⚬ ————

"Where is she?"

Thad's question roared back to Cade on the street even though Lily's uncle had charged ahead of him into the courtyard of the inn, where the smoke of an outdoor fire stained the sky gray. Thad had helped him hurry back from the provost office. After Cade revealed where he'd found the cipher disk, O'Henry had directed them to return and question Beth while he ordered a search of the town.

Cade still couldn't believe Lily's uncle was not only acquainted with the provost marshal—he'd been passing him information for some time. Thus, the first names. Thad had also suspected the saboteurs were sharing intelligence through someone at the inn, but he'd expected the middleman to be a local citizen, not a member of his own family.

"How could I have missed this?" he'd asked in an agonized tone as they'd left the provost.

As Cade limped into the courtyard, Thad's ferocity as he faced down his daughter revealed as much anger at himself as at her. Beth stood frozen, facing her father with a large basket on her hip. Next to her, a black girl with an alert expression held a long paddle over a boiling cauldron of linens. This must be Mika, whom Lily had mentioned but whom he'd never met.

Beth fluttered her thin dark lashes at her father. "Where is who?"

Thad latched on to her arm. "Don't play coy with me, young lady. You know who I mean. Your cousin!"

"Why, she went out on an errand. I don't know what—"

"Stop it!" Her father shook her arm. "We know you've been passing messages for the saboteurs. The lieutenant found the cipher wheel hidden in your attic room." Thad jerked his head toward Cade, who hobbled up next to him.

Cade panted to catch his breath. "We don't actually know—"

"We do know. The only question is if my wife shares her guilt." Thad pinned Beth with an unwavering gaze. "Even if you resent Lily, how could you turn her over to the likes of Alex LaFleur?"

"What?" The pink that had stained Beth's cheeks when her father first accosted her drained away, leaving her skin even paler than usual. If Cade was not mistaken, a sign of genuine shock.

"That's right. Lily's been taken." At Thad's announcement, Beth dropped her basket and covered her mouth. "And the provost marshal expects LaFleur will attempt to get her out of the area quickly, probably by river."

Never had Cade felt so helpless. O'Henry had spoken with the harbormaster the day before, who had not known if LaFleur had yet regained possession of his steamer from the Confederacy. Even if he hadn't, his many connections would make travel on the Mississippi simple.

Cade stepped forward, placing his hand on Thad's arm until he released Beth's. "Please, Beth." Lily had described her as wounded and insecure. Perhaps she'd respond better to pleading, which he was more than willing to do if it would save Lily—even though his first impulse might also be to shake the truth from the girl. "Lily went to the authorities yesterday about LaFleur being back in town and what she overheard in that meeting before the *Sultana* was sunk. They haven't been able to locate him yet." After he and Thad left, the provost marshal had gone to find the Pinkertons. Hopefully, the detectives were on their way back from Crowley's Ridge, since they had likely also discovered that LaFleur was still near Mound City. "We have to find Lily before he skips town again. Where is he? Where can we find your cousin? If you know anything at all, you have to tell us."

Beth licked her lips and looked between Cade and her father as tears filled her eyes.

"Think carefully, girl." The warning came like a soft growl from Thad. "This may be your last chance to avoid the same fate as that saboteur."

"It's true," Beth wailed. She cupped her hands beneath her chin. "I do know LaFleur, but I didn't have to tell him about Lily. He already realized she was onto him. He figured she'd recognize him when he saw her outside the inn. He's been watching her. One of his spies followed her to the provost office a couple days ago."

Thad angled his chin to one side. "Are you saying you had nothing to do with her disappearance?"

"No. Nothing!" Beth shook her head fervently.

A thud drew their attention behind her. The girl had dropped the laundry paddle against the rim of the cauldron and stood with her hands on her hips and a glower on her face.

"Mika? What is it?" Thad asked.

She pressed her lips together as though fighting what might escape. Finally, the words won out. "Maybe you should ask Miss Beth where she went this mornin'. She said it was to see the reverend's wife, but she was more scared than upset. And now I don't think it was about the judge."

"Beth? Where did you go?" Thad's tone had dropped to deadly calm. "And don't lie to me. You're a terrible liar."

Beth drew in a tremulous breath, then her hands burst from beneath her chin. "Yes! I warned LaFleur. But I had no choice. He knew the message I'd received for him had gone missing. It must've fallen out of my cloak when this girl took it without asking." She whirled to glare at Mika, whose lips parted. Beth turned back to Cade. "And then I heard you talking early this morning. I knew you'd found not only the message but also the cipher wheel."

Cade gasped as another piece of the puzzle slid into place. "That's why you were in my room that first night. You came for the cipher wheel."

She balled her hands. "And if you'd drunk enough broth, you never would've known, and all this never would've happened!"

Cade's stomach soured. He'd been right about the morphine and right to suspect Beth. "You never drugged the other men, did you? Just me."

Before she could respond, Thad moved toward her, hands extended as if he would seize her. "You dare blame him when you betrayed your own flesh and blood?"

Beth shrank back. "I had no choice, Father. If Frenchie's whole operation had been compromised and it was my fault, I don't know what he'd do to me."

The operation? Did she know the plan for the *Lady Jane*? Whatever it was would happen tomorrow, but Lily could be taken away from Mound City today—if she hadn't already been. Cade ran his hand over his face. "So you turned Lily over to LaFleur instead." What would a man like that do to her? He couldn't bear to answer the question. They had to stop talking and find her.

Thad groaned, the sound capturing the anguish of a parent wrestling with his own failure. "Why would you do that? You wanted her out of the way with Cecil that badly?"

"No!" Beth's luminous eyes swung back to Thad, pleading. "Frenchie was supposed to rough her up a bit, frighten her. Take the message. Not kidnap her." A tear slid down her cheek. "I don't know what he's doing."

"But you do know where he might be holding her." Cade spoke evenly, though every nerve pulsed for action.

She swallowed audibly. "If I tell you, will you promise to ask the provost marshal for leniency?"

Chapter Twenty-Two

❧

"Wakey, wakey." Something soft landed on Lily's chest. "Time to get dressed."

The oily masculine voice, sliding over the distant undertones of a steamboat's bell and feminine conversation from somewhere below, seemed faintly familiar. The shiver that ran down her body warned her before her memory did.

Before her eyes fluttered open and focused on Alex LaFleur.

Lily bolted upright. What was she doing in bed? And in his presence? The grin on LaFleur's hawklike features mocked her confusion, especially when the room spun around her and she had to clamp her hand over her mouth.

He snickered. "Now don't go doing that again. I'm not going to clean up after you as Tilly did." But with a loud scrape, he toed the metal basin on the floor closer to the side of her cot. *His* cot, for it reeked of him.

Oh, yes…it came back to her now—the alley, the madam, and the captain Tilly had mentioned. Alex. LaFleur or one of his henchmen must have brought Lily here, and he must be the captain. After all, Cecil had said the saboteur captained his own steamboat before the war.

Forcing herself to take slow breaths, Lily willed both the nausea and the panic back down…down to a place she could deal with them later, for she could not show weakness in front of this man. Even if she was his prisoner. He hadn't killed her, so she might as well find out what he intended to do with her. Only then could she make a plan. *Please, God, help me.*

She let her hand fall to the mattress and forced herself to meet LaFleur's glittering dark eyes. "What do you want with me?"

One side of his thin mouth cocked up. "Right now? For you to put on the gown I brought for you and make yourself presentable. You, my dear, are going on a journey. An adventure." He winked at her, then pulled a gold watch from a pocket in his royal-blue silk vest. He dressed like a dandy, with the same gambler-style hat she'd seen him wear at the inn over his long, slicked-back hair, a pinstriped shirt, fitted black trousers, and riding boots with chestnut-colored tops. A leather pistol belt hung below his vest. "And hurry up about it. We need to introduce you to the other ladies."

What other ladies? The ones she'd heard talking on the floor below… and the madam? Her midsection clenching, Lily picked up the satin bodice that lay in her lap atop a folded skirt, the slick folds of which slid away from her grasp. A garish garment trimmed with black lace, it laced up the back and would drape in pleated folds below the shoulders. "I'm not wearing this." She shoved both bodice and skirt onto the floor.

In a single, fluid move, LaFleur scooped up the clothing and tossed it back into her face. "You'll wear that, or you'll wear your undergarments. It matters not to me. But that prim old rag you're in now is going in the furnace before we leave."

Lily sucked in a breath. She swung her legs to the floor, grasping the edge of the cot. "I'm not going anywhere with you."

"I don't see as you have any say in the matter. Not since you chose to insert yourself into my business." LaFleur strode to a nearby table, where he poured some whiskey from a crystal decanter into a glass. He cut her a glance as he took a sip. "You know too much. I can hardly leave you at loose ends."

So they'd been right that the saboteurs had concocted a plot against the *Lady Jane*. Maybe she could bluff her way out of this. She pushed to her feet, glancing around for her basket, which was nowhere in sight. If they'd gone through it, which they most certainly would have, they'd not only discovered the encoded note and cipher wheel but also read the message she and Cade had decoded. She could hardly claim ignorance, but perhaps she could bargain. "If you let me go now, you could get away. I have no proof against you."

Turning from bolting back his drink, the man they called Frenchie narrowed his eyes at her. "You'd run straight to the authorities with your tale, where you were headed when I intercepted you. You take me for a fool, Miss Lily?"

"No." When her legs trembled, Lily braced herself against the bed. "It would be my word against yours. With no evidence, the authorities have no reason to hold you. But if you keep me, you've added kidnapping to your crimes. They'll track you until they find you."

Cade would make certain of that. But had Cade even realized she'd failed to return to the inn? She should have made a plan to check in with him. For all he knew, she was hard at work in the kitchen or guest rooms. How long before he worried enough to look for her? And when he realized she was missing, who could he turn to for help?

Lily swallowed. She should have told Mika and Martha about her errand. Why hadn't she trusted them? Because with the recent tensions in the inn, she hadn't wanted them to know where she'd gone in case her aunt or cousin questioned them.

"As though they'd take my word over yours." LaFleur thunked the glass back on the table and crossed the floor, stopping before her and twisting a loose lock of Lily's hair around his index finger. "With a pretty, innocent little face like this and such a spotless reputation." He released her hair, but the grin that spread over his face made her catch her breath. "Not so spotless for long. You see, your dear cousin Beth did me a favor. I've had my eye on you since you spurned my advances at River Rest."

Lily gasped. "Beth did this?" While she'd known Beth was most likely the go-between for LaFleur and his men, she'd never have thought her cousin would surrender her to their clutches.

A cackle spilled from LaFleur's lips. "Isn't it delicious? Came to see me quite early this morning, more than willing to sacrifice your hide to save hers after she lost the message intended for my St. Louis contact—that fat little wealthy merchant I met at your uncle's inn that day. Lucky for her, I wasn't as mad as she thought I'd be. Her tattling gave me the excuse I'd been waiting for to make you mine."

No! Alarm bolted through her, energizing her weak limbs. Lily darted toward the door, but she'd barely gotten past LaFleur before his arm caught her waist like a heavy boom in a lumberyard and swung her back onto the bed. She fell with a cry in a heap of petticoats. When she attempted to spring back up, he shoved her harder, then leaped atop her, wrestling her down flat.

"Stop! Don't touch me." The terror of the assault when she was sixteen came flooding back, giving her unnatural strength as she bucked and twisted her way from beneath him.

He flung his leg over her, and she aimed a knee jab at his groin. With a guttural groan, he crumpled.

Lily lunged from the bed and stumbled upright. The world tilted and her stomach surged, but she forced herself to put one foot in front of the other. She'd almost made it to the door—a glimpse of a mostly empty warehouse space with daylight streaming through the large windows just beyond—when an unmistakable click halted her. Cold horror washed her from head to toe. Lily slowly turned as LaFleur struggled to his feet, though he still bent at the waist with the arm that held his pistol cradled close against his body.

"That's right." He spoke through clenched teeth, grimacing. "I'd rethink that if I were you. Now just come back over here." He wagged the weapon away from the door. "And take off that dress. You need some lessons on how to treat a man before I put you in with my other girls."

"No!" The floor tilted and the darkness closed in again. Her worst nightmare was about to come true. She could *not* faint. But Lily swayed, and her knees went slack.

LaFleur was there to catch her before she fell, one arm going around her waist while with the other hand he tucked his pistol into the holster on his hip. The horror of his hot mouth nuzzling her neck infused her with the strength to push back and call out for help.

Her assailant shushed her, laughing with sick pleasure. "No one is coming, my sweet. You're one of my girls now, so I can do with you as I please." His fingers worked the top buttons of her bodice loose.

After so many years of guarding her safety and virtue above all else, this couldn't be her fate. She refused to surrender. But LaFleur anticipated her every move, pinning her arms and covering her mouth with his hard lips, his teeth nipping at her like a hungry dog's. Lily whimpered and shrank inside, desperate to escape the shameful act this man would force on her. *Oh, God, help me. Please send help.*

LaFleur bent to sweep his arm beneath her, presumably to carry her to the bed.

A loud *crack* sounded from below. Shouts and feminine screams followed. A gunshot? Her heartbeat stuttered. Had someone come to rescue her?

Hope surged through Lily, renewing her determination. As her captor straightened and turned his head toward the door, she balled her fist and drove it toward his eye with all the force she could muster. She made solid contact with the bony socket. Pain traveled from each knuckle down the nerves into her arm, but LaFleur's head snapped back. Seizing her opening, she lunged for the door.

Not fast enough. He grabbed her around the waist and threw her to the floor. She landed hard on her backside. Her petticoats cushioned her fall, but the heels of her hands throbbed.

"You worthless wench." The fury in his eyes as he loomed over her confirmed she'd just worsened her fate.

Lily scooted away, scrambling to get to her feet. "Help! Someone, help!"

"Alex!" A woman's sharp voice from the doorway, punctuated by another gunshot, silenced Lily's pleas and drew LaFleur back around. Madam Tilly stood there in her green dress and a plumed black hat, her painted eyes wide. "Get her and let's go. We've been discovered. We have to get the girls to the dock."

———————◆◆●————————

"Was that a gunshot?" About a block from the inn, Cade stopped to cock his head. Without a hat, he squinted in the bright light. The sun beat down, its noon radiance blinding his unaccustomed eyes and its heat plastering his cotton shirt to his body.

Thad's alarmed gaze met his. "I think so. And coming from near the warehouse Beth told us about. Come on. Hurry."

As they picked up their pace down the dirt street, Cade groaned his frustration when his hobbling steps fell behind Lily's uncle's. Had O'Henry's men located LaFleur before they did? Even with the pistol Thad had provided tucked into his waistband, even if he could manage to fire the dang thing, he'd hardly be any help if he caused both of them to arrive too late.

Muttering under his breath, Cade flung his crutch away. It clattered against a brick storefront, eliciting a jump and a glare from a portly woman in widow's weeds a few paces ahead. When Thad gaped back at him, he made a shooing motion. "Go ahead. Run. I'll be right behind you." He hoped.

Thad surged forward, darting around servants with shopping baskets, a mustached barber sweeping the boardwalk in front of his business, and a newsboy in a navy wool kepi singsonging the latest headlines from the corner.

Cade managed to keep Lily's uncle in sight. His loping pace brought only a dull ache to his hip, but that could be due to the numbing effects of the energy thrumming through him. The provost's men wouldn't intentionally put Lily in danger, but hadn't she told him how often this uncivil war had harmed innocent civilians?

At last, the two-story brick warehouse Beth had described near the dock came into view, its long windows that weren't broken out, streaked, and dingy. Tall weeds sprouted around the perimeter. Thad was trying the double door beneath the raised, pedimented porch that fronted on the street. It must have been locked, for he ran back to meet Cade, puffing.

"Let's check the shipping doors on the river side."

Cade nodded and drew his pistol in his left hand, allowing Thad to take the lead again. The man peeked around the side of the building facing the Mississippi before turning the corner. The massive wooden doors in the center of the warehouse stood open with no one in sight.

Thad tossed a frown over his shoulder. "Where are they?" Still, he climbed onto the loading dock with caution and swung the barrel of his pistol into the dark opening before proceeding. After a quick look inside, he turned back to Cade. "Seems clear."

Cade assessed the ground beneath the platform, and his heart plummeted. He motioned with his weapon. "Wagon tracks. Recent, from the looks of it."

Thad blew out a breath as he lowered his head. "We don't know anything yet." He meant that LaFleur had gotten away with Lily. "Let's check the building first." His expression pleaded for Cade to not go running after the wagon.

Cade nodded, but his thudding heartbeat warned him of what they might find inside. He climbed the steps to the loading dock and followed Thad into a large open space with crates and barrels stacked against the walls. The place smelled of rum and gunpowder. Thad motioned toward the stairs on one side that led to the second story. They'd made it most of the way there when heavy breathing from behind a stack of crates halted their steps.

Thad trained his weapon on the spot. "Who's there? Come out with your hands up. We're armed."

"Well, I'm afraid I can't do that, seein' as how I've already been shot." The lazy drawl, so unexpected with its hint of humor, made Cade's head snap toward Thad.

The man lowered his pistol, his features going slack. "Cecil, is that you?" He stepped around the stack of crates. "What happened, man?"

Cade hurried over and his jaw dropped. At Thad's feet, an unkempt, bearded man sprawled, unconscious or dead. Blood stained several slashes in his woolen vest and linen trousers.

A second man slumped against the crates, shot through the right shoulder. Lily's Confederate. With his left hand, Cecil pressed a kerchief to the wound, though it was already soaked through with his own blood, while near his slackened right hand lay a bowie knife—the weapon used on the first man? Must have been…for he would have been required to surrender his firearms along with his partisans.

Despite his dire predicament, a crooked grin split Cecil's face as he looked up at Thad. "What happened is, my luck ran out." His chest gyrated with a wheezing laugh. "Made it all the way through the war without takin' a single bullet, but wouldn't you know, I get shot a week after I get home, chasin' a girl."

"Where is Lily?" Stuffing his pistol back into his waistband, Cade stepped around LaFleur's fallen man to Cecil's side.

Cecil eyed him, and his mouth turned down. "You again."

"Where is she?" Cade knelt as he repeated himself, bracing his weight with his good hand, then reaching around his neck to remove his sling. The man's bandana was done for. Cade laid the sopping cloth aside and placed his wadded sling against the wound instead. "Here. Hold this in place."

The former partisan winced as he complied, lashes fluttering as his lids slid closed. "LaFleur's got her. Took her with the other girls in a wagon."

Cade blinked at him. "Other girls?"

"Prostitutes." Cecil's green eyes opened, flashing, the word he spit slicing into Cade's chest like shrapnel.

Thad stepped closer. "Where to?"

"His steamer, I expect. I heard some of the men talkin' about it—the *New Republic*. You've got to hurry." He spoke with intensity. "They'll leave early knowin' we're onto them. Soon as they can get up steam."

Cade struggled to his feet. "Who told you to come here?"

"Timber. His friend overheard Frenchie's plan to take Lily."

Even as Cecil answered, a groan came from behind Thad, who whirled, raising his pistol. Something scraped across the floor, and a canvas sack fell off a crate with a puff of flour, revealing a lanky, gray-haired man who sat up on the other side. "Oh, my head." He gingerly touched his temple, where a sizable lump had already turned dark red.

"Timber." Thad let the name out on a rush of breath.

"Thad?" The older man frowned at Lily's uncle, then looked around too quickly and moaned again. "Did they get away?"

"Yes, and you've got to go after them. Now." Cecil barked out the order, though his voice rasped. His bloody fingers wrapped around Cade's ankle, drawing his attention back to Cecil's pleading gaze. "When I got here, that blackguard had her upstairs. She was callin' out for help. She was terrified."

Cecil was banking on him understanding all that meant. Had LaFleur already harmed Lily? Cade's chest constricted, and he nodded. "We'll find her. And we'll send help back for you." That Cecil had tried to save Lily even after she spurned him—that such anguish filled his face even now—left no doubt that he truly loved her. But he wasn't the only one.

Cade would fulfill the promise that Lily's childhood sweetheart couldn't—or he would die trying.

Chapter Twenty-Three

Identifying the *New Republic* presented no challenge, even if her name had not been painted in large red letters on her side-wheel casing. She was the only steamboat at the Mound City dock. Save for her name and taller decks, the *New Republic* could have been *Sultana's* twin, from the mostly open main deck where steerage surrounded the furnace and boilers to the steam huffing from the twin smokestacks fore of the inset Texas cabin. Atop it, the pilot moved about the open-sided pilothouse. The wagon that Cecil had said had taken LaFleur's girls to the riverfront was nowhere in sight, and the last passengers were crossing the gangway onto the main deck's bow.

Within minutes, dock workers would release the mooring line, the giant twin paddlewheels would churn, and the *New Republic* would chug north, taking her precious cargo with her. Yet Cade's entire body was frozen beside the harbormaster's office. And not because Timber had pleaded for a moment to catch his breath after their dash to the dock, where he now stood in the shade of the shack, bent over with his head between his hands. No. Cade had not been prepared for the terror that gripped him at the thought of boarding that steamer.

God, help me.

Lily was on that boat, facing a fate worse than death.

Thad shifted from one foot to the other. "Now's the time, before they raise the gangway."

"They's not gonna let us on without a ticket." As Timber mumbled his response, Cade leaned close. Was he slurring his speech?

He laid his hand on the older man's back. "You feeling nauseous? Dizzy?" He'd warned against the effects of a concussion, but Timber had insisted they needed another able-bodied man—though Cade wasn't too sure Cecil's injured friend qualified any more than Cade himself did.

"Naw." Hands on his knees, the former scout pushed himself into an upright position. "Just a splittin' headache. I'll be fine."

Thad tipped his head toward the uniformed man standing at the head of the gangway. "You two distract the ticket agent while I board."

"What if they shove off before you find Lily? We can't let you go alone." Cade was getting on that boat even if he had to throw himself aboard, but some backup would be helpful. No telling how many lackeys LaFleur employed. And they should expect all the crew and employees would answer to him as well. Cade scanned the light crowd on the docks. "Any chance O'Henry and the Pinkertons might show up?"

Thad's mouth went flat. "Probably not back from Crowley's Ridge yet. And how would they know to come here? No, it's just us. So do either of you have a better plan?" Thad switched his gaze between them, his middle finger tapping spastically on his pistol holster.

Cade gave a single nod. "We'll get you on, then we'll follow." One way or another. Though the irony that chances were good he'd perish on a steamboat after surviving the sinking of the *Sultana* was not lost on him. At least this way, he'd have a good reason. A reason worth dying for.

Timber removed his hat to swipe the sweat from his forehead. "I'm not above knockin' some men into the river, but turns out, I think I do have a better idea."

"Well, out with it!" Thad threw his arm upward.

Unruffled, Timber resettled his fedora and continued in a leisurely drawl that resembled Cecil's. "LaFleur doesn't know I'm involved in any of this. Last he saw me, before the surrender when he went crazy with revenge, I was on his side. I'll send word through that ticket master instead, tell him I have an urgent message for the captain."

Cade tugged on his goatee. "And what will that message be?"

"No idea." He shrugged. "Hopefully, I won't have to come up with anything. Once I get on board, I'll go straight to find out where he's keepin' the women. They won't leave port as long as Frenchie's expectin' me."

"That might work. But you'll have to move fast." Thad worked his jaw back and forth a moment before nodding. "I'll go with you."

"No." Cade edged forward. "I'll go."

"Shooting left-handed? I don't think so."

Timber flicked his fingers toward Lily's uncle. "The lieutenant's right, Thad. They'll recognize you, but him they've never seen. Even injured, he'll be more help than nothin'. 'Sides, he seems as eager to rescue Lily as you." His wink drew Cade's startled notice. How much had Cecil told him?

Thad puffed his chest out. "I'm not just going to sit here—"

"'Course you're not. You're gonna cover us. We may well need it." The lanky scout broke from the shade of the building, adding over his shoulder, "Come on, Yankee man. Let's go get our girl."

The bright sun on his face told Cade he'd followed without being conscious of movement. Thankfully, it also blinded him from studying the steamer as Timber sauntered up to the ticketing agent and struck a casual pose, one hand on his hip. But the blood thumping through Cade's ears reminded him he was near to once again setting foot on a floating prison. Above the sound, above even Timber's friendly but no-nonsense introduction, a single name split the air. His. In a voice that wrenched his heart with its combination of familiarity and fear.

"Cade!"

His head jerked up. On the hurricane deck where the Texas cabin perched above the raised skylights of the main saloon, a slender man with long, dark hair attempted to wrestle a struggling blond woman away from the knee-high railing, propelling her toward the steps of one of the crew cabins. "Lily!"

Cade shoved the ticketing agent out of his way and sprinted across the gangway. A startled gent in a top hat leaped from his path as he bounded for the outside stairs to the second boiler deck. He ran as though he'd never been hurt, never been in prison, nothing but strength shooting through his limbs. His feet thundered on the wooden steps. His heart pounded. His vision cleared…with one single focus.

Then a gunshot cracked from the dock. A moment later, a body streaked down from the hurricane deck. As it hurtled toward the planks, a woman's scream pierced the air. Cade hesitated only long enough to ascertain it was a man rather than a woman who fell—not even looking over the side when the thud sounded from below, along with a chorus of gasps and cries—before he rounded the turn and sought the next flight of stairs.

He came out on the hurricane deck with the force of a mad bull. A good thing, since a red-bearded stranger was charging toward him with equal determination. Lowering his head, Cade plowed into him with his left shoulder. Pain exploded across his back, but his momentum sent his opponent sailing sideways and backward into the Texas cabin wall. His head snapped forward before he sank onto the deck. Which was clear behind him.

No more assailants but also no more Lily. She should be directly in Cade's view. Where was she?

"Cade!" Thad bellowed from the docks. "Cade! Help her!"

What did he mean? As Cade ran to the low railing, shooting broke out, both from the lower decks of the boat and the dock. More gunmen than just Thad on the landing. But the puffs of gray gunpowder were not what drew his eye. He went cold all over when he looked over, for there, dangling from the outer edge of the rail fore of the wheel casing, was Lily. LaFleur must have pulled her over as he fell. Her skirts flapped in the stiff river breeze as she grunted and attempted to wedge one black boot against the deck.

"Lily!"

Her name burst from him, but he shouldn't have let it, for her head turned his way, and her foot lost purchase. She gave a strangled cry as her legs swung into the open space of the boiler deck's balcony below. With a crack and a shrill scream from Lily, a section of the wooden railing gave way and pulled outward—along with Cade's heart.

———————◆◆◆———————

The railing dropped her several feet as it fell flat but somehow remained attached at the bottom. Not for long. Not with her weight on it. On instinct, Lily swung her lower body toward the steamer, grasping for the deck. Just when she managed to take hold, the rail pulled free and hurtled past her head. She flailed as for a horrible moment she dangled by one hand from the side of the massive steamer.

And then Cade's fingers closed around her wrist. "I've got you. Grab the deck."

He knelt above her, his good hand clutching hers, the elbow of his bandaged arm planted on the planks. Lily whimpered. If only she could gain purchase with her feet against the side of the boat. But the open balcony below made that impossible. And if only someone on the next deck down would hasten to her aid. But the shouts and firing of pistols told her that wasn't likely. She had to do this. And she had to rely on the man she loved—despite his injuries.

God, help us.

Lily lunged and got both hands on the deck, but the swinging of her body with its heavy skirts and the sweat slickening her fingers ultimately loosened her hold. She clung by the tips to the edge, Cade's grasp on her wrist the only thing anchoring her.

She panted. "I can't hold on!"

"Take my other hand."

Her eyes shot open wide. "No!" Even with her safety—maybe her life—hanging in the balance, she knew what that meant.

Cade extended his bandaged hand. "You have to. I'll pull you up."

Still she hesitated, her mind flashing back and forth between the options. The fall probably wouldn't kill her. Would it? Wouldn't those odds be better than—

"Lily, you must!"

Her wet, aching fingers slipped. She wouldn't have a choice, after all. A bizarre sense of relief filled her, followed by blinding panic as she let go. And then two hands closed around both of hers.

The cry in her ears wasn't hers, but Cade's, as her weight snapped his arms and hands taut, those fractured bones that would have just begun to heal. But he didn't let go. He leaned back with a tremendous groan, countering her fall, pulling her shoulders and upper body over the edge of the deck until she could take hold. She scrambled onto all fours as he collapsed next to her.

Cheers from their unseen audience below barely registered. Lily flung her arms around Cade, gratitude for the solid surface beneath her and panic for her rescuer triggering near-hysterical tears. She frantically stroked his head and shoulders, searching for an opening to assess the damage. "What have you done? Oh, what have you done?"

His face still tilted down, he opened his good arm to her, and she snuggled against him. "The only thing I could do." But his agonized expression and the way he clutched his other arm to his side testified of the cost. And his back—he'd surely broken open the barely healing skin.

Lily dashed tears from her eyes. "Oh, Cade. It's much worse now, isn't it? You should have let me fall."

His gaze swept up to hers with a silencing ferocity. "Never."

Love such as she'd not dared to imagine swept Lily's breath from her chest, her heart with it. She drew his head to hers, though her tears blinded her. Didn't matter. She'd never in her life seen things so clearly. "Then I hope you know what you've bought with your sacrifice. You're never getting rid of me, Cade Palmer."

Chapter Twenty-Four

Lily had cried so inconsolably as Dr. Courtner examined Cade's injuries that he'd finally sent her from the room. He couldn't bear her heartbreak, and neither could he assuage her guilt—not with the elderly physician present, and not with his poking and prodding eliciting almost as much pain as had bolted through him when he'd seized Lily's hands and dragged her over the side of the boat. He'd be honest with her once the doctor left, but she didn't need to see him like this.

Not that she was far enough away that she might not overhear his sharp intakes of breath and the groans he attempted to bite back. The creaking of the floor right outside his attic room told him she paced the landing, after delivering the basin of ice water his arm now rested in. He sat on the edge of the bed while Dr. Courtner applied a salve and bandages to his back. The man knew better this time than to try to press him to take morphine. He told Cade he'd only broken open the new skin in several places, and those ought to heal, but his predictions about Cade's fractures were decidedly less hopeful.

"It seems that since your hands took most of the strain, the lower portion of your radius did not displace, which is a small mercy, indeed," he said as he began the process of rebandaging. "Not that you didn't possibly reopen the fracture. And likely trigger some calcification and malformation."

"I know. I know, Doctor." Hearing it spoken aloud roused that old side of him that warred against the unnatural peace he'd experienced even in the moment of injury.

"But your hand…" Dr. Courtner shook his head, tying off the bandage on said appendage. "Well, I'm at a loss as much as I was before about the damage this did. I really wish we had an expert in the area to render an opinion. You deserve it, after what you did for that young lady. And not just for her but for however many other girls were not on that steamer by choice. I hear some of them were awfully young."

"Indeed. Thank God, they're free of LaFleur's evil clutches now." Cade had to marvel at how the Almighty's plan had saved so many more people than just Lily—although it would have been worth it for her alone.

It had all happened so fast. He barely remembered his blind rush to Lily's side. Timber Sutton had made it up to the hurricane deck minutes after Cade pulled her back over the edge. After the shooting stopped, Timber had helped Cade down to the dock. They'd later been told O'Henry and the Pinkertons had rushed there after learning a widow named Mrs. Tilly Wharton had resided with several young women in LaFleur's cabin in Crowley's Ridge—and O'Henry had recalled from the harbormaster's log that a woman by the same name was registered as owner of a steamer scheduled to arrive today at Mound City. Thank God, they'd gotten there in time to divert LaFleur's men after Thad shot LaFleur, giving Cade the opportunity to reach Lily.

O'Henry had gathered the gaudily clad women into the saloon for questioning while the Pinkertons secured LaFleur's remaining accomplices. Two of his henchmen had been shot. One had died. Two others were captured. Outside on the dock, their leader lay dead in a pool of his own blood, his neck broken.

On the way back to the hotel, Lily had related to her uncle and Cade what the scoundrel had intended for her—and how Cecil's intervention as well as theirs had saved her from that fate.

Dr. Courtner grunted. "Thanks to God, yes. And to you. A true hero, you are."

Cade extended his arm for the doctor to begin winding the linen strips around his wrist. "Not just me, Dr. Courtner. Lily played as much a part as I did, and we couldn't have done it without Thad, Timber, O'Henry, even Cecil Duke. How is he, by the way?"

"Resting in a room below. I got the bullet out before I came to see you. He's weak from blood loss, but he should recover with no permanent injury."

Cade let out a soft breath of relief. The last thing he needed if he hoped to start a life with Lily was the gallant partisan's death or disability on his conscience. Or hers. "He was willing to risk everything for Lily, just as I was. And those Pinkertons—we would have never gotten out of there alive without them. I was scared spitless to go on that boat—until I saw LaFleur with Lily. So I'm not a hero. Not really. What I am is a man in love."

The man's bushy eyebrows ascended at the same moment a gasp sounded from the landing. Dr. Courtner chuckled and spoke loudly. "Well, I hope she feels the same way, because you're going to need all the help you can get. That and a miracle if you ever hope to practice—"

Cade had no need to silence the doctor this time, as the door flew open and framed Lily in the threshold, half of her hair escaping her bun and her eyes wild. "I certainly do feel the same way." The force of her words alone could have knocked Cade over if he wasn't already seated. The surge of warmth her pronouncement invoked momentarily deadened all pain.

Dr. Courtner shifted on his seat to take Lily in. "I suppose there's no keeping you out this time?"

"None at all." She remained standing with one hand on the doorknob, her gaze fixed on Cade.

"Then perhaps you'd like to finish up here. Throw the water out and use just the ice—"

"Yes, yes." Lily came forward and nudged Dr. Courtner from his chair.

He snorted but with more amusement than rancor. "I can see my services are no longer required." He stood and gathered his medical supplies, stuffing them into his black bag. "I'll be back tomorrow to check on you, Lieutenant. Meanwhile, I'll see what I can do to make certain you're on the last steamer north, the one leaving Wednesday."

"Thank you, sir." That would give him four full days to recuperate—and hopefully, for Lily to make necessary arrangements. Cade extended his left hand to shake the doctor's, who paused to do so with a nod of respect. Lily drained the water from the basin into the washstand and placed the container on the bed at Cade's side. Then, after she sat down and the physician slipped out the door, Cade rested his bandaged arm over the ice. He turned and reached for her hand with his other. "So you heard what I said."

She dipped her head and caught her lower lip between her teeth. "Are you upset? I couldn't bring myself to leave your side."

"No. I'm glad." He leaned forward. "It makes what I want to say next easier. Because I feel the same. I can't leave your side."

Lily exhaled a quick little breath, and her brows rose.

Cade pressed on. "Before all this, when you got back from the provost office, I was going to ask you to come with me to Cincinnati. You and Jacob. I know this happened fast, and not everyone is going to understand. And I don't know exactly what the future will look like. Maybe eventually I will use my medical training again in some way, God willing. But I'm thinking it's more likely I'll be behind a pulpit than an operating table." He held up his bandaged hand with a soft grunt of a chuckle.

"How can you make light of that?" Lily reached for the still-loose end of the bandage, wove it around his arm, and fiddled with it in an attempt to tie it off—though how she could see to do so past the burgeoning moisture in her eyes remained a mystery. Her touch and voice were gentle, full of regret. "I can't bear it that it's my fault you've lost your chance to be a surgeon, after all you've been through."

"It's not your fault."

She stopped, and her chin wobbled. "I would not have taken your hand, Cade. I had already decided."

"I know that. And so had I." Cade touched her jaw to stop its trembling. "There was no decision to make, really. That's how much I love you."

With a hiccuping gasp, Lily cupped his face instead and pressed her lips to his, their sweetness like a balm to his soul. "I love you too, Cade."

She drew back, adding with a soft laugh, "And I don't care what anyone says or thinks, because there could be no truer test of our feelings than a moment like that."

"A moment of life or death."

"Where we both chose the other." She sniffled and wiped a stray tear.

Lowering his bandaged arm onto the ice again, Cade ducked his head, momentarily overcome with emotion himself. *Thank You, God.* "It's what was meant to be, Lily. I know that now. I have peace with it. I didn't even need Dr. Courtner's assessment…because it doesn't matter either way. If my father will take me back, take me under his wing, that's where I'm content to be. Both fathers, earthly and heavenly." He looked up, and she searched his eyes.

"Truly?"

"Truly." Cade allowed a smile to lift his lips. "With one condition." Not for God, because God didn't treat with conditions. It was all or nothing—Cade knew that now. This condition was for her, but he'd no qualms about begging, bribing, or pleading for her to meet it.

"What's that?"

"That you're by my side as my wife."

Lily sucked in her breath. "You mean that?"

"You didn't think I'd ask you to come along to Ohio like so much baggage, did you?"

Her hand flew to her mouth. "I didn't dare to hope you'd ask me that yet. Maybe down the road…"

"Well, I'm asking now. We know we're in love. I need you by my side to face this uncertain future. And you need a place to go. Not just to go but to thrive." Cade laced his fingers through hers. When she quirked up a brow and pursed her lips in obvious confusion, he couldn't contain his smile. "You had a dream of opening a seamstress shop that you thought died with your friend leaving Memphis."

"Yes…?" Lily drew out the word, cocking her head.

"How would you feel about serving Yankee customers?"

She squeezed his hand. "If they're anything like you, I'll sew for them for free!"

"No need to do that." Cade chuckled, though he shifted his weight as the drying strips on his back started to pull and burn. "Remember I told you that my brother-in-law is a silk importer?" He waited until she nodded. "Well, there's plenty of room in his warehouse for a shop where you could display and fit customers in the finest creations made from his best cloth."

This time, with a strangled cry, Lily covered her whole face. "Oh, Cade. Would he really do such a thing for me? If we were married? How do I deserve that?"

He pulled her hands down. "You deserve it whether you marry me or not. I'm just hoping you take this beat-up prodigal Yankee into the bargain."

She shook her head slowly. "You're not the bargain. You're worth far more than that. You're the priceless prize the river washed up on my shore."

"Then we agree that what the enemy meant for evil, God has used for good."

"Oh yes, we do."

Cade wanted nothing more than to drop to one knee and propose to this woman with the solemnity the occasion demanded. Then, if she consented to marry him, to stand and sweep her into his arms and kiss her with the passion that surged in his chest. The time would come for that. For now, he settled for tugging her to the bed at his side. He needed her closer, right that moment. She set aside the basin of ice and came to him. He stroked her hair back over her shoulder and whispered against her ear.

"Lily Livingston, will you do me the honor of becoming my wife?"

An hour later, Lily pulled the door to Cade's room shut behind her, making sure the latch didn't click and wake him. She leaned against the solid wood for a moment and closed her eyes. Though the setback and probable lasting effects of his reinjury still weighed on her, the bliss of new love now overshadowed it.

She was engaged! Lily's eyes flew open, and she stifled a squeal against her knuckles. Cade had promised they'd pick out any ring she wanted when they got to Cincinnati—next week! Or perhaps his mother would gift them with one of her own. He'd told her that and so many other things after she'd helped him into his sling, then to settle onto his side. And she'd shyly yielded to his request that she rest beside him.

They'd both been through so much, and yet she could hardly allow her weary body the repose it begged for, not when her mind and her heart raced each other like two Kentucky thoroughbreds. Cade growled when he couldn't use his injured hand to touch her—he'd had to stop himself several times—but he more than made up for the lack with the soft kisses he rained over her face and against her neck as they made plans for the future. His ragged breathing rather than his tiredness had finally prompted her to rise.

Lily touched her swollen lips, which bent upward in a satisfied smile. She didn't fear him. In fact, the lack of a need to fear—not just due to his injury, but even more due to his character—had freed her to acknowledge her own desire for the man. And that was why she'd needed to leave. She hadn't wanted to stop kissing him. That he'd be well enough to fulfill that passion when they wed this fall fed her yearning for a future she'd never dared to dream she'd feel.

For now, the man needed to rest. And Lily needed to seek out Mika… because she had something important to ask her. She dashed down the stairs and gave a cry of delight upon discovering the girl alone in the kitchen.

Mika jumped, clattering the teapot in a knit cozy she grasped onto a tea tray, then whirled around. "Oh, Miss Lily!" She darted forward as if to embrace her but stopped short, as constrained by the barriers of race and class as if an invisible wall separated them. A bubble of a sob escaped her. "I'm so glad you're all right."

Lily laughed and threw her arms around the dear girl. No more walls. "Thank you, Mika. Me too. And I have great news, wonderful news!"

"What?" Mika drew back, her eyes wide. "The lieutenant's gonna be all right?"

"I think he will, with God's grace. Even if that means preaching rather than doctoring, Cade has found peace with that." Lily seized Mika's hands. "What's more, he's asked me to marry him. Jacob and I are going to Cincinnati with him next week!" She'd yet to tell Jacob, but from the way he'd flung himself at both Lily and Cade upon their return, she didn't expect much resistance. Especially when he learned his life would no longer consist of a litany of thankless chores.

A gasp, and Mika covered her mouth. She batted her thick fringe of dark lashes. "You're leaving?"

"Yes, we are, and we want you to come too." Lily touched Mika's arm, speaking rapidly to ward off the inevitable onset of tears. "Cade has agreed. Will you come?"

"As your...servant?" Mika slowly lowered her hands.

Lily nodded. "I'll pay you as my maid for now." Apparently, Cade's family was comfortably off. Whatever challenges might lie ahead, her lifetime of financial struggles appeared to be over. "But I'll open a seamstress shop after we get settled. You can work there, if you want. Or find a job someplace else, with the Palmers' help. Imagine all the possibilities in a city the size of Cincinnati. You can do whatever you want to do, Mika. It's a fresh start for all of us."

"Oh, Miss Lily." Mika's shoulders curled forward with the breathy exclamation. She stared past Lily into some distant future. "You offer more than I dared to dream of. And yet, I'd have to leave my parents." Her face crumpled.

"That's true, but a steamer trip down the river is no big feat for a free woman of independent means." Lily's wink had the desired effect—the instant brightening of the girl's countenance. "Think about it. Talk to Martha and Joss. You have until Wednesday morning to decide."

Mika's face relaxed into a grin. "Thank you, Miss Lily. I will. Although I think I already know what my answer will be."

"I was hoping you'd say that. Now, what can I do to help?" She had far too much energy to sit around. Lily turned to the tea tray. "Who is this for?"

"For Cap'n Duke. The missus said I need to take him some tea and toast."

"Oh." Lily went limp.

How could she have forgotten about Cecil? Though LaFleur and

Madam Tilly had ushered her out of the warehouse before she saw who had attacked the guards, Cade had told her what Cecil had done to try to save her—armed only with a knife. Desperation might have emboldened his amorous advances past his normal gentlemanly reserve the day Cade had intervened, but in the end, Cecil had proved every bit as gallant as in her girlhood dreams.

Remorse flooded her...and responsibility. She owed him her heartfelt thanks and her honesty about her plans for the future. Their long, shared history deserved a respectful closure.

"I'll take it."

"Yes, miss." Mika's solemn tone reflected her understanding of the sensitive situation. She hurried over to the oven and pulled out two pieces of toast, which she transferred to the waiting plate. After Lily added the jar of honey, Mika handed her the tray. "I'll pray God gives you the right words."

Lily broke into a smile. "Thank you, Mika. I need it." The girl could become a valuable friend and ally as she matured, if she chose to go to Ohio with them. *When* she chose to go. For something told Lily that Mika's independence and sense of adventure wouldn't allow her to do otherwise.

She'd started to turn away when a wail from the next room halted her in place. Her gaze swung back to Mika's. "Who is that?"

Mika's mouth pressed flat, and then she whispered, "Miss Beth."

Lily's eyes widened. "What's happening?"

"That Yankee man ask her lots of questions, ever since you and the lieutenant were with the doctor."

"The provost marshal?" So much had happened while she basked in her new fiancé's arms. She should have expected that O'Henry would begin his investigation immediately.

Mika gave a nod. "The missus and Mr. Thad be in there with her." She stepped closer and spoke low and soft. "I heard them ask if she can leave the area—stay with her cousin in St. Louis rather than go to jail for helpin' that scoundrel, Frenchie."

"What about Judge Winkler? The authorities might be lenient if she was engaged to a federal employee."

Mika pulled a face, moving aside. "She says she won't marry him."

Maybe Beth was heeding Lily's advice to wait until a man she could love in return came along.

LaFleur had died rather than face justice, and several men had been shot due to Beth's actions—not to mention, Cade's reinjury and her own near demise. But somehow, maybe because the whole world had just opened up to her, Lily couldn't find it in her heart to wish a prison sentence on her cousin. Yes, her actions had been selfish, her loyalties misguided, but the years of belittling and loneliness had whittled her into the type of bitter and hollow person susceptible to the devil's schemes.

Lily heaved a breath and asked the good Lord for grace. Then she asked, "Do they think Aunt Susanna was involved?"

Mika didn't even attempt to feign ignorance. Lily's trust that the servants knew everything of importance that went on with the family proved founded. "She claims she wasn't. And Mama says they don't seem to have anything on her."

Lily nodded. "I see. But that doesn't mean she's innocent." Even if she had never passed a message or otherwise aided a saboteur.

Mika's face hardened with understanding and agreement. "No, miss, it doesn't."

"I suppose I'll have my own moment with Mr. O'Henry soon." He'd want a statement, and she wanted to know if the risks they'd taken had paid off, saving even more lives than the women on the *New Republic*. Had the message they'd intercepted stopped the plot against the *Lady Jane*? Lily sighed. "For now, I need to speak with Cecil."

Chapter Twenty-Five

From where he reclined on several pillows, Cecil gave Lily that halfway grin when she stepped into the doorway. "I've been hopin' every knock was yours. Although I admit, this isn't exactly how I pictured you first seein' me in bed." He waved his long fingers at the bandage over his chest.

How did he manage to flirt a flush onto her face, even when she was here to say goodbye? His broad, bare, golden-haired torso didn't help matters. Ah, it would have been so easy to let him romance her.

And miss the biggest love of her life. Cecil's misstep couldn't have been timed better, warning her of the selfish tendencies beneath his charm.

Lifting her chin, Lily strode forward with the tray. "Aunt Susanna sends you tea and toast."

"Will you feed it to me?"

She narrowed her eyes. "I believe at least one of your hands is working just fine."

"Ah, that it is."

Much like her lieutenant's upstairs. Lily suppressed a smirk and slid the tray next to him on the bed rather than on the table where he couldn't reach it. "But I will help you with your tea. Honey?"

He chuckled as though the word was an endearment rather than a question. "Yes, please."

Lily leaned over to pour the hot liquid into the cup, then swirl in a dollop of sweetener from the grooved ladle. She offered the drink handle first. Cecil took it with a wry glance, then raised it for a sip. When her gaze lowered to the small red stain on his bandage, her heart softened as fast as butter in a hot skillet. "You're here because of me. I'm so sorry, Cecil."

"Now, now." He set the teacup on the tray. "There's no call to wax sentimental, my dear. I only did what any other gentleman would do when his girl was in danger."

"But that's just it." Lily pulled the nearby chair over to the edge of the bed and settled herself on it. "I'm not your girl. Not anymore. You knew that going in. And yet still…you went. With nothing but a knife."

Cecil flicked his index finger up. "Never underestimate a Southern boy with a knife."

Laughter bubbled from her lips despite her solemn resolve. "Oh, you are impossible not to love."

His face angled back toward her. "So you admit, you do love me?"

Lily drew a breath. She wouldn't pretend her statement had been a faux pas. But neither would she tantalize him with one more moment of false hope. "Yes. I love you, Cecil. You've been my friend for over twenty years, and my twin loved you like a brother. So that makes you like a brother to me."

"You love me like a brother." He drew the conclusion in a flat, disbelieving tone.

"I do. And with a lifetime of love."

Cecil's face tightened. "You're just saying that because of what happened last time I saw you. I lost control, Lily. I was coming to tell you how sorry I was when Timber told me Frenchie had taken you. You've got to understand, I've waited for you for four years—no, longer than that. Ever since I saved you from that boy—"

"So you became just like him? And no better than Frenchie?" All tenderness had fled from her tone. She'd not countenance yet another man's excuses of why he had the right to assault her.

"No. I never would've…forced you. Never. Don't you know that? I just wanted you to kiss me back with the fervor I felt for you."

The sincerity he displayed, the shamefaced plea in his last statement, paved her anger over with a layer of sympathy. "But I couldn't do that, Cecil. Don't you see? No matter how hard you kissed me." As her voice trailed off, she opened her hands in her lap.

"Why not, Lily?"

He was going to make her say it. She met his eyes but spoke softly. "You know why. Because of the man upstairs."

"You're in love with a Yankee with nothing to show for himself."

"Oh, he has plenty to show for himself." Though each enumeration of Cade's good qualities would repeatedly stab Cecil's fragile ego and possibly anger him again. And that was not how Lily wanted them to part. "But so do you, and that's what I'm trying to tell you. Because of your loyalty and now your bravery, I owe you a debt I can never repay."

Cecil shook his head slowly, his golden hair brushing his shoulders. "It's not yours to repay. It was mine, my promise to discharge, and I did. Not just for Hamp but also for you. I love you, Lily. Can you ever forgive me?"

Leaning forward, she reached for his hand. "Cecil, your sacrifice for me atoned for your honor a hundred times over. If you hadn't come when you did, LaFleur would've had his way with me." She paused. Shuddered at the memory of how close her call had been. "You could've been killed. I'm so thankful you weren't, because I want to always think of you here in Crittenden County, making your family farm thrive again, leading the way in the community. Eventually, finding love. Be that man, Cecil. The one who shows others the way into the future."

"You want to think of me here? *Eventually*, you want me to find love?" His brows crumpled his forehead as he searched her eyes. Had he heard anything else she'd said?

Lily sat back, freeing her hand. "That's right. Jacob and I will be leaving next week, going to Cincinnati. Cade has asked me to marry him."

"You can't have accepted." Cecil struggled upright. "Lily, you barely know the man. You can't leave with him. I won't let you."

"You won't let me? Cecil, you don't have that power." Partially rising,

Lily gently eased him back onto the pillows. "And not because you're injured. Because that's for me to decide and you to accept." She laid her hand on his forehead, offering a brief, soothing touch as she smoothed his hair back. "You'll just have to trust me, though of course, I'll stay in touch with Uncle Thad, and I'm sure he'd give you updates. Maybe, when things have healed more in our country, I'll come back for visits." When her aunt was able to forget Lily was the reason her daughter was sent away, and only if Beth herself found her way.

Cecil caught her hand. "You're makin' a mistake, Lily. Even if you don't marry me, please don't go. You belong here. Not with them."

She allowed her fingers to linger in his. "I'm so sorry, Cecil. I never should've let you assume I'd always be yours. I didn't know any better back then. The truth is you deserve a woman who will admire and love everything about you. As I told Beth, you shouldn't settle for anything less."

"But I already found that kind of love." The thickness of tears swelled Cecil's words, and her heart squeezed as he kissed her hand. Had he not understood her? How could she be clearer without being cruel? "If you leave, I'll never be Lucky Cecil Duke again."

Didn't he know he already no longer was? His continued self-focus gave her the strength to gently tug her hand free and whisper, "Goodbye, Cecil."

God be with you. She'd pray he could find a new identity in Christ, one that would help him face the changing world unfolding around them.

The next afternoon, Lily was helping Martha and Mika serve after-church diners when Aunt Susanna stopped her from dishing out stew with a hand on her shoulder. Lily's heart skipped a beat as she turned to take in her aunt's pale skin and puffy, reddened eyes.

The provost marshal had insisted that Beth remain in the local jail until she could testify in the trials of LaFleur's men. That decision had prompted the wail Lily and Mika heard. Only after Beth testified against the saboteurs would O'Henry honor his agreement to send her to relatives in St. Louis. In her absence, Lily's aunt had actually been waiting tables, but she'd avoided looking at or speaking to Lily.

Now she said, "The provost marshal is here to see you. He's in the private dining room."

Lily exhaled and smoothed her hands over her skirt. The moment she'd anticipated had come, though she'd expected a summons to the provost office instead. "Thank you."

"Take him some stew."

"Of course. A good idea." Lily reached up to untie her apron, but as her aunt started to turn away, Lily touched her arm. "Aunt Susanna?" When the woman faced her again, her mouth drawn tight, Lily fumbled for words. "I just want you to know that I'm sorry about Beth."

Surprise flooded her aunt's features. "*You're* sorry? My daughter's actions almost got you killed. Along with a lot of other people."

Was her aunt actually bordering on an apology? That she hadn't expected. "Yes, but she got caught up with some bad people. I think, at first, she felt she was helping a cause she believed in." And vainly grasping for admiration from dangerous men. "I'm relieved that Mr. O'Henry will grant a pardon in exchange for her testimony. Maybe in St. Louis, Beth can start over."

"She'll have to." Aunt Susanna's sharp features congealed. "She's shamed this family beyond repair. If it's up to me, she'll never return to Mound City."

Lily gasped. "Aunt Susanna—"

But the woman had turned, her spine stiff, and marched across the kitchen for another tray of plates containing the midday meal. With a pit in her stomach, Lily bit the inside of her cheek as Aunt Susanna strode through the doorway. Her aunt seemed angrier that Beth had gotten caught than that she'd broken the law in the first place. She had to realize that her own burning zeal for the Confederate cause had driven her daughter into the arms of spies and saboteurs—no doubt, seeking her mother's approval as much as the men's.

Laying her apron on the table, Lily released a sigh. Soon enough, the dysfunctions of the Livingstons would no longer be her problem. She, Jacob, and Cade would create a new life in Cincinnati. But it broke her heart to leave what remained of her family in such shambles.

As she entered the private dining room with her tray of stew and coffee, the reason she'd been called here instead of to the provost office became clear. "Cade!" she cried as she hurried forward.

He sat at the table, his splinted arm in its sling cradled against his fresh white shirt. The faint lines of pain etched on his features—clearly visible due to the shave she'd very much enjoyed giving him that morning—crinkled into a smile when she called his name.

O'Henry perked up and sniffed the air. "Is that coffee? Real coffee?"

"It certainly is." Lily placed the tray on the wide table in front of him, just on the other side of his stacks of papers. She passed him a steaming mug, then slid the one she'd intended for herself to Cade, sharing an intimate smile when their fingers brushed.

"My, I can use this." Without benefit of cream or sweetener, O'Henry slurped down several appreciative swallows of the fragrant brew. "Forgive me for taking you away from the kitchen, Miss Lily, but I wanted to record your statement as soon as I finished the lieutenant's."

"I was expecting to be interviewed, but I admit, I'm surprised to see my fiancé out of his room this morning." As much as that new term might thrill her insides, Lily couldn't decide who to level her chiding glare at—Cade or the provost marshal.

Cade leaned forward. "It was my decision to come downstairs, Lily. This is official business, of the most important sort, not something I want to discuss from my bed."

She considered him a moment, admiration rising again. Then she gave a brief nod. "I understand. You might as well have a bowl of stew before you go back up." Lily distributed the servings to the men, then went around the table to sit at Cade's side.

"Actually, Miss Lily, I have some information I'd like to share with both of you before I take your statement." O'Henry shoveled in a quick bite of stew, then shuffled his papers.

Lily exchanged a glance with Cade. "We're eager to hear anything you're free to share. And I'd like to start by thanking you, sir, for your clemency to my cousin." She ignored the wry expression Cade fixed on her as he paused with a bite of stew halfway to his mouth.

"Yes, well…" The provost marshal sighed and shook his head. "That she got caught up in all this is a shame."

Cade's spoon clunked against his bowl. "That may be, but she knew what she was doing. Why does everyone keep acting as though she was some mindless pawn? If she hadn't run to LaFleur and told him we'd decoded the missing message, none of this would have happened. She put loyalty to him over loyalty to her own family."

Lily turned a quelling look on Cade. Why was he bringing this personal issue up now, in front of O'Henry? "We talked about this. She must have felt the Confederate guerillas were her family. I should have done more to connect with her. Then maybe I could have headed some of this off."

"What you should do is stop shouldering her blame."

The provost marshal cleared his throat, breaking in. "The fact is Miss Beth actually possessed little information of any value. She merely acted as a go-between for the saboteurs, passing messages and arranging meetings."

"But she did encode the message for LaFleur's contact, right?" Cade opened his hand. "Otherwise, she wouldn't have needed the cipher wheel."

"She did. That's why I'm keeping her under arrest and requiring her testimony for exoneration." O'Henry's chair creaked as he shifted his weight. "She planned to pass the message to a nephew of the St. Louis contact, a wealthy merchant we've identified as Dennis Stevenson."

Lily glanced at Cade. "The middle-aged man I saw here with Frenchie—LaFleur." She turned back to the provost marshal. "So does that mean that when we intercepted the message, the plot was averted?"

O'Henry rubbed his bristled chin, raising his ginger brows of the same hue. "Unfortunately, one of LaFleur's men who talked in hopes of leniency verified that his boss sent another message as soon as your cousin informed him of the loss of the first. And it did reach Stevenson in time." He waited until Lily and Cade both gaped at him before he broke into a grin. "But so did my telegraph to the St. Louis office, thanks to you. Our agents there intercepted a coal torpedo on the barge where the *Lady Jane* would have taken on fuel. The Union officials returning from Lincoln's funeral steamed safely back to Memphis yesterday evening."

"Oh, thank God." Lily let her shoulders contact the back of her chair. Sagging wasn't really an option in a corset.

"Turns out, it was a good thing the plot got to that point. We were able to take Stevenson and his nephew into custody too." O'Henry scooped another heaping bite of stew to his mouth.

Cade had gone unnaturally still. After a moment during which the sound of O'Henry chewing overlaid the hum of conversation from the next room, he spoke softly. "If they found a coal torpedo intended for the *Lady Jane*, does that mean they did plant one here in Memphis for the *Sultana*?"

Lily stared at him, her stomach bottoming out.

The provost marshal swallowed and wiped his mouth with his napkin. "LaFleur's henchman who sang vows it was so, though, of course, he claims he had no part in it. He says LaFleur was acting on orders from Charlie Dale."

Cade's left hand tightened into a fist atop the table.

Lily laid her hand over his. "That means we got them, Cade. We helped bring to justice those who killed so many good men."

"Actually, I'm not convinced that's so." O'Henry slid his bowl away and leaned back from the table.

Lily turned a frown on him. "What do you mean?"

"Charlie Dale," Cade interjected before the officer could answer. "You've got to go after him now. If he's truly the mastermind behind all this, he won't stop with this setback."

O'Henry took a quick sip of coffee. "We'd love nothing more, and believe me, we have men investigating Dale. But I'm still not convinced he or LaFleur had anything to do with the *Sultana*."

Lily shook her head. "You just said his man confessed."

"Folk will say all sorts of things when they get caught…to curry favor, to divert attention, or even to gain notoriety. This whole thing with the *Lady Jane* could have been an attempt to make a statement, to raise doubts and build fear after the *Sultana* sank by other means. Do you know who the Washburn Commission is interviewing today, over there across the river?" O'Henry leaned toward Lily.

"No." How would she have any idea, given the recent turn of events here in Mound City?

"John Witzig, supervising inspector of steamboats. He's been here since the fourth. And he's telling anyone who will listen that the explosion was caused by an excess of steam. You'll quickly realize why that's significant."

Not quickly enough, apparently. Lily's beleaguered brain scrambled to keep up. When she fixed a blank look on Cade, he lowered the hand that had been rubbing his chin and said, "Sabotage would have exonerated his inspectors."

"Exactly so. And look at this." O'Henry plucked a newspaper from one of his stacks and plopped it down before them, facing their direction. *The Chicago Tribune*, from Friday, May fifth. His square nail underlined a paragraph in a long feature about the *Sultana*. "This article places blame everywhere *but* on sabotage. An agreement between the captain and the quartermaster to overload the boat with troops for a kickback while other boats sat idle. A boiler which had not been examined or tested since it was patched. Even that the *Sultana* may have been running at a higher amount of steam pressure than allowed by law. Read this bit aloud."

Lily was closest, so she leaned forward and gave voice to the portion indicated. "'These facts are sufficient to give the lie to the canard, stated by the mate, that the explosion must have been arisen from an infernal machine. The infernal machine that exploded the boiler and sent so many souls into eternity, carrying bereavement and mourning into thousands of Western homes, was undoubtedly, the bribe—the greenbacks paid by the officers of the *Sultana* to the Quartermaster for the transportation of the troops.'"

She sat back, and silence fell over their little assembly. Deep and sudden grief swamped her, and she covered her face. "This is awful. All these theories, and will we ever know the truth?"

The provost marshal spoke again, his voice softer. "The location of the explosion, at the top and rear of the boilers, and not near the fire-boxes, points to the likelihood that mechanical malfunction caused the *Sultana's* demise." He firmed his mouth and glanced between them. "We may never know the exact details, or all of the how and why. I suspect this is something that will be investigated and debated for years to come."

"But if they think these Union officers were responsible, whether for bribes or overcrowding or not repairing a boiler properly, they'll go after them, right? They won't let them just get away with it?" Desperation nudged Lily's questions into a higher pitch than she'd intended. When Cade's fingers brushed her skirt, her hand fluttered back up to her mouth.

O'Henry had the grace to take her seriously. "Yes, Miss Lily, that is the aim of all these investigations." A frown flitted over his face. "I must admit, I was hoping that the fact that the evidence now points away from sabotage would come as a relief to you."

"It does. It does." As if in defiance of her words, a sob bubbled up in Lily's throat, and she turned toward Cade. He cast an anguished glance at the provost marshal.

"Um, I'll give you a minute." The older man's chair scraped across the floor as he rose. "Let Miss Lily compose herself before we start her interview."

Once the door closed behind him, Cade stood and held out his hand. Lily rose, and he drew her against his left side. She let her tears fall onto his soft white collar while he stroked her arm. He murmured against her hair, "Do you want to tell me what this is about?"

"You don't know?" She wiped her face, then dried her hands on her skirt. "So many people could be culpable in this tragedy, but from what I'm hearing, there isn't enough evidence to bring any of them to justice."

"That's a problem for the army and the government, though, isn't it?"

Lily peered at him. "Do you really believe all these committees will come to a consensus and bring the right people to trial? How can you be calm about this when you were so determined that Beth get what she deserved?"

"You're right." Cade grimaced. "I should show more mercy for your cousin. I suppose the family betrayal hits me deeper…for obvious reasons."

She nodded, resting her hand on his chest. "I can understand that."

A sheepish smile twisted his face. "Apparently, you saving my life made me protective of you really fast."

Lily shrugged. "You want justice for me just as I want it for you." How strange and wonderful to think she had someone fighting in her corner again.

"I want it for me too. You know how torn up I was when I learned James had died. I still want answers, for him and all the other men even more than for myself." Cade leaned against the table, pulling her against him. "But when I settled things with God, I gave what happened in Andersonville as well as with the *Sultana* over to Him. When this fell into our laps, we did our parts, and now we have to let the officials do theirs. Even if they do it imperfectly, there is a perfect God waiting at the end of this. And He'll see justice done."

"Yes, He will." As peace settled her heart and mind, Lily laid her head against Cade's shoulder. "And that allows us to move forward without bitterness."

"That's right." He lifted her chin and sought her gaze. "You know, Lily, when I started home from Vicksburg, I was a broken man who thought God had abandoned me. I was determined to make my own way in life, but I was on the wrong path. And then you pulled me out of that river, and everything changed. My own will had to sink with the *Sultana* for me to be able to see the wonderful future God had planned. With you." His thumb caressed her jaw.

She smiled, her heart overflowing with love. "Your will may have sunk with the *Sultana*, but hope certainly didn't."

"No." He lowered his soft lips to hers, teasing her with visions of the future. "Hope is rising."

Epilogue

The long, high, steady blast from the twin smokestacks of the *Marble City* signaled that they were underway, heading north from the Memphis docks with the fifth and final group of *Sultana* survivors. The boat moved so smoothly that only the changing shoreline confirmed their departure. Nevertheless, Lily sought Cade's hand as she looked up at him. She might be leaving the only home she'd ever known while he resumed the journey toward his, but how must he feel, venturing once again onto the wide Mississippi?

The darting of his eyes betrayed the same anxiety he'd displayed when they'd first set foot aboard the *Rosedella* to ferry across to Memphis, then again when they'd traversed the gangway onto *Marble City*. But his expression remained calm, and he squeezed her hand. So far, so good, then.

As they slid past the little trio that had accompanied them from Mound City—Uncle Thad, Martha, and Joss—Lily freed her hand to wave one more time. Her brother jumped up and down at her side, flailing his arms so widely he almost struck a petite lady in a massive silk bonnet and even wider hoopskirt standing behind him.

"Well, I never," the woman grumbled, but Lily let the infraction go with only a pat on Jacob's shoulder. She could be nothing but glad he was embracing this new adventure so wholeheartedly.

Mika, on the other hand, blubbered uncontrollably, her hand extended toward her mother, whose kerchief covered most of her face and whose shoulders shook. A moment of doubt crept over Lily. Had she done the right thing, inviting Mika along? Luring her with promises of a brighter future? She was so young, and the world could be so cruel.

A glance at the many recuperating Union soldiers on deck reassured Lily. These men and tens of thousands more had sacrificed life, limb, and health so people like Mika could have that future. The sense of rightness that filled Lily brought a rush of tears to her eyes.

Thank You, Lord.

Even as she comforted Mika, Lily battled her own fears. When their loved ones blurred from sight, she peeked at Cade, smoothing her hand down the fitted blue bodice of the neat linen traveling outfit with its pagoda sleeves and tucked rear peplum that Aunt Susanna had gifted her with—from her own wardrobe, no less. The outfit, though rendered without an excess of sentimentality or even speech, had still gone far as a gesture of conciliation. Lily had accepted it with profuse thanks. She would wear it today and upon their arrival in Cincinnati to buoy her confidence, donning more modest apparel for the train journey between Cairo, Illinois, and Camp Chase, Ohio, where Cade and the other men would officially muster out. But arriving dressed like a lady could only ease her mind so far about what awaited her in Cincinnati.

Cade instantly read the apprehension in her eyes. "What is it, my dear?"

"Are you sure your parents will approve of me?" She couldn't help that the insecurity tumbled out.

"Of course they will. I read you their response when we telegraphed them on Monday. They're beside themselves with excitement."

Lily quirked up one side of her mouth. "They're excited to see *you*. And it probably didn't hurt that you mentioned you were coming home to embrace your 'true calling.' They would've known exactly what that meant." Though she'd thought the idea a good one herself.

Cade chuckled, tweaking her chin with his index finger. "The main thing I *mentioned* was that I'd be bringing my fiancée and her little brother."

"That's me!" Jacob waved his arm as he rotated around to face them. "Are you sure I get my own room?"

"Completely sure. You'll even get a pick of several."

Jacob wahooed, but Lily's eyes widened. Cade had explained that while his father drew a modest salary from the church, he'd inherited family money earned through railroad ventures. But just how big *was* the Palmer home? The probability that she'd be expected to mingle with polite society—Northerners, at that—had Lily struggling to swallow past a sudden obstruction in her throat.

"You too." Cade gently touched Mika's shoulder. "You won't have to stay in the servants' quarters if you're more comfortable near Lily."

"Thank you, sir. I would be." Mika swiped moisture from her cheeks and angled to face them, her chin tucked. "And Lieutenant?"

"Yes, Mika?"

"Do you think there's any chance that doctor friend of yours might need a helper, sometime down the road? Even if you don't doctor anymore? I know I'm not qualified to be a nurse, but I could learn. I could clean and do laundry and run errands—"

Mika's eyes went wide when Cade held up his hand, but then he smiled. "If that's what you want to do, I'd be more than happy to inquire for you."

Her lips parting, Mika sought Lily's approval, which she gave with a nod.

"Oh, thank you, Lieutenant Palmer. I'd be grateful for life."

"There's no need for that." Cade patted her shoulder. "Just flourish for life, whatever you do."

"Look, Mika, there's a tugboat." Oblivious to their momentous conversation, Jacob grabbed hold of the girl's arm and pulled her toward the bow of the *Marble City*. Mika's bonnet blew back from her head, held only by the ribbons knotted beneath her chin as she followed her young charge into the stiff wind.

"Stay close," Lily called after them, then she turned to Cade with a sigh. "That was good of you, Cade. It's truly amazing that your folks were happy enough about your return to not protest you dragging a penniless, simple Southern girl and her little brother along. Not to mention, a freed slave. I can only imagine what they must think."

A breath rushed out of Cade, and his expression softened. He raised his hand to her cheek. "What they must think is that the prodigal returns, and he's found the love of his life. Now stop this fretting, Lily. They're going to love you. Amelia too. She's always wanted a sister."

"Will you tell me about them? All you can think of." Lily wrapped her hand around Cade's arm and gave it a gentle shake. "I want to know everything."

"Yes, but relax. We have the whole journey ahead of us."

But first, they had to get past the wreck of the *Sultana*. A glance toward the bow confirmed that the low-lying mound in the collection of Paddy's Hen and Chicken Islands where the boat had gone down was coming up far too soon. "No better time to start than now. By the time we reach Ohio, I want to have heard every significant achievement and adventure from your childhood. Why don't we find a table in the saloon and order some tea?"

She tugged on his arm, but he tugged back. When she looked up, he slid his hand behind her neck and brought his face down to hers right there on deck. A tingle started at her crown and worked all the way down to her toes as his mouth moved over hers, aligning them body, heart, and spirit.

When he raised his head, she asked with a gasp, "What was that for?"

"Because I know what you're doing. And I appreciate it, but I don't need it."

"What am I doing?"

"Trying to divert my attention. And while you're very good at that, I'm really all right, Lily." His eyes begged for her to trust him. "I'd much rather mark this moment with reverence than pretend it isn't happening. I think we owe James and the others that much."

Lily's heart gave a dull thud. "Of course, you're right."

"You only thought to spare me. But with you and God in my life, I'm stronger now. Strong enough to face the past—and the future— head-on." He turned and offered her his arm. "Shall we join Mika and Jacob on the bow?"

"Yes. Let's." She wrapped her fingers around the sleeve of the coat he wore with one arm inserted and the other side draped over the top of his sling—no vest yet. If he could be this brave, so could she. No more looking back. And no more fretting about how she would fit into Cincinnati society. As long as he was by her side, she could face anything.

Lily huddled on the bow of *Marble City* with her little group of sojourners. As they passed Hen's Island, as yet wreckage strewn but with only the jack staff marking the resting place of the *Sultana*—the Stars and Bars still proudly waving at its tip—Cade suggested they bow their heads for a moment of silence. Then he prayed aloud, committing to God the families of all those who had perished in the waters below as well as those now steaming their way to a brighter future.

Author's Note

The first novel I ever wrote was set during the Civil War, inspired by travels to historic sites of the Southeast with my parents and scribbled in my eleven-year-old hand in spiral-bound notebooks. Fresh out of college with my new degree in journalism with a minor in history on my shelf, I searched for a publisher for yet another Civil War trilogy. That search ended with a callback from my then-dream publisher saying, "Almost but not quite."

Fast-forward another decade or so. I was a young mom writing for magazines and directing a volunteer 1800s dance group when my Georgia Gold Series, literary-style historical fiction set between the Cherokee Removal and Reconstruction, found a home with Canterbury House Publishing. Since then, as I've grown as both an author and an editor, I've followed social and publishing trends and written everything from Revolutionary War romances to Hallmark-style contemporaries, everything *but* Civil War–era stories… until this one. It doesn't feel like an accident that the first stand-alone my hardworking agent, Linda S. Glaz, was able to place with a larger publisher was set in 1865. It feels a lot like coming home.

Some of that also has to do with the fact that I love writing stories that illustrate how God can bring healing and redemption out of the most difficult circumstances. I also endeavor to work as much real history as possible into the plots of my novels. These principles certainly applied to *When Hope Sank*. With *Destruction of the Steamboat Sultana* by Gene Eric Salecker as my primary source, accompanied by a research trip to Marion and Memphis, I attempted to reflect events accurately, from the hours before the *Sultana* explosion to the early investigations following the tragedy. The numbers presented in the story—2,130 aboard, 961 survivors, and 1,169 deaths—reflect the findings of Mr. Salecker's meticulous in-person research. As staggering as this event was, newspaper coverage quickly turned to Lincoln's funeral and the arrest of his assassin, John Wilkes Booth. With over 600,000 lives lost in the war, citizens had long ago exceeded their capacity for suffering and death.

However, the investigations into the explosion of the *Sultana* did lead to a general being relieved of command and a captain being court-martialed. There were so many officials suspected of bribery or negligence that many feel justice was never achieved. If you'd like to try to untangle the culpability of those involved, again, I recommend Mr. Salecker's book, as well as *The Sultana Tragedy* by Jerry Potter.

The plottings of Alex LaFleur and associates were a fictionalized extension of the very real activity of spies and saboteurs in and around Mound City, Arkansas. And the very real suspicion cast upon Charlie Dale, a.k.a. Robert Lowden/Louden, in the firing of the *Sultana*. Dale was indeed a Confederate agent, saboteur, blockade runner, and captain from St. Louis who carried messages between General Sterling Price and Confederate regulars and bushwhackers (and upon whose exploits I based LaFleur's, though with LaFleur as an underling).

In May 1888, the *Memphis Daily Appeal* ran a sensational article in which a man named William Streetor claimed that Charlie Dale had confessed he used a coal torpedo to fire the *Sultana*, along with half a dozen other steamboats on the Mississippi. The coal torpedo had been invented by Thomas Edgeworth Courtenay, also a Southern-sympathizing saboteur from St. Louis.

While many coincidences do link the activities of these men, other facts serve to counter Streetor's story. According to Salecker, Streetor claimed he worked with Dale some three years after the war. But Dale died in New Orleans in 1867. Actual evidence confirms that Dale fired far less than a dozen boats, maybe as few as one.

There were also physical challenges to consider in getting an explosive aboard the *Sultana*. Had Dale put the torpedo on at Memphis, it would have been buried when the steamer took on a thousand bushels of coal from the barges just upriver and could not have been shoveled into the furnace until hundreds of miles away, not a mere seven. Had it been put on at the coal barges north of the city, the saboteur would likely have been spotted by the loyal Union employees.

Finally, one man who read the 1888 article came forward saying he knew Charlie Dale but that he was nowhere near Memphis at the time of the *Sultana* explosion.

While questions remain as to what did cause the explosion and a number of factors may have contributed, such as the overcrowding and the failure to properly distribute the *Sultana*'s load, the consensus over time lends toward a combination of the dangerous design of tubular boilers and over-pressurized steam against an inferior quality of iron used in the repair. Those wanting to learn more can do so in a number of published accounts of the tragedy, plus a visit to the Sultana Disaster Museum in Marion, Arkansas. I'd like to thank Melody Walker, director of planning and operations, for her kind assistance during my visit and for beta reading my story for accuracy regarding the *Sultana*.

If you do visit, keep in mind that nothing remains of the towns of Mound City and Hopefield. While the historical marker says that Union soldiers burned Mound City in 1863, the *Encyclopedia of Arkansas* clarified that it was a few homes, whereas Hopefield was thoroughly fired. For my story, I made Mound City a bit larger than it probably was during the time period.

Another thing the modern visitor should note is that the Mississippi River has changed course over the years, partly to do with the sinking of the *Sultana* and partly to do with later levees. Hopefield and Mound City Chutes, now lakes, once brought river access to the towns on the Arkansas side.

For the medical portions of this story, I also owe special thanks to my living historian friend, Rachel Smith, RN, NP-C, BSN, MSN, and a member of the Society of Civil War Surgeons, who has spent over twenty years researching medicine of the mid-1800s. She checked over my research, added to it from original medical textbooks, and served as a beta reader to ensure I got the treatments for burn injuries and fractures as close to correct as possible.

Special thanks are also due to my other beta readers, faithful members of my launch team, including Gretchen Elm, Kimberly Porter Bowie, Karen Jennings, and Jennie Webb.

After all the research and all the writing and editing, I hope you've enjoyed this beautiful love story based on shared faith and sacrifice. If you did, your reviews let publishers know my stories are worth continuing to publish. I notice and treasure each one. Please visit me at https://www.deniseweimerbooks.com, where you can find my other stories set between the Revolutionary War and modern times. I'd also love to connect on social media and through my once-a-month newsletter, where I conduct giveaways, polls, and cover reveals, and I give behind-the-scenes glimpses of my many historical adventures.

Monthly e-mail list: http://eepurl.com/dFfSfn

https://www.facebook.com/denise.weimer1

https://twitter.com/denise_weimer

https://www.bookbub.com/profile/denise-weimer

North Georgia native **Denise Weimer** has authored over fifteen traditionally published novels and a number of novellas—historical and contemporary romance, romantic suspense, and time slip. As a freelance editor and Acquisitions & Editorial Liaison for Wild Heart Books, she's helped other authors reach their publishing dreams. A wife and mother of two daughters, Denise always pauses for coffee, chocolate, and old houses.

A Day to Remember

A new series of exciting novels featuring historic American disasters that changed landscapes and multiple lives. Whether by nature or by man, these disasters changed history and were a day to be remembered.

When the Waters Came
By Candice Sue Patterson
May 31, 1889

Pastor Montgomery Childs struggles to tend his humble flock in Johnstown, Pennsylvania, while seething at the evil practices among the rich and privileged on Lake Conemaugh. Like Noah, Monty prays for justice, but he never expects God to send a flood. Annamae Worthington comes to help the newly formed Red Cross deal with the aftermath of the failure of South Fork Dam, never imagining the horrors she will encounter. As Monty and Annamae work together distributing supplies, housing survivors, and preparing the dead, a kinship forms between them. But when an investigation into the collapsed dam points to the South Fork Fishing and Hunting Club, secrets emerge that may tear them apart.

Paperback / 978–1–63609–758–9

When the Flames Ravaged
By Rhonda Dragomir
July 6, 1944

World War II Gold Star widow, Evelyn Halstead is taken in by her brother and soothed by the love of his wife and children. Evelyn refuses to cower in grief, so on a sweltering July day in 1944, the family attends the Ringling Brothers and Barnum & Bailey Circus in Hartford. When a blaze ignites the big top, Evelyn fears she will lose all that remains of her life, while Hank Webb, who hides from his murky past behind grease paint as Fraidy Freddie the clown, steps out of the shadows to help save lives and return hope to Evelyn.

Paperback / 978–1–63609–786–2